HER DEADLY HOMECOMING

A Carolina McKay Thriller

TONY URBAN
DREW STRICKLAND

PACKANACK
publishing

Copyright © 2020 by Packanack Publishing, Tony Urban & Drew Strickland

Visit Tony on the web: http://tonyurbanauthor.com

Visit Drew on the web: http://drewstricklandbooks.com

Cover by Jonathan Schuler: http://www.schulercreativelab.com/

All rights reserved.

No part of this book may be reproduced in any form or by any electronic or mechanical means, including information storage and retrieval systems, without written permission from the author, except for the use of brief quotations in a book review.

This is a work of fiction. Names, characters, businesses, places, events, locales, and incidents are either the products of the author's imagination or used in a fictitious manner. Any resemblance to actual persons, living or dead, or actual events is purely coincidental.

For mom,
Because without your continual support and encouragement, none of this would be possible.
—Tony

***

For Sara,
It's always been us and always will be.
—Drew

"Buzzards got to eat; same as worms."

— JOSEY WALES

"Birds born in a cage think flying is an illness."

— ALEJANDRO JODOROWSKY

FOREWORD

"Her Deadly Homecoming" is the first book of my new crime thriller series in which Drew Strickland and I follow the adventures and exploits of ex-police detective, Carolina Wren McKay. The books don't necessarily need to be read in order, but there are bits of backstory which are best enjoyed if you start at the beginning.

We're really excited to share Carolina with the world and hope you enjoy reading her stories as much as we've enjoyed writing them!

— Tony Urban

CHAPTER ONE

Abigail Chalmers had spent the better part of her life alone in the woods. As she was pushing eighty, that meant many a year wandering through the mountains and hollers of southern West Virginia, yet she couldn't recall a single time she had felt afraid.

Until today.

She told herself she was being silly. There was nothing in these hills to fear. Nothing worse than a little poison oak, anyway. It was time to push away the old lady worrying and get back to searching the forest floor. Time to resume her chore of harvesting ginseng.

Ahead, she spied a scattering of red berries and green leaves. Hallelujah!

The season was only two weeks old, and she'd already snared half a pound. If she could double that today, she'd be up five hundred dollars. That was a lot of money for a widow who survived on social security and by the grace of the church's food pantry.

Before she moved toward it, another wave of unease washed across her body, making her frail arms break out in goosebumps that commingled with her liver spots.

She wasn't alone. She was certain of it.

"Who's out there?" She scanned the woods around her, trying to find anything amiss, but came up empty.

The only answer to her query came in the form of a swift breeze that caressed her bare neck and sent a shiver down her stooped spine. She pulled the bobby pins, freeing her hair from the loose bun and let her white locks tumble down. The coverage they provided was sparse but better than nothing.

Time to get on with the getting on, she told herself.

As she moved toward the ginseng, the wicker basket she had looped over her forearm rocked back and forth. Back and forth. Her breath came out in shallow puffs, visible against the cool morning temperatures.

Fall was her favorite season largely because of these crisp hours when the air was pure, sent straight from God's own lungs, and she refused to let her nerves spoil an otherwise glorious day.

Abigail let out a little laugh, feeling ridiculous for being such a scaredy-cat. When she reached the first plant, she knelt and set the basket next to her. She eased the small spade into the dirt, careful as a surgeon as she circled the plant and brought it up.

The root was thick and gnarled - a prize for certain. Before depositing it into the basket, she pinched off the berries and returned them to the Earth where, Lord be with her, she would harvest them once more somewhere down the line.

She moved to the next plant, scooting herself over instead of standing up, and dug into the ground. Just as she pulled it up, a *snap* sounded to the north. She shot her eyes in that direction and set the plant aside.

The land there sloped downward, vanishing into a small gully. On any other day, she'd have been able to convince herself the noise was a raccoon. Or a rabbit. Maybe even a skunk if her luck was bad. Something small and harmless that she could dismiss and go about her work. But not today.

As she walked toward the sound, she gripped the handle of the digger tight enough to turn her knuckles ghost white. The sun was in the midst of its lazy ascent, casting long shadows that transformed the forest floor into a checkerboard of irregular shapes. Moving through them was like traversing a maze, only the walls were figments of her imagination.

Maybe that's all it is, she tried to convince herself. The addled mind of an old woman. Nothing more.

Then the smell attacked. Her nostrils furled in revolt as the odor invaded her airways, and her free hand shot to her face, covering her nose and mouth.

But it was too late. The sickly sweet, fetid aroma was inside her now and impossible to escape.

A deer, she assured herself. One that took a bad shot from a poacher and survived long enough to run off, only to die soon thereafter. It wouldn't be the first time she'd found such a scene in these woods, and it wouldn't be the last, either.

As she reached the edge of the ravine and peered into the abyss, she could see nothing but a labyrinth of kudzu. The crooked vines had overtaken the ground, turning it into an ocean of green. Underneath the vegetation, an invisible creek babbled.

A person could disappear in there, Abigail thought. Never to be seen again.

A *caw* echoed above her, interrupting her speculation. She stared up and saw four buzzards circling. Gliding black silhouettes patrolling the cobalt sky. *Nature's garbage men*, her father has always called the birds and she smiled at both the memory and the man she'd lost more than five decades prior.

Abigail decided she didn't need to go any further. The smell and the buzzards were proof enough. She'd spent enough time worrying over nothing. It was time to return to the harvest.

She turned away from the gully, took one step forward, and attempted a second. But her trailing foot caught in an exposed tree root, and the sudden impediment dropped her aged body to the dirt.

Her knee collided with a rock, sending a lightning bolt up her leg. She jerked back, away from the pain, but that was a mistake.

She felt herself tumbling backward but was unable to slow, let alone stop, her descent. On her third reverse somersault, she felt something tear in her ankle. Another burst of misery. And still, she was falling.

Thoughts of dying in this little-seen patch of the planet rolled through her head as her body bounced and ricocheted three more times. And then she landed in a soft, wet pile of death.

Abigail was alive, but whatever she had fallen into was not. The aroma from the top of the hill was a summer bouquet compared to the revolting redolence that had nearly swallowed her up.

A squadron of flies dive-bombed her face, angry over her sudden appearance. She swatted them away, trying to right herself, trying to get her bearings.

Abigail planted her right hand on the ground, but it wasn't the ground at all. Her palm sunk into something dense and moist and warm. She didn't want to know what the source of this terrible, foreign feeling could be, but she was in it—wrist-deep. Turning a blind eye would solve nothing.

When Abigail looked toward her hand, she realized it was buried in a rotting torso. Not that of a deer, but of a person. She retracted her arm, but the body protested, and her hand came free with a hungry, sucking sound.

Abigail wiped her palm against the ground, desperate to cleanse herself of the gore. During her frantic gesticulations, she saw the face to which the body belonged.

And then she screamed.

CHAPTER TWO

Mornings were always terrible, and this one was no exception.

Carolina laid face-down on the mattress, trying to ignore her cramping stomach. The thin sheet that covered her stuck to her clammy skin like a second layer of flesh. Through squinted eyes, she found daylight invading the dirty windows of the panel van.

For the last few months, she had turned sleeping into a contest. Always trying to better how many z's she could capture. To date, her greatest achievement was waking after 2 p.m. Now, she fumbled for her cell phone, found it, and checked the time: 7:17 a.m.

Why the hell was she awake?

Tap, tap, tap.

Tap, tap, tap.

The sound was small, but incessant—audible version of Chinese water torture.

Tap, tap, tap.

Only one person could be that damned annoying, and her already-sour mood took a southern detour.

She spoke through the fixed rear windows that overlooked her twin mattress. "What do you want, Mom?"

"I made French toast for breakfast. Your favorite." Her mother's flinty voice penetrated the metal shell of the van Carolina had transformed into a home on wheels earlier in the year. This was supposed to be her safe space, but nothing was safe from Beatrice Boothe.

"That was my favorite when I was ten. Now, I prefer coffee and quiet."

"Coffee, I have."

She could picture her mother standing out there, a smug smirk on her aging face as she tried not to laugh at her own joke. Seeing that expression, while her own head throbbed, was the last way Carolina wanted to start the day.

She squeezed her eyes closed, not wanting to let the rest of the world in. She yearned for privacy and rest. Why had she thought she'd get either by coming home? Carolina shook her head, at a loss with not only the situation but her entire life.

"If you think I'm going to tolerate you parking this...monstrosity in my driveway and living like a hobo and not even get some small talk in return, you're sadly mistaken."

"I'm tired. Leave me alone."

"Carolina Wren McKay! You may be thirty-four years old, but I am still your mother."

Oh, great. Playing both the mother and the first, middle, and last name cards at the same time? She was in deep shit now.

"I'm not asking for much. Just some company. Now, get your hiney up and inside my house."

There was no use fighting. The battle was lost.

Carolina opened her eyes, the sunlight battering her face as she rolled onto her right side. That movement caused her shoulder to scream in pain, and she sat up in a hurry, which sent waves of nausea radiating through her midsection.

As the morning fog cleared from her head, she saw Bea's face through the grime. Despite the filth, Carolina could tell her mother was smiling, and that made everything even worse.

She rolled off the mattress, stepping on a pile of unwashed clothes and empty fast-food wrappers while moving to the sliding side door. The walking path through her makeshift tiny home was so narrow that she almost knocked a mug reading Charm City Cafe off the counter and onto the floor, catching it only an instant before it fell.

Thank God. That was her lucky mug.

She clutched it tightly in her hand as she opened the door. Bea had teleported there, causing Carolina to flinch in surprise. Her mother tried to peek around her, to spy into the van she called home, but Carolina did her best job of blocking the view. She pushed the mug toward her mother.

"Coffee. Please."

"Inside," Bea said.

Carolina took in how much older her mother appeared since she'd last seen her. How long had it been? Four years? Maybe five? It mattered not as somewhere in that period, Father Time had finally caught up with the woman who'd often been referred to as the most eligible widow in Dupray, West Virginia.

Her pale, red hair now carried painterly strokes of white. Deep lines etched the corners of her eyes and mouth. And the skin under her chin had taken on the old-lady wattle that seemed to afflict everyone who wasn't a frequent flyer at the plastic surgeon's office. She looked older than her 61 years.

Bea's eyes hadn't changed, though. They were piercing green, the color of a black hills spruce, and they were as judgmental as ever.

"You need to wash these windows," Bea said as she dragged a finger across the glass. "I could write my name in the dirt."

"I'm not sure that's worth a brag. It's only three letters, after all."

Bea uttered a forced, fake laugh. "Always with the sarcasm."

"What can I say? It comes naturally." Carolina realized her mother had given up on inspecting the van's interior and had turned her gaze on her. Her hand drifted to the ragged scar above her armpit, covering it.

Carolina wore nothing but panties and a tank top that sagged halfway to her knees, and she felt exposed. Vulnerable. "I'll be over in a minute. As soon as I change."

Bea pinched her mouth closed, biting back a derisive comment. Carolina made a shooing gesture with her hands, directing her mother toward the sprawling but aged stone house that stood twenty yards away.

"All right. I'm going," Bea said, but Carolina waited until she'd turned and had begun her retreat before sliding back into the van.

She grabbed a pair of jeans from the floor and gave them a quick smell. Good for another week. Two if she didn't get close to anyone. Then, she grabbed a cardigan which was amongst the few clean clothes she had stacked and folded in a hamper beside the mattress. When she pulled it on, the pain deep in her shoulder gave her a nagging jolt.

Still here, in case you forgot about me.

Yeah, I didn't forget, she thought.

She opened a cabinet, where a few plates and cups were stacked in no discernible order, and she pushed them to the side. Behind them was the orange bottle she needed.

The only way to start the day.

The bottle was so full of pills that it barely rattled as she popped the lid and rolled two tablets into her palm. Carolina threw them straight to the back of her throat and swallowed them dry, then returned the bottle to its place, the label staring back at her accusingly.

Oxycodone. Take one tablet every twelve hours as needed for pain.

Who are you to judge me?

CHAPTER THREE

She hated coffee. Always had. But since the shooting, and the little pills which held the misery at bay, she found it was the only thing that kept her plumbing functional. Carolina held the mug just under her nose, trying to ignore the bitter aroma before she took a long swallow.

"Tell me your plan, darling," Bea instructed as she eased into the chair across from her, and Carolina saw her wince. Her mother's arthritis was worse in the mornings and she considered telling her that there was medicine for that but knew such a comment would only open up a line of discussion she preferred to avoid.

Carolina downed another swig before setting aside the mug. Her eyes wandered across the wooden kitchen table, and she could see faint outlines from homework she'd completed twenty years earlier. They say that you can never go home again. But maybe, the truth is that you just don't want to.

"My plan?" Carolina finally asked, feeling her mother's eyes boring a hole straight into her soul.

"Yes, your plan. For your life now."

She used every bit of self-control she possessed to not fly into a rage but still felt the need to get her point across. "Give me a fucking break already."

Bea didn't flinch. "You're still young. And you'd be pretty if you took better care of yourself."

Zing! One for team Bea.

"You've got potential, Carolina, and you need to decide what you're going to do with the rest of your life."

"What do you suggest? Tell me, oh wise one." Carolina began to regret agreeing to coffee. Hell, she regretted pulling her van onto her mother's property, and it hadn't even been 36 hours.

Bea acted like she'd wanted to end up broken and unemployed. Taking a medical retirement before she hit the downhill side of her thirties. Cut off from the one thing in life she enjoyed. Running home with her proverbial tail tucked. None of this was her choice. She wasn't to blame. The only person who was at fault was--

Carolina squeezed her eyes shut, pushing that memory inside her brain's black hole. Reliving the past would drive her insane. Better to ignore it. To pretend it never happened.

Like that was possible.

As her frustrations grew, so did the pain that gnawed away at her shoulder like a feral animal. She knew the pills would kick in soon; she only had to wait this out.

"Maybe look for another job," Bea suggested.

"I don't need one; I get all the money I need from my disability pension," Carolina said. "It's not like I have a lot of overhead."

"Not for the money. For a purpose. For a reason to go on."

"I think reasons to live are overrated. Think of the Neanderthals. Did Zog or Gak need bullshit careers? Hell, no. All they wanted out of life was not to get trampled by a woolly mammoth. And they did just fine."

"The Neanderthals went extinct." A satisfied grin tugged at the corners of Bea's mouth. "Have you ever considered teaching? I could use my connections and get you hired at the university. At least on a trial basis."

"What am I supposed to teach? How to get shot and fuck up your career? I don't think that would look appealing on the curriculum."

"Maybe you'd enjoy it. Maybe you'd even meet somebody."

"Like a man?"

"Or a woman," Bea said. "I went to an all-girls college, remember? I experimented."

Make it stop. "I did not need to know that. And just because I was a cop doesn't mean I'm a lesbian."

"Well, if you're too contemptible to find a reason to go on, I'll have to find one for you." She grabbed a small spiral-bound notepad and pencil. "What would you say is your greatest skill?"

"Are you interviewing me now?"

"Answer the question."

Carolina considered it. "I'm an excellent liar."

Her mother's eyes narrowed. "I don't believe that's an asset."

Before Carolina could respond, footsteps thudded against the wooden stairs that led to the front door. Whoever it was didn't bother with a knock.

"Expecting someone?" Carolina asked.

Bea opened her mouth but didn't get to speak before Lester Fenech appeared in the dining room. He was preoccupied with buttoning his tan uniform shirt, which meant that Carolina saw him first.

"Before you yell at me, I meant to pick up the creamer you asked for but forgot all about it." Four buttons still to go when he glanced up.

When his eyes found Carolina, he first smiled, then hurriedly cinched the top of his shirt closed, covering exposed, pale flesh and wiry white hairs.

Carolina suppressed a grin at his embarrassment. His presence flipped the light switch on her mood. Gone was the annoyance, the simmering anger. In their place was an emotion that had been a rare visitor to her world over the past year. Happiness.

Because Lester Fenech was the first man that she'd ever loved.

"Carolina Wren," he said, his face a mix of surprise and glee. "As I live and breathe."

He'd changed more than she could hardly believe. His once mahogany but now all salt, no pepper, hair was longer. Down to his shoulders in the back. Even though it had thinned out on top, he carried enough confidence that it looked cool rather than desperate.

A smattering of porcelain stubble covered his chin and cheeks. Wrinkles had invaded his face, and they were especially harsh around and under his cornflower-blue eyes.

Those eyes, Carolina thought, were still gentle but also perpetually sad. He had the look of a man who seemed on the verge of weeping at the drop of a dime. She supposed he had a right to that sadness, though; he earned it the hard way.

God, he looks so old.

It wasn't only the passage of time. He looked worn out and beaten down. As if life had kicked him in the balls, then rolled him around in the dirt and sucker-punched him in the kidneys for shits and giggles. He wore baggy blue jeans that were held up by a black leather belt and prayer. And at his side, a silver Smith & Wesson .357 glistened in its holster.

Some of her cheer at seeing him faded, but she tried not to let on.

As he moved toward her, he slipped on his white cowboy hat, the badge pinned to the center shiny like a new penny.

"Guilty as charged, Sheriff," Carolina said as she rose from the chair because she knew a hug was coming her way.

And she was right. His arms felt good around her. Strong and comforting, and welcome. His Old Spice cologne conjured more memories, better ones, and she squeezed him back.

But all good things come to an end, and he eventually released her. "I'm sorry I didn't make it to see you in the hospital; I wanted to. We wanted to." He threw a glance at Bea. "But--"

She waved away his concern. "I wasn't fit for company; believe me."

"Still, though..."

Yeah. Still.

"Hey, I got someone you need to see." Lester turned back to the front door, which he'd left hanging open, and unleashed a shrill wolf-whistle. On cue, a furry blur bounded inside and raced toward the kitchen.

A pure-white Great Pyrenees that appeared to weigh at least one hundred pounds planted his front paws on Lester's chest, licking his face.

"Oh my God," Carolina said. "Is that Ghost?" As soon as the words left her mouth, she realized how foolish they were. Ghost was old when she still called this house home, and that was a few lifetimes ago in big dog years.

"No," Lester said. "I lost Ghost a long piece back. This guy is Yeti." He gently pushed the dog off himself. "Go say hello to Carolina. She's good people."

Yeti went to her, full of dumb, unquestioning friendliness, and lapped at her hand with his sandpaper tongue.

"Hey, guy. You're a handsome one," Carolina said as she looked into the animal's earnest, chestnut-colored eyes. She missed dogs and buried her face in his fur as she loved on him.

"You know I don't appreciate that dog in my house," Bea said.

Lester's smile shifted to a perturbed scowl. "He's just visiting. And speaking of visiting, why didn't you tell me Carolina was home?" He didn't wait for an answer before looking back to Carolina. "That your van out front?" He made a lazy gesture toward the driveway.

She nodded. "More fuel-efficient than an RV."

"I thought maybe it was the plumber. Come to handle that running toilet your mother keeps nagging me to fix."

"A lot of good it does me," Bea said.

"She thinks I have nothing better to do with my time than fiddle with her plumbing."

"Please. I don't want to hear anything about you servicing my mother's pipes," Carolina said.

Lester's face flared beet red, and the resulting smile revealed aging, but natural teeth and pulled the skin tighter, firming up his jowls.

"God, is it good to see you," he said.

"Same," Carolina said. And she meant it.

He grabbed her again, renewing the embrace. This time he caught her unexpectedly, and his arms went around her shoulders. A red-hot poker of pain burned, but she endured it because this man was the father she'd always wanted, even though it never quite worked out.

"Bea didn't tell me you were going to stop by, either," she said. "She's full of secrets this morning." She shot her mother a smirk, enjoying the low-key dig. One for team Carolina.

"I'd never miss my Wednesday morning breakfast date with your mother."

Carolina raised an eyebrow. "But this is Tuesday."

"Is it?" he asked, eyes narrowing. "Must've looked at the calendar wrong. Your mother talked me into that laser eye surgery a couple years back. I ditched my bifocals, but now, my near vision isn't worth a damn."

"At least you can decipher the road signs," Bea said as she gathered Carolina's dirty dish and silverware and deposited the lot of it into the sink.

"I'd prefer to be able to read the daily news."

"Such a complainer."

They bickered like an old married couple, and Carolina briefly wondered why they'd never taken that step. Probably for the best it didn't happen, as none of her mother's four marriages lasted beyond the gift of cotton stage.

Lester was on the verge of responding; then, something visibly clicked, and he changed course. "Never mind that now, Bea. I actually just stopped by on my way to a crime scene. A body's been found in Poverty Hollow; so, I can't stay."

"Oh, Lester. I bought an extra carton of eggs." Bea rested her hand atop them like a dollar and forty-nine cents worth of jumbos outranked a human life.

"They'll hold til next week, I'm sure."

He was eager to move on, but Carolina didn't want to let go just yet. "Let me drive you."

He looked at her, surprised. She didn't really expect him to take her up on the offer but needed an excuse to get out of this house and away from her mother. "We can catch up on the way." She flashed her winningest smile.

"You sure, hon?"

"One hundred percent."

"Well, all right then. But we need to book it."

"That won't be a problem."

Bea was about to add Carolina's mug to the other dirty dishes, but she swooped in and snatched it from her hand. "That's mine," she said, chugging the remaining swill.

"I was just going to wash it."

"Doesn't need it. Coffee's self-cleansing."

Lester gave Bea a peck on the cheek. "Sorry, Bea. I'll make it up to you. Cross my heart."

Bea rolled her eyes, but Lester didn't see it as he was headed to the door, Yeti trailing on his heels.

Carolina noticed, though, and she knew it was meant for the both of them. "What? You told me to find something to do."

"I was hoping for something more worthwhile than being a taxi driver."

"Beggars and choosers, Mom. Beggars and choosers."

CHAPTER FOUR

"Abigail Chalmers called it in," Lester said. He adjusted his posture as he sunk deeper into the worn fabric seats of the van. In the back, Yeti lounged on her mattress. She knew she would be breathing in dog hair for weeks but didn't mind.

Carolina kept her eyes forward, speeding along at fifteen miles over the limit as she took Lester where he needed to go. The road was almost empty. Not a surprise. Only the unending curves and dips kept her from driving even faster.

"She was out digging ginseng," Lester continued. "You remember her?"

Carolina thought she did. "Small woman. Nose like a wood shaving. Corner booth at the farmer's market?"

Lester chuckled. "That's the one."

"She found the body?"

He nodded. "Quite a mess over it, too."

He rolled down the passenger-side window, allowing some fresh air inside, and Carolina wondered if that was because the van stank. She tried to remember the last time she'd washed the sheets and laundry but could only recall an afternoon in a laundromat in Wilmington a month back. Not a good sign.

"The deceased is a young woman. And the body was mutilated. In a purposeful way."

Carolina's ears perked up. She'd expected this hullabaloo to be over an accidental death. Maybe a suicide. But she knew Lester was hinting at more.

"Abigail told dispatch all that? I never took her as that perceptive."

"She's not. Some of the deputies are on the scene already. Johnny's the one that notified me and filled me in."

"Johnny Moore? Isn't he the janitor?"

Lester tried to cover a laugh with a cough. "He was promoted after Anse Medley retired."

"But he's a fucking idiot."

"What can I say, Carolina? There aren't a plethora of folks signing up to be deputies when the starting pay's a buck less an hour than they'd earn at Dollar General. We take who we can get and do our best with 'em."

Carolina gave a derisive snort.

"Mayhap you want to apply?" Lester asked. "If you do, I'll fast-track your application. I do have an in with the town council."

"I'm retired."

"Damn waste. Goddamn waste."

She didn't want to get into this and tried to steer the conversation back to the matter at hand.

"So, Johnny Moore's handling a potential murder scene?" She'd have been less surprised if he told her monkeys were experimenting with nuclear fusion in the closet where the Sheriff's department kept the body bags and crime-scene tape.

Lester shook his head. "No. Elven's running the scene."

"Elven Hallie?" she asked. "He's a cop now?" That was a surprise.

Lester nodded. "A damn good one."

"Shit," Carolina said. "I figured he'd be running his daddy's coal mine and sipping brandy with Dupray's upper class."

"Dupray doesn't have an upper class. And that mine ran dry eight years ago. Sent a hell of a lot of prideful men to the welfare office."

All of that was news to her. Last she knew, the Hallie Mining Company was Dupray's biggest employer, and Elven was a cocky asshole who seemed to have no purpose other than living off his parent's fortune.

"I guess a lot can change in fifteen years," she said.

"You got that right."

She rounded a sharp curve, taking it a bit too fast. In the back, Yeti gave a grumpy growl.

"The only problem with Elven is that he knows he's the best I've got and isn't afraid to let everyone else know, too."

She was still getting over the fact that one man she thought a rube and one she thought a trust fund brat were the law in these parts when Lester shifted back to the case.

"Johnny told me something else about the scene. Something that struck me as too much of a coincidence to be a coincidence."

"Yeah?" Carolina asked. "What's that?"

"He said the girl, the dead girl..."

As if he'd be referring to any other girl.

Carolina waited for the pregnant pause to pass. He hesitated a while, so long that she began to wonder if he was having a senior moment. After he spoke, she realized a brain fart would have been preferable.

"She didn't have any eyelids," Lester said.

Carolina felt her stomach seize. Now Lester's hesitation made sense. But this was not a path she wanted to walk down.

"Probably animal predation. Or insect activity. Eyes go pretty early on." She hoped the cop-speak would be enough to make him keep him from trading his cowboy hat for one of the tinfoil variety.

"Maybe." His voice trailed off, and she knew from that single word that he wasn't letting go of this. If nineteen years hadn't been long enough for him to move on, she doubted he ever would.

Ahead, two deputy's vehicles and a silver hearse were parked in the mud at the end of a dirt road that transitioned into a poor excuse for a hiking path that, in turn, led into the woods. She saw movement through the brush, took a closer look, and then found Johnny Moore pushing through a thicket of laurel with one hand and zipping his fly with the other.

He didn't top five-and-a-half feet in height but might have broken that in circumference. A WVU beanie was pulled halfway over his eyes. He stared down at his zipper, which was clogged with his underwear. The predicament kept him oblivious to the van's arrival on the scene until Carolina pulled it to a stop less than ten feet from him.

He glanced up with confused, dull eyes and stared through the window to see who had come within a first down of running him over.

"Fucking Johnny." Carolina left the engine idle and waited for Lester to exit, but he lingered with his fingers curled around the door handle.

"Why don't you come with me?" Lester asked.

"To the crime scene?"

"You came this far. Check things out with me. Give me your input. It wouldn't be the first time."

When she was a teenager and had expressed to him her interest in a career in law enforcement, Lester made a habit of showing her case files and discussing investigations. But those were for petty crimes. Burglary, auto theft. It was a game. This... was not.

"I don't know, Lester. You've got two deputies here already. I think that's plenty."

Ahead, Johnny cupped a hand to his mouth and bellowed. "This is police business. No media allowed."

Carolina shook her head. "Well, one deputy and Johnny."

"Come on." Lester stared with those sad, wounded eyes. "What if it's him? What if he's back?"

Another wave of dread hit her like a freight train. The last time Lester had gone down this rabbit hole, he'd barely emerged with his life. She couldn't see him endure that again. And she couldn't handle his baggage on top of her own.

"Lester, it's been too long. Whoever murdered Diana is either in prison or six feet under. You know that."

She could read his face like a book. He wasn't buying it, but he loved her enough that he didn't want to worry her. He put on a crooked and fake smile. "Yeah. I know. Suppose I just got to thinking."

Johnny was coming toward her window now. He rapped it with his bare knuckles, but Carolina ignored him.

"You could still help me, though," Lester said, desperation saturating his voice. "You're damn good at what you do, Carolina."

"Did."

"What?"

"I was good at what I *did*. Emphasis on past tense."

He shook his head. "Fine. Don't worry about me; I'll get a ride back with Johnny." Lester climbed out of the vehicle but paused before shutting the door.

"Even if you don't want to help yourself, you can still help other people." He waited for a response that she didn't volunteer. "All right, then." He slammed the door shut, and Carolina watched him walk up to Johnny. The two men began to converse, then turned to the forest and disappeared into it.

CHAPTER FIVE

19 Years Earlier

"Have you heard?" The girl asked Carolina before she'd even set her tray on the lunch table.

Today was Friday. Fiesta Pizza Day. Even though the crust was soggy, and she had a sneaking suspicion that the meat was leftovers from Taco Tuesday, fiesta pizza was her favorite of the offerings doled out at Dupray Junior High.

"Heard what?" Not that she cared to hear whatever gossip Maggie Smidt's tongue was wagging. It was usually about the love lives of classmates or the lack thereof—either that or Maggie bragging about who she'd been able to bully into an eating disorder.

Carolina didn't even like the girl, but survival in the lion's den that was high school meant you have to live by the 'Keep your enemies closer' mantra. If you weren't Maggie's friend, you were her target. So, Carolina tolerated her.

"They found a body near the college!" Maggie's eyes were almost feral with glee over the chance to spread such salacious news.

"A body? Who?" This was certainly more interesting than hearing about how Bethany broke up with Peter because he kissed Kaylie behind the field house.

"They don't know yet. A girl." Maggie scanned the lunchroom as other classmates filtered in, and Carolina knew she was waiting for her audience to grow. For the other half-dozen girls who comprised their clique to join the crowd, but so far, it was just the two of them.

Maggie sighed, resigning herself to having only Carolina to share the gossip with. "I heard that she was all cut up. Throat slashed. Eyes gouged out. Like in one of those horror movies!"

Now that was unexpected. A murder? In Dupray County, where nothing interesting ever happened? Her mind spun over the possibilities.

"Did they arrest anyone?"

Maggie shook her head, sending her permed curls bobbing. "Nope. The killer's still out there!"

Damn, this was exciting. Scary, too, a little, but as a 15-year-old girl, Carolina still lived in a world where she was impervious. Where bad things only happened to other people.

She watched as Maggie took a nibble of her pizza, cheddar cheese embedding itself in her silver braces. Not a good look, and Carolina bit her lip to keep herself from laughing.

"That's terrible," Carolina finally said, feeling as if it was expected to say something about how tragic this news was.

Then, Heather and Shannon sashayed up to the table. Shannon had passed on the fiesta pizza, instead opting for the salad. She had been eating rabbit food ever since Maggie had told her she was looking chunky.

"Have you heard?" Maggie repeated, and the cycle began anew.

Carolina didn't pay attention this time. All she could think about was the dead girl—the murdered girl—and the fact that whoever killed her was still out there. She wondered if Lester was at the crime scene now, investigating. And she couldn't wait to see him and ask him all about it. He'd protest. Tell her that she was too *young to hear it, but she knew she could get it out of him sooner or later.*

As Carolina's mind reeled with possibilities, Mrs. Beardslee shuffled into the lunchroom. Her makeup, usually magazine perfect, looked like an oil slick around her eyes as she inspected the room.

Something was up. Carolina wondered if Mrs. Beardslee, who wasn't her favorite teacher but was in her top five, knew the victim in some way. Maybe she was even related.

Carolina was on the verge of approaching her to pepper her with questions when the tall, lithe woman made a sharp right and moved toward a table where a group of kids everyone thought of as the goths dined.

"Oh shit," Maggie said. "Look!"

The other girls now homed in on Beardslee, too. She went to Brittany Mason's side and rested her trembling hand on the waifish girl's shoulder. Brittany was a year younger than Carolina, but if you believed the rumors (and most did), she was willing to open her legs for a pack of Newports or a six-pack of Old Milwaukee.

Her short hair was spiked and dyed impossible black. Her eyes were raccoon-esque, while the rest of her skin was fish-belly white.

Mrs. Beardslee leaned into the girl, whispering something in her ear, which was pierced in multiple places. And then Brittany's facial expression changed from smug to shocked.

"Bullshit!" she screamed the word, and the cafeteria went silent as a library.

Everyone stared at the burgeoning scene. Beardslee tried to embrace Brittany, but the girl shoved her away, hard. The teacher stumbled backward, her long legs becoming entwined in the plastic seats, and she fell to the floor.

"You're a fucking liar!" Brittany yelled. "My sister's not dead!"

Mr. Horving, a rotund, bespectacled man who was a few years past retirement age, rushed toward her, his plus-sized movements drawing laughter from many in the room, including the girls around Carolina.

But she didn't laugh. Her excited curiosity had waned, replaced with a sick dread. Because now, the dead girl wasn't the anonymous, movie-star figment her imagination had created. Now she was a real person.

A person with family. With a sister who loved her.

Mr. Horving grabbed Beardslee's hands and helped her to her feet, but Brittany wasn't waiting around. As she dashed from the lunchroom, Carolina saw that the girl, usually the epitome of dazed and confused, was sobbing.

This wasn't fun anymore. And Carolina was more convinced than ever to insinuate herself into the situation and do whatever she could to discover what had happened.

CHAPTER SIX

The morning dew soaked through his boots and wetted his feet as he walked. Each footstep sunk an inch or more into the damp ground. That wouldn't last long, though.

Fall would hit any day now, and with it would come the cold that would harden the soil and turn the canopy of the forest into a watercolor painting of oranges and yellows.

Lester's mind drifted. Thinking about the damnable past. About his daughter and what had been done to her.

Johnny rambled beside him, but Lester only caught every third or fourth word. Even those were enough to piece together what the man was trying to convey, which was that Elven was pissed that Johnny had called him to the scene.

That was not a surprise.

As yellow tape, Elven Hallie, and Abigail Chalmers came into view through the ash and poplar trees, Lester wished Carolina hadn't spurned his request. He would have appreciated not just her help but her advice. Her detachment. He needed her to tell him whether or not he was being crazy.

Sobbing sounds made him focus on the matter at hand. He

realized they were coming from Abigail, who sat on an uprooted tree. A basket sat beside her feet, one of which was wrapped in a flesh-colored bandage that stretched to her knee.

Lester ducked under the crime scene tape and nodded to the crying woman.

"Sorry you had to experience this, Abigail. Never easy finding a body—especially one that met a premature end."

She stared through him like he wasn't even there. He tried a reassuring smile, but that was difficult given the circumstances. Instead, he turned to the gully where Elven stood, his back turned. He had a small camera raised to his face and occupied his time by photographing the scene.

Lester turned to Johnny. "Do me a favor?"

"What's that, Sheriff?"

Johnny was the only deputy, hell, maybe the only person in the county, that addressed him as sheriff. Lester had asked him several times to stop, but the man never had. He saw little sense telling him again now. "Distract Elven for a few minutes."

Johnny's heavy brows furrowed like two black caterpillars preparing for coitus. "Why, Sheriff?"

Lester sighed. Apparently, that was enough, and Johnny took the hint to just do it.

"Hey, Elven."

Elven Hallie turned. He wore mirrored sunglasses, although the sun had no chance of penetrating the dense blanket of foliage above. When he saw Lester, his face froze, and Lester knew he was itching to lob a snide comment like a hand grenade, but he had enough sense and professionalism to avoid causing a scene within the scene. "What do you want, Johnny?"

Johnny paused. He hadn't planned that far ahead and was anything but nimble of mind. "I think I saw some evidence down the path a ways, and... I... I don't got no gloves with me."

Elven was tall, a few inches taller than Lester, who loathed looking up to the man. He was nearing forty but looked younger. He pushed a few locks of sand-colored hair off his forehead as he approached with a movie-star smile. He's too handsome for his own good, Lester thought.

"Morning," Elven said.

"That it is," Lester replied.

"You didn't need to bother yourself, running all the way out here. I have the situation under control."

"I'm sure you do."

Johnny grabbed hold of Elven's shirt sleeve, giving it a hesitant tug. "It's over that way," he said, pointing to the east.

Elven cast a smirk at Lester before following his colleague.

Lester continued on to where the ground disappeared downhill. When he reached the edge, he peered into the ravine where Phil Driscoll knelt beside the reason he was here and not enjoying Bea's cooking and company.

"Lester. Good to see you, as always." Phil tipped a finger in his direction. In addition to his role as coroner, Driscoll multi-tasked as Dupray's lone doctor and owned the Driscoll Family Funeral Home. A man of many talents.

His dark, beady eyes looked disproportionately small in his large head. A coarse, gray beard covered the bottom half of his face. But up top, he was as bald and white as a cue ball.

"How'd you beat me here?" Lester asked. Did Elven alert every asshole in the county except him?

"Hallie gave me a ring. I wasn't far. One of Hoyt Andersson's brood got pink eye a few days back, and now the lot of 'em are flush with it. I went to their place so they wouldn't contaminate the whole damned town."

"Wise choice," Lester said.

Lester looked toward the body, or what he could see of it, which wasn't much. He began crab-walking down the hill, planting each step carefully so as to not go ass over head and cement his reputation as a cop who'd hung around too long.

"You recognize the deceased?" Lester asked when he made it half-way.

He could only see her feet, legs, and waist. Her shirt was bloody and pulled askew, revealing gray-green skin that looked as tight as mylar stretched across a drum. Crystal-clear water washed over the bottom two-thirds of the body, giving it an unending bath. Nevertheless, the stench this close was enough that Lester was now glad he'd missed breakfast.

"I do not. Maybe you'll have better luck," Driscoll said.

Another few steps, and Lester was at the bottom and breathing a bit easier. He stopped at Phil's side, and both were near the dead girl's lower extremities.

He could see her better now. A hot pink ring pierced her distended navel. Had she been alive, he might have thought she was in her second trimester. But she was dead, and he knew better. There was a ragged hole where Abigail Chalmers' hand had implanted itself earlier in the morning.

Lester wasn't concerned with any of that. What he wanted to see were her eyes.

But they were gone. Not just the eyelids, either. All that remained were two cavities, empty aside from the maggots that overflowed and spilled onto her cheeks and into her brown hair, where they looked like writhing grains of rice.

"Jesus," Lester said.

"I don't think he's anywhere near." Phil crouched beside the body, one of his knees giving off a firecracker pop. "Look familiar to you?"

"Can't say she does. But I don't know the young ones as well as I used to."

Driscoll pointed to the corpse's neck, where a gash extended from one side to the other. "I'm no M.E., but here's your fatal wound. There are a few bits and bobs." He motioned to various scratches and gashes on the body. "All postmortem. Probably happened when she was dumped. Plus, the animals have been at her."

Lester saw that, too. The tips of her fingers had been gnawed upon, and one of her toes was completely missing. A small chunk of flesh had been excised from her upper arm. Just a bite, though, as if the coyote or fox sampled the entree and didn't like the taste. There were also several smaller tears, which he knew were the work of the buzzards he'd observed circling above during his trek in.

Foamy blood had leaked from her nose and mouth in a way that reminded Lester of shaking up a bottle of soda pop and watching it blow. Her features, even in death, were delicate. So damn young, he thought. Early twenties. About the same age as--

He stopped himself from thinking that through. He couldn't go there. Not now. Not here. He needed to be in charge and keep his shit together. "How long do you reckon she's been here?"

Phil shrugged. "Four, five days, judging from the decomp."

"Her eyes. You think that was done to her by the killer?"

Driscoll winced, and Lester regretted the question, but it was in the air now. No way to unblow that balloon. "I'd say it's more likely to blame nature. Carrion like soft tissue. They could peck away, then the flies set in..."

"You can't rule it out, though."

Phil shifted on his feet, and Lester knew he was trying to come up with an answer that would placate him. "I'm sorry, Lester, but it's not clear. It's possible, but—"

"It's highly unlikely," Elven said. His voice had more of a southern drawl than you'd expect from someone who came from money and spent his college years at Wheeling. Lester sometimes wondered if he played up the *Aw shucks* routine to endear himself to the common folk.

Lester looked up and saw Elven standing at the top of the hill. He'd removed his shades, and even at a distance, Lester could see his hazel eyes glimmer.

"I don't like to make assumptions without investigating every possibility," Lester said.

Elven pocketed the camera he'd been holding. "Neither do I. But you don't need to go searching for ghosts in every case, Lester. Ever hear of Occam's Razor?"

That was a new one, and rather than prove himself ignorant, Lester stayed quiet.

"It's a theory that says the most likely explanation is usually correct. Now, we could have a serial killer who hasn't made a peep since I was rushing for fifteen hundred yards and leading the Dupray Deacons to a mediocre six-and-four record, or we could have a girl who was in the wrong place at the right time and ended up robbed, killed, and dumped. Which do you think is more apt to be true?"

He was right, of course. But part of being a cop was trusting your gut, and Lester's gut told him that someone who picks up a random girl to rob and murder doesn't usually haul the body half a mile into the woods. Especially not in a corner of Dupray county that was so far off the grid that few people knew it existed.

"Besides," Elven said. "This girl's not posed."

"Posed?" a woman's voice asked.

All the men looked past Elven and saw Carolina approaching.

"My goodness. Carolina McKay," Elven said with a laugh. "Is it really you?"

"The one and only," she said, giving him a nod. "It's been a long time, Elven."

"Too long. I read about your heroics in Baltimore. Surprised your head can still fit through doorways these days."

"Don't believe everything you read." She peered into the ravine, to Lester, to the body. "All right if I join you?"

Lester nodded. "Watch your step; soil's loose."

"I will. I saw Abigail's leg. You sure it's not broken, Doc?"

Driscoll shook his head. "Bad sprain."

Elven cocked his head, eyes narrow and bemused. "I'm curious. What exactly are you doing at my crime scene? We're outside your jurisdiction, are we not?"

"She's here because I asked her to be here. As a consultant,"

Lester said. He was still in charge, whether Elven liked it or not. At least until the next election.

"Just what we need," Elven said.

"I'm retired, and I heard you're understaffed," Carolina said. "Think of me as free labor." She started down the hill, making the trip much quicker and easier than Lester. When she reached the bottom, she took another glance up at Elven. "What were you saying about posed?"

"Lester's got it in his head that this unfortunate soul is related to our last rash of murders. But those girls were posed after death."

Carolina, with one eyebrow raised, looked at Lester. "You never told me about that."

Lester hated having withheld it from her all these years. "We kept that private," he muttered.

She leaned into Lester and whispered, "I expect to be filled in later."

"Of course."

Carolina crouched to get a better look at the body, and Lester pointed out the girl's face. "Look at her eyes."

"What's left of them." Her voice was cool, and he knew she was upset with him. He also knew the woman well enough not to push it.

"What do you think was used to cut her throat, Doc?"

Driscoll considered it. "My guess would be a box cutter."

Carolina nodded. "Sounds about right."

Elven cleared his throat loud enough for the sound to roll down the ravine. "If you're going to take over, Carolina, do you mind if I head back to town? Might be an expired meter that I can attend to."

Lester saw the woman smirk.

"Did I step on your toes, deputy?"

"Not at all," Elven said. "I just don't like to waste resources."

Carolina stood, crossing her arms. "If this is your scene, can you tell me the victim's name?"

"No ID, and none of us recognizes her. So, unless you've become clairvoyant since the last time that I saw you--"

"It's Jennifer Millstrom. She's twenty-two years old. Student at McDowell University. Organ donor." She looked to the decaying corpse. "Though, I doubt that's going to be useful anymore."

"How the--"

Carolina cut Elven off by displaying a rhinestone-bedazzled billfold which she held in her gloved hand. "Found this near a puddle of piss."

Elven glared at Johnny. His shoulders sagged, sheepish. "My bad," Johnny said. "Hey, Carolina." He gave a small wave.

"Hi Johnny," she said. "Also, there's forty-two bucks and a Visa card inside her wallet; so, I guess that shoots the shit out of your robbery theory, Elven."

Lester bit back a smile as he pulled out an evidence bag. She dropped the billfold into it.

"Thanks for that," Elven said. "Some of us have a few things to learn about observation." He strode toward Johnny, who looked like a toddler ready for his paddling.

Lester grabbed Carolina's hand and pulled her a few feet away from Driscoll. He lowered his voice as he spoke. "Does this mean you'll help me out?" he asked.

"I only walked out here because you left your dog in my van."

"Oh. Put him in Johnny's car. It's the one with the smashed-up bumper."

"I have to say that handing Elven's ass to him was even more fun than I'd hoped."

Lester had enjoyed it, too. "Will you at least consider it?"

Carolina took a deep breath and looked at the dead girl. Lester saw the look in her eyes and recognized it; that look was the past colliding with the present. "I need to clear my head before I commit to anything."

Before he could respond, she scrambled up the hill and out of sight. Even though she'd made no promises, he knew he could count on her.

CHAPTER SEVEN

The park was deserted, just as she'd hoped it would be. As it was a school day, Carolina had planned on no kids being around, running and yelling, and utilizing the playground equipment. Upon arriving, she realized they probably had little use for this place on the weekends, either.

A small slide had turned pumpkin orange with rust. The monkey bars were missing every other rung. The swing set had one working swing while the second hung from a broken chain, the rubber dangling and drawing random lines in the sand underneath as it swayed in the breeze.

No joy to be found here.

The shrubbery and rhododendrons had been consumed by kudzu, creating an unending sea of drab greenery. It reminded Carolina of a documentary she'd once watched, something called *Life After People*, where nature reclaimed the world after humanity came to an end.

From what she'd seen during her drive into Dupray, West Virginia, that wasn't far off. The town had been far from bustling during her youth, but it had something akin to small-town charm, albeit in a sad, desperate way.

There had been mom-and-pop businesses, a bowling alley, and a two-screen movie theatre. Half a dozen restaurants and diners had lined the main street, intermixed between the bank, two pharmacies, a gas station, a bar, and a grocery store.

All that remained of the town that once was were the pharmacies, one pizza joint/diner, and the bar. The grocery store was gone, replaced by a Dollar General with no fresh produce or meat to be found. All the quaint businesses she'd thought were so kitschy and boring as a teen were either razed or covered with plywood upon which *Closed* and *Out of Biz* had been spray-painted in sloppy, careless fonts.

Dupray was like a ghost town, but worse. Because people still tried to live and make a living amid the slow, miserable death throes. She could imagine the town leaders promising hope and coming prosperity. Ensuring everyone that good times would return as soon as they found a new vein to mine. Or pitching Dupray as a possible tourist destination where families could experience *Wild, Wonderful, West Virginia* up close and personal. All lies.

During her years in Baltimore, she often wondered why she had fled the simple life for the madness of the city. Now, she realized that small towns like Dupray existed in their own special version of crazy. A world where time moved on, but people lingered. A place where there was no future, only the past.

Somewhere to her right, a bird tweeted. That bird, not her pessimistic philosophizing, had been her reason for coming there; so, she tried to push aside her thoughts and find the source of the chirping. Her eyes scanned the foliage, unsuccessfully at first, and then she found it: a red-breasted nuthatch.

It wasn't a rare find, but it would do. She opened her notebook, took out her pencil, and began sketching. She was no John James Audobon, but she could get her point across. And the drawing wasn't the point, anyway. The reason she was here, focusing on a tiny, ordinary *Sitta canadensis,* was to clear her mind.

Bea taught ornithology at the university—had since before Carolina was born. Her mother's obsession was how she ended up with her name: Carolina Wren. Her younger, half-sister, Scarlet Tanager, fell victim, too. Many times, Carolina thanked God that she didn't have a brother. The thought of having a sibling named Hawk or Falcon was too much to bear.

Despite their constantly butting heads, Carolina inherited Bea's bird obsession and spent days in the woods and at the creeksides, searching out Bohemian waxwings, Pine grosbeaks, and Hoary redpolls.

One of her greatest moments was spotting, at the age of 14, a male Painted bunting feeding in a farmer's field. She'd watched the bird, which would have looked more at home in the jungles of South America, for the better part of an hour, enthralled. And at peace.

Birdwatching not only served as the lone common string tethering her to her mother, but it also taught her self-control. She learned to slow down and take her time. It showed her how to pay attention to the smallest of details.

As she began to draw the short, stout bird, it flitted to the ground, its sharp beak pecking the dirt as it hunted for a lunch of bugs or spiders. With the outline finished, she added the smaller features. The transition of its feathers. Its stubby tail.

She relished the silence of the process.

That was very short-lived as panting and steady, jogging footsteps came from Carolina's right. The bird gave up on sourcing a meal and flew into the vegetation, vanishing.

Shit.

Carolina tried to gather her things together in a hurry, but she wasn't fast enough. A female jogger with a pitbull at her side emerged from the trail and made a turn in her direction. She wore a pink-and-blue velour tracksuit and wireless headphones that protruded from her ears like alien antennae.

She paid Carolina no attention as she stopped at the trail end and checked her Apple watch. That was just as well, as Carolina was in no mood for small talk with a stranger.

The woman looked to be in her late twenties, with a mop of bleached-blonde hair and a toned body that was evident even through her outfit. She was the type to down green smoothies of dubious origin for breakfast. Carolina would stick with French toast.

The dog kept watch at the woman's side, its muscular frame shaking as it panted and caught its breath. Carolina was a self-professed dog person, but even she didn't think that one looked friendly. It was the ears. They were clipped and jutted from its skull like horns. People that did that should be shot.

She was half-into a standing position, halfway to a clean getaway, when the woman saw her. At first, she gave a curt wave, the kind people do so as not to appear rude, even though they are, but then she smiled.

"Carolina?"

Damn. She wasn't up for Old Home Week and thought about lying, but it was clear she'd been made. "Yes?"

"It's me, Margaret." She waved her hand. "Maggie, from school!"

Her mind quickly connected the dots. Even though they'd been casual friends from sixth grade to senior year, they hadn't shared a word since the day after graduation, when Carolina left Dupray for what she thought would be forever. They were the same age, give or take nine months. So, how did Maggie look so damned young?

"Oh, hi. Long time no see."

"You're telling me!" Maggie dropped onto the bench beside her.

Carolina could smell fruity body wash intermixed with perspiration. The dog flopped at her feet and stared as it kept guard without emotion.

"When did you get back in town? How come you didn't call me?" She didn't wait for an answer, instead leaning in for a hug.

Unlike the shared embrace with Lester, this one was unexpected and unwelcome. Carolina felt her body stiffen and hoped the old friend wasn't offended.

"Sorry, I'm all sweaty, but you know, gotta keep that figure." She let go and looked Carolina up and down. "You... look great."

Carolina didn't need to be a cop to know that was a lie.

"Have you heard?" Margaret asked. It immediately took Carolina back to high school, where the teen version of Maggie was the first to spread, and often create, gossip.

"Heard what?"

"They found a body!" Margaret wrinkled her nose and faked a shiver. "Allen called me before I left to walk Stanley. I guess he heard about it from Sam down at the foundry, who got a call from Lois after she talked to..."

Carolina didn't care to listen. None of the names Maggie threw out meant anything to her; she wanted more than even to extricate herself from this conversation as soon as possible. But her former friend's mouth still ran like the proverbial flapper on a duck's ass, and there was no pause that would have allowed her to cut in and say, *Sorry, but I don't want to speak to you, and I'll be leaving now.*

"Reminds me of back in high school. Remember those murders? I guess that's a dumb question. Who could forget, right?"

Carolina shrugged. "It did make—"

"Oh my God, that's right. You're like a cop now, aren't you? A big detective in Baltimore, right? We're all so proud of you! Are you helping with the case?"

Carolina tucked her pad under her arm and rose to her feet. The dog, who she presumed was Stanley, inspected her, wary. His whip of a tail never budged, and she half-expected him to launch himself and tear out her throat. That might have been preferable to enduring more of Maggie's nattering.

"I'm not a detective anymore. And I really better—"

"Uh-huh," Maggie said. She clicked her headphones and held up a finger to Carolina. *Shush.* "Yeah, I'm on my way. The house is ready for the walk-through."

She put her finger down and looked back to Carolina. "Sorry about that. Duty calls, you know? But it was great seeing you! We should really catch up. Maybe this weekend?"

Carolina nodded. "Maybe."

"Great! Give me a call. Your mom has my number if you don't," she said just before jogging away. Stanley cast one more wary glance back, and Carolina realized the dog might not be vicious after all. Maybe he just wanted away from his owner. And who could blame him?

Alone again on the bench and in the park, she scanned that area for birds, but Maggie's blathering had chased them all away. Her brief moment of relaxation was spent, not to be returned.

She'd come back to Dupray to find peace, but instead, she found a homicide investigation. Maybe it was an omen.

Sitting on the sidelines had never been her style. So, she took a deep breath and picked up her phone.

She dialed, and it rang only once.

"Lester," she said. "I'm in."

CHAPTER EIGHT

THE SOBBING LASTED THE BETTER PART OF TEN MINUTES. THAT was always the worst, and after more than four decades on the job, the aftermath of having told someone their loved one was dead hadn't gotten any easier.

It didn't matter how the deceased met his or her end. Car crash. Drug overdose. Workplace accident. Death by misadventure. It always played out the same.

A knock on the door. Faces that grew anxious and worried when they saw the badge. Then came the forced platitudes: *I'm afraid I have some bad news. I'm sorry to have to tell you this.* Something gentle to prepare them for the hammer that was about to fall as you ruined their lives.

But the sobbing was the worst, and he still didn't know how to handle it, so he let them get it out and waited for it to end. Sooner or later, it always did.

"Who would want to hurt my Jenny?" Amy Millstrom blotted her eyes with an already saturated tissue.

"I don't know just yet. If you can answer a few questions for me, that might help find out."

She nodded, putting on a facade of composure. Amy Millstrom had been a young mother and was still in her early forties. If you could see past the pain, she was prettier than average, with brunette hair that hung in loose curls past her shoulders. Lester was surprised to see that her ring finger was barren.

"I'll do my best," she said.

"When was the last time you spoke with Jennifer?"

She didn't need to think about it. "Last Sunday. She had dinner with us."

And died, most likely, on Monday, Lester thought.

"Us?" He hadn't seen any signs of a man's presence in this house, which was decked out in Home Interior chachkis, teddy bears, and angel figurines.

"My mother and I live together. Jenny did, too, when she wasn't in school."

"She stayed at the university, then?"

Amy nodded. "Said she wanted the college experience. But between tuition and room and board, it cost her so much that she worked almost every waking minute she wasn't in class."

"Where did she work?"

"The dollar store down in Jolo. Took every shift they'd give her."

He knew a trip to that store, in the southernmost part of the county, would be in his future and jotted that down. "Did she have a boyfriend that you knew of?"

"Last summer she dated a boy: Teddy Voley. Everyone called him Buzz because they buzzed off all his hair when he enlisted. But he was shipped overseas—Germany, I think. They didn't last long after that."

"Is he still there? In Germany?"

"As far as I know."

"And she hadn't been on a date since then?"

"She said she didn't have time." She swallowed. "How was she killed? I mean, was it at least quick, or did she suffer?"

He hated that question. The internal debate as to how much he could lie without it being unethical. "She was stabbed. And it's hard to say for certain, but I do believe she probably went fast after that." God, he hoped.

More inquiries would follow if he wasn't quick. She'd want details. To know when she could see the body. He had to hurry now.

"Did Jenny ever tell you about trouble with anyone? Maybe a classmate who wanted to take her out and wouldn't take no for an answer? A coworker who was too friendly for his own good?"

Another shake of the head. "No. Everyone liked Jenny. She was a good girl."

"I'm sure she was."

The faucets that were her eyes came on again. "Where is she now? She's not still laying somewhere out there, is she?"

"No, ma'am. She's at Driscoll's. You can call Phil, and he'll walk you through everything."

She again attempted to use the tissue, which was too far gone to do any good. He pulled a handkerchief from his back pocket and passed it to her.

"Is Jenny's father in the picture?"

"He died in the mine when she was still in diapers."

And back to sobbing. He knew there was nothing more to gain here. "Is there anything I can do for you before I go?"

Amy shook her head and tried to speak, but no words came out. He gave her a pat on the shoulder and left her to her grief.

Before he made it out of the house, a tired, halting voice came from above: the voice of God—if God was an elderly woman who'd chain-smoked away the best years of her life. "Sheriff Fenech?"

He peered up a staircase and found an elderly woman in a housecoat perched unsteadily on the steps. Her white hair had thinned to the point where her liver-spotted skull shone through, and her head looked too large for her frail body. It all came together in a way that reminded him of a baby bird.

"Yes, ma'am," he said.

"I'm Mary, Jenny's gramma. I heard most of your conversation with my daughter." She beckoned him with a crooked hand. "I hate to be a bother, but I traverse these stairs as infrequently as possible. Will you come to me?"

He nodded. "Of course. And I'm very sorry for your loss." Such hollow, worthless words.

"As am I." She shuffled out of sight.

Lester ascended the stairs, turning in the direction the old woman had gone. He saw her slip through an open door and followed.

He found her sitting on the edge of a twin bed covered in a pristine log cabin quilt filled with vibrant pinks and purples. The color scheme of the bedspread matched that of the room. Posters for boy bands, letters spelling out JENNY, and random photographs filled the walls.

Mary peeled one of those pictures free and held it in her hands, staring at it.

"This is Jenny. From what I heard, I doubt she looked this pretty when you saw her today." She extended it to Lester.

He looked at the photo, which was of Jenny and Mary sitting side by side on the porch of this very house. Jenny had her arm around her grandmother's frail shoulders and a perfect smile on her face. She was right; Jenny didn't look like that anymore. The girl in the pictures was gone.

He went to hand it back to her to the woman, but she held up her palm.

"You keep that with you so that you don't forget she was alive once."

"I won't forget that, ma'am. I promise."

She reached to him and laid her hand atop his. "I know you won't. Because you know all too well how unfair life is."

He fought back a shiver. It always unnerved him when people remembered Diana's death, and he was put in the shoes of the victim.

"This is her room, you know," Mary said.

"I gathered as much." Lester stepped to a dresser, where a mirror and a variety of makeup tools littered the top. Also, there was a worn bible, a few pieces of costume jewelry, and an assortment of paperback romance novels.

Intermixed with them, he saw a thin booklet with a faux-leather cover. Stamped in gold were the words *My Diary*. Upon flipping through the pages, he saw it hadn't been updated in over two years, and he set it aside.

Then his attention went to the photographs, which made something of a timeline of the girl's short life: Jenny in her AYSO soccer uniform. Jenny in a prom dress. Jenny eating funnel cake at the county fair. Jenny sitting under a banner that declared *Sweet Sixteen*.

She didn't even get started, Lester thought. Why did life have to be so damned cruel?

"I lost my husband thirty-three years ago," Mary said, drawing his attention. "Helped my daughter bury hers when Jenny was still in diapers. Add in two sisters and a brother, and I have plenty of experience with dying. But someone murdering our Jenny... Tell me, Sheriff, how do you get past that?"

Lester considered it. He thought about offering something trite and reassuring but opted for the truth. "You don't," he said. "You just find a way to muddle through."

Tears leaked from her eyes as she wept silently.

"I'll do everything I can to bring the person that did this to them to justice." He caught himself, that word—*them*—but too late to call it back. Mary either didn't notice or understand, for she only shared a sad smile, squeezed his hand, and didn't comment further.

CHAPTER NINE

Carolina followed Lester toward Bea's house, struggling to keep up with his long strides.

"Phil Driscoll faxed over his report, such that it is," Lester held a stack of files in one hand and tapped the thinnest of them with the other.

"Fax, Lester? Please tell me your department has email by now."

"Fax, email, same difference," he said.

Carolina smirked. "Not really."

He held the door open for her.

"What were his findings?" she asked.

"Not much we didn't know. Cause of death was blood loss due to the neck wound. Nothing to indicate she was harmed in any other way before she expired."

"Was she raped?" Carolina asked.

"No obvious signs."

"But the creek could have done a number on that," Carolina said.

He nodded as he dropped the files onto an otherwise empty coffee table. "If you see Elven, don't mention to him that I gave you these files, all right?"

She spread out the folders, then plopped herself into the extra-large, green leather sofa that was comfortable but hideous. She glanced at Lester, who stood on the opposite side of the table.

"Why would he care?"

"Because he thinks I'm a paranoid fool. They all do. You're the only one that can see this is connected to Diana. And the others."

Carolina flinched when he said the name. Diana was Lester's daughter. six years older and impossibly sweet, pretty, and perfect. Carolina had idolized her growing up, had wanted to be her.

Diana's death had been the beginning of the end of everything decent in her life. For the last fifteen years, she'd tried to forget the girl existed, and she hated herself for that.

Carolina swallowed hard. She didn't want to let him down, but she wasn't going to lie to him. "Honestly, Lester, I'm not convinced that they're related. I'm looking into it because…"

Her words trailed off. She didn't know why she was going down this rabbit hole with him. Other than pity, and she wasn't about to say that aloud.

Instead, she changed the subject. "Who cares what Elven Hallie thinks, anyway? You're his boss. Fire his ass if he gives you shit."

Lester laughed. "You've never really liked him, have you?"

Carolina looked up from the files. "He's an arrogant prick. What's to like?"

He cocked his head. "He's not all that bad, truth be told. Just overeager."

"Whatever. You're still in charge, though. So, I say, fuck him."

Lester cleared his throat of phlegm, then swallowed it down. "It's not that simple."

"How so?" She could tell by the look on his face that this was a different kind of serious.

"I'm not running for reelection. I've already announced that I'm done when my term's up."

Carolina fell back into the leather and took a breath. "Shit," she said when she exhaled. Lester had been Sheriff for over forty years. It was what he lived for, and she'd assumed he'd go to his grave with the badge pinned to his shirt. "Why in the hell are you doing that?"

"I see myself every morning in the mirror, Carolina. I'm about used up. And I... I suppose I realized there are other things I can do with my life."

"Like what? Play pinochle at the senior center and pull weeds in Bea's garden? That's not a euphemism, by the way."

He grinned.

"Bullshit. Tell me the truth if you want my help on this."

Lester scooted an ottoman with garish floral print away from a chair and used it as a makeshift seat. He leaned into the coffee table with his elbows. "They want me out, Carolina."

"Who?"

"The town."

"Why?"

He looked away from her eyes, shameful. "The last couple years have been... rough. You remember the Starcher clan?"

Carolina nodded. They were a shady bunch but had an almost Robin Hood-esque reputation in Dupray.

"Hollis, the patriarch, he's got it in everyone's head that I'm going past my prime. Hell, maybe he's right. I'm not sure of much of anything these days."

"This town loves you."

"At one time. Now, when I walk down the street, I see they look at me. Same way you look at your favorite horse when he gets fat and swaybacked and needs put out to pasture. It's my time. I'm done in November, and I already endorsed Elven as my replacement."

"November? That's barely a month-and-a-half away."

He nodded. "I'm aware."

This wasn't possible. "I never took you for the quitting type."

"Neither did I. But life has a way of making a man reconsider himself."

CHAPTER TEN

Lester shifted in his seat, anxious and embarrassed. She didn't like seeing that look on him. She didn't want to think of him as weak. It wasn't right what they were doing to him; he'd given so much of his life, his heart, to this town and its people.

"I see the wheels turning, Carolina. But I'll have none of it, do you understand me? I'm a grown man, and I make my own decisions. So, what I need from you is your advice on this case. Help me go out with some dignity."

And that was it. She had to respect Lester's wishes, but she didn't have to like it. And she'd be sure to give Elven shit over it the next time she ran into him.

"I'll do everything I can for you."

"I know you will. And I hope you know how much that means to me."

He grabbed one of the older files; its manilla cover had gone caramel over the years. He held it but couldn't bring himself to open the cover.

"Sometimes it seems like yesterday, and other times, it feels like a made-up memory of a life that never was." Lester turned his gaze to the floor. "Not sure if that makes any sense."

She knew exactly what he meant. Being so close to a case, being *involved* in a case that remained unsolved was the worst thing that could happen to a cop. It was like vermin feasting on your soul with a hunger that never ceased.

Maybe—probably—Lester was wrong about it being the same killer, but she would do her best to find out what was going on and put an end to at least one of his regrets.

"Now, fill me in on this posing business."

Lester glanced at the folders. "There are photos, but in broad strokes, the girls were placed in a kneeling position. Their heads were tilted back. Almost like they were genuflecting."

"Why didn't you tell me?"

He scowled. "You were a teenager, Carolina. I told you too much the way it was. And we'd agreed to keep that within the department, just in case we had to weed out any false confessions."

That made sense, and her annoyance over being left out of the loop faded. She noticed Lester glancing at Bea's antique Grandfather clock.

"I hate to run out on you, but it's been a long day, and I still have to head to Jolo and stop by Millstrom's place of work." Lester stood and put on his big cowboy hat.

That was an hour's drive in the daylight. Lester already looked exhausted, and the thought of him spending that much time on the county's shitty roads scared her.

"Let me do that."

He raised an eyebrow. "Pardon?"

"I'll go to Jolo. Question her coworkers. No reason I can't handle that much."

"You really want to do that?"

She didn't, but it was better than wondering whether he'd make it there and back in one piece. "I do. But it might help if I had some sort of ID."

Without hesitation, Lester unpinned the badge from his shirt and handed it to her. "Be warned, though; Elven catches you with that, he's liable to arrest you for impersonating an officer of the law."

"And I'm liable to punch him in the dick."

That garnered a laugh, one that sounded like music in her ears.

"I'd pay good money to see that." He stepped into the light of the window, and for a brief moment, she saw his younger self and not the worn-down, tired shadow she'd come home to.

He nodded toward the files. "When you have a chance, take a good look through those, and tell me what I missed. By God, I hope there's something. I've never been so eager to be wrong."

"I'll do my best." She smiled as she watched him leave the room, then waited until she heard the front door open and close before taking the deep tan file he'd been fidgeting with and opening it.

There, on the front page, was Lester's murdered daughter sprawled on an autopsy table. The mortal wound was the gash on her neck, but that seemed pale in comparison to how she'd been mutilated after death.

Diana Fenech's eyelids had been cut off, leaving behind ragged bits of skin and lifeless eyes which never closed. Eyes that stared into your soul and pleaded for justice. For retribution.

Carolina had never seen Diana like that, but now, she'd never be able to unsee it. And Lester's obsession made sense.

She flipped to the next photo. It was Diana naked, and on her knees, eyes cast skyward. Lester had compared the pose to genuflecting, but that was much too clean. To her, this had no resemblance to a religious act of contrition. It looked sexual, as if the dead girl were being forced into submission.

She opened the other files: Darlene Mason and Rhonda Seese. Both featured the same garish wounds as Diana. Finally, she opened the newest and thinnest file: Jennifer Millstrom.

Her photos were printed on copy paper and of poor quality. Although her body was much further gone than the others, and even though her eyes were missing entirely, when you put them all side by side, it was impossible to ignore the similarities.

Carolina gave the notes a speed read. Ages were similar. All were college students. All were brunettes. All had been killed by having their throats cut. All had trauma to their eyes.

The main difference, aside from the posing or lack thereof, was that Jenny Millstrom was clothed, while the others were all found nude. However, the first three victims showed no sign of sexual assault, leading to the assumption that the killer was impotent.

Carolina was so caught up in reviewing the case files that she didn't know her mother had entered the room until she heard the Bea emit a light squeak, like a mouse that had just fallen prey to an aggressive tomcat. She scrambled to hide the photos, but the damage was done.

Bea's face had gone the color of ash. After taking a moment to regroup, she finally spoke. "Get that filth out of my house!"

Carolina jumped to her feet, shoving the papers together in a haphazard pile. "I'm sorry. I—"

"I don't want excuses!"

Carolina was already out of her seat. Despite her differences with her mother, she cursed herself for being so careless and letting Bea see those crime scene photos. No one should be forced to live with that implanted in their psyche.

"What are you even doing with those?" Bea asked.

"Lester asked for my help."

Bea closed her eyes, tilting her head back. "That man... He's like a dog that has lost its bone but refuses to stop looking for it, although it's long gone." She opened her eyes and stared at Carolina. "What are you thinking, encouraging that nonsense?"

"I don't know if it's nonsense. Not yet." She held the files close to her chest, feeling too much like the child in the relationship for her liking. "There are enough similarities that it would be foolish to write them off without investigating."

Bea bit her lips, turning the surrounding tissue white. Carolina hadn't seen her this upset since her rebellious teenage years. "Let the dead rest," she said. "You and Lester both."

With that, Carolina was out the door.

CHAPTER ELEVEN

Jolo's lone market was surprisingly busy for almost 9 p.m. Carolina waited in line behind four shoppers until she reached the cashier. Her name tag read Candy, and she was barely tall enough to see over the counter. When she realized Carolina wasn't there to buy Doritos or Red Bull or generic toilet paper, she turned her bored eyes up to look at her face.

"Cigs or snuff?" she asked.

What kind of woman chews snuff? "Neither." Carolina set the badge on the Formica, tapping it for effect. "Did you know Jenny Millstrom?"

Candy snarled, revealing several missing teeth. "Bitch hasn't shown up for any of her shifts since last Tuesday. That's why I'm working evenings when I'm supposed to be day shift only. No calls, no nothing."

That fit the timeline they'd put together. "She has a good enough excuse."

"Oh yeah? What's that?"

Carolina took a quick scan of her surroundings to ensure no one was within earshot. All clear. "She's dead."

Candy's right eye grew wide, but her left was lazy and remained half-closed. "No shit?"

"None whatsoever," Carolina said. "Are you the manager?"

Candy nodded. "For the last three years."

"Is there someone else that can run the register while we talk?"

Another nod. "Wait here."

She did and, after a moment, a man in his thirties, with a case of dandruff so bad it looked like a snow squall was brewing around his skull, slipped behind the counter. He eyed Carolina, shy but curious. His badge declared him Stu.

"You with the sheriff's office?" he asked.

"That's what it says on the badge." See, she didn't even have to lie.

"I always thought it would be fun to be a cop," Stu said. "Is it?"

"It has its moments."

"Candy told me Jenny was dead," Stu said. "What happened to her?"

Before she could answer, Candy appeared at Carolina's left. "Outside," she said. "I took my break early for you."

She followed the diminutive woman out the automatic doors and into the night, which had turned cool after sunset. Arc sodium floods gave the parking lot a green hue and made Candy look as if she was in the midst of a bad case of the stomach flu.

"So, what do you want from me?" she asked as she lit a cigarette, sucking the first drag in so far it obfuscated her soul.

"I want to know what you can tell anything you can about Jenny."

"Any certain place you want me to start? I mean, I can tell you how she used to mix M&Ms with Sour Patch Kids, all in one mouthful, but I doubt that'll help."

"Try whatever you think is pertinent."

Candy took another puff, exhaling smoke rings that drifted a few feet before dissipating. "She's worked here for about a year. Rarely late. Only called off two or three times until, well, you know."

Nothing helpful so far. "What was her personality like? Outgoing? Timid?"

"She was fine with the customers. Friendly but didn't slow down the line with chit-chat. Professional, you know? Not their best friend." Candy pushed the cigarette toward her. "Want a drag?"

"Thanks, but I don't smoke."

"Don't know what you're missing." The tip flared orange as ash spread down the tube.

Sure I do: Cancer. Emphysema. Heart disease. "What about friends?"

"Not many. Not to badmouth the dead, but she could be uppity. She didn't even go to the Fourth of July family picnic we had last summer, and we roasted a whole hog." There was disdain in her voice, as if passing on pulled pork was akin to blasphemy. "Said she had plans with her boyfriend."

"The boyfriend," Carolina flipped through Lester's notes. "Was that Ted Voley?"

Candy finished off her cigarette and shook her head. She ground out the butt on the bottom of her shoe. "They broke up before then. This was an old dude. Manx something. Builds houses."

Carolina made a note of this. "Her mother didn't mention him."

"I doubt she would," Candy said, lighting another smoke. "Guy's got a wife and a couple kids."

"Really?" Maybe this was worth the drive, after all.

"Yeah. I tried telling Jenny, married dudes are bad news, but she wouldn't hear it. Said he loved her and was going to leave his wife for her." She snorted. "Like they don't all say that, right?"

That was the truth. "She ever have trouble with any of the customers here? Any men come around and pay her more attention than she wanted, maybe?"

"Never said anything to me if they did."

"How about the walking snowglobe in there?"

Candy gave a phlegmy laugh. "Stu? He runs from spiders."

With no further questions in mind, Carolina dismissed her. The cashier took residence under the light and puffed away.

Carolina grabbed her phone, ready to call Lester, only to see there was no signal. Probably just as well as she hoped he was in bed, getting some much overdue rest. Word of Jenny Millstrom's lover could wait until the morning.

CHAPTER TWELVE

IT WAS 4 A.M., AND CAROLINA COULDN'T SLEEP. SHE SAT CROSS-legged on her mattress with the files laid out in front of her. A 40-watt bulb in a bedside lamp was the only illumination, but that was all right. She could see enough to read.

She'd read the case files so many times that she had memorized. Names, places, dates. The investigation was thorough but sterile. It wasn't that Lester had done a bad job. To the contrary, he'd poked his nose into nooks she would never have considered. What was missing, however, was the substance of the victims. They were crude outlines when she needed a painting.

To figure out why they died, she needed to know what made them alike, aside from their approximate age and color of their hair. She needed to find the thread that tied them together, then see if Jenny Millstrom fit the same mold.

There was only one place to start. And it was at the beginning. With the family of the first victim.

Darlene Mason.

The last time Carolina had investigated these killings, she was 15 years old. She hoped she did a better job this time around.

CHAPTER THIRTEEN

Vanessa Wehner loathed league night at Rumsen Lanes, Dupray's bowling alley. Even though close was 2 a.m., afterward, she had to gather together hundreds of beer cans and half-eaten bags of pretzels that people had been too lazy to toss into the oversized garbage bins. Then she had to mop the floors that, by the end of the night, were so sticky that it felt like she was walking on duct tape.

By the time she locked the doors, it was after four, so late that she wondered if going to sleep when she got home was even worth the effort. It was her damn bad luck that she had a 10 a.m. class that same day.

All that annoyance and exhaustion for nine bucks an hour hardly seemed worth it, but working was a necessary evil. While her parents paid her tuition, room and board were on her, and every dollar counted. Besides, every once in a blue moon, a dude would be drunk enough or horny enough, or both, to give her a nice tip as she was shutting the place down and herding them outside.

This wasn't her lucky night, though. No tips. Just aggravation.

The pole lights lit up the parking lot like it was a high-school football field on a Friday night. Her Accord was the only vehicle in the gravel lot, and she made a beeline to it.

Vanessa never thought herself a scaredy-cat, but this was the part of the job she hated most. She was alone out here, at least a quarter-mile from any homes or businesses. And every man who bowled knew she ended the night just like this.

Isolated. Vulnerable.

When she took the job, her father had offered to give her what he called a *purse pistol* to use for protection, but Vanessa was convinced she was as likely to shoot her own foot off as any potential assailant, should trouble arise.

She did, however, keep a small, emergency canister of bear spray in her purse. At least that she was confident she could use as intended and not blast herself in the eyes.

On most nights, she wasn't so paranoid, but the story of the murdered girl was all over the news, and rumors at the college were that she was a student. Her name hadn't released yet, and all day, Vanessa had wondered if she knew her. It was a small school, and the odds were good.

Since when did things like this happen in Dupray? It was supposed to be a safe place. That was pretty much the only thing the county had going for it. It was supposed to be the type of town where you didn't lock your doors, not the kind where you needed to carry a rape whistle.

She sidled up next to her car while digging through her purse for her keys and not finding them. God, she hated the thing. It was like a bottomless pit. She pulled it open as far as the seams would allow, letting the floodlights brighten the inside.

Gum. Phone. Compact. Billfold. Tampons. Change. More gum. Bear spray. A bottle of Motrin. A small, plastic baggie with enough marijuana to make two joints if she was lucky. But no keys.

Damn it.

She kept rummaging, hands at the bottom of the purse, when she heard movement.

Crunching in the gravel.

Footsteps.

Vanessa spun around, pressing herself against her Honda as her eyes scanned the parking lot. Nothing to the left. Nothing straight ahead.

She looked to the right, where the lot met the woods. Where the overhead lights faded to black.

And she saw movement.

She jumped, and a startled *Ah* spilled from her mouth as her purse spilled from her hands. It landed upside down, dumping its contents into the shale.

Double damn it.

Crouching down, she felt for the bear spray while keeping her eyes locked toward the point of the movement. It was still now. Everything was quiet again.

And that was worse.

Because whoever was out there was being careful.

Her hands found the bear spray, and her finger curled around the trigger. Now, she was ready.

"You come any closer, and I'll blind you!" She screamed, trying to sound tough, but fear contaminated her voice and betrayed her.

She heard more noise. Faster now. Running.

And then she saw it. A buck with four measly points bounding across the edge of the lot as it dipped in and out of the light.

"You bastard," she said, laughing at herself. Stupid deer.

As she returned the junk to her purse, finding her keys in the process, Vanessa could feel her heartbeat returning to a normal level.

She unlocked her Accord, tossed her purse onto the passenger seat, and dropped behind the wheel as she pulled the door closed.

Another laugh and a shake of her head. How had she let herself get so spooked by a damn deer?

She started the car, then flicked on the headlights, but ahead of her lay a blurry haze. Like she'd forgotten to put her contacts in.

Then she realized her windshield was fogged. From the inside.

Vanessa leaned forward, dragging her right hand across the glass, wiping clear lines through the moisture. Another few swipes, and the world was clear again.

She eased back into the seat and reached for the shifter when--

Someone grabbed a fistful of her hair.

Her head was pinned to the headrest—tightly, painfully. She tried to jerk herself free but had no success.

This isn't happening.

She reached for her purse, hand digging inside, clawing, desperate.

Gum. Compact. Lipstick. Gum.

Where's the damn bear spray?

Motrin. Pot.

Then she felt cold steel against her throat.

Then she saw her blood spray the interior of the windshield.

Then she felt it running down her neck and chest.

I'm dying, she thought.

And she was right.

CHAPTER FOURTEEN

The Manx homestead was impressive by southern West Virginia standards. Two stories of whitewashed brick, a multi-gabled roof, an immaculate lawn, and shrubbery. Lester thought it felt out of place, though. That it would have looked more appropriate nestled within a New York suburb, somewhere with a history of middle-class prosperity. Here, it was a sore thumb.

Where the driveway met the county road, a CNC cut metal sign read *Manx Commercial and Residential Construction, LLC*. It didn't exactly roll off the tongue, but Lester supposed it got the point across.

He steered the Blazer up the long, curved drive, idling it beside a champagne quartz BMW with a custom license plate: TROFYWIF. That made him smirk. He glanced at Yeti, who sat upright, taking in the view.

"Lifestyles of the rich and the famous, huh, boy?"

The dog looked at him but seemed unimpressed.

After shutting off the engine, Lester headed to the front door, which seemed obnoxious at a height of ten feet. A wrought-iron knocker of a bull with a ring through its nose awaited, and as he used it, he wondered when doorbells went out of style.

A few seconds passed before the door opened. Behind it, a woman with a towel wrapped around her head peeked out.

"Hello?" she asked. Her cadence was husky, a smoker's voice for sure.

"Mrs. Manx?"

She nodded. "SueAnn."

"I'm Sheriff Fenech. Would your husband happen to be home?"

SueAnn Manx opened the door further. When she moved, he noticed she was on the thicker side, and she wore sweatpants that were a size too big. A plain, white t-shirt that stretched to her thighs to cover up the middle-age spread.

"He's at work. They're building a big lodge out on Andalusian Ridge." She pulled the towel off her head, allowing her long, damp hair to spill free and used the fabric to wring out some of the moisture.

"Andalusian," Lester said. "That's a kind of horse, isn't it?"

She shrugged her shoulders, eyes wary. "What do you need to see Warren about?"

He debated how much to say. It wasn't his purpose to ruin a marriage, but he didn't care to lie to a woman who was already on the receiving end of more deception than fair.

"I need to ask him a few questions about someone he might know."

"Who's that?" She ran her fingers through the clumps of hair, separating them. "Maybe I can help you."

He knew she didn't want to help. She was fishing for information. "I doubt that, miss. I appreciate your time this morning and apologize for the bother."

Lester half-turned, hoping to make a clean getaway, but SueAnn wasn't going to allow that.

"I got a right to know," she said.

He supposed she did. "Did you watch the news this morning?"

She nodded.

"Then did you see the story about the body found in Poverty Hollow?"

SueAnn Manx sucked in a mouthful of air that whistled as it passed through a small gap in her front teeth. "What's that got to do with Warren?"

"We have reason to believe he knew her."

"Knew her how?"

"I really can't say," Lester said.

"Was he fucking her?" Hurt and anger intermingled on her face.

"Has he had affairs before?"

She was slow to respond, slow enough that an answer wasn't needed.

"Can you tell me where your husband was this past Thursday and Friday?"

"He stays on the job site Monday through Thursday. Said it saves a small fortune on gas not having to commute."

Lester wasn't a walking map, but he doubted Andalusian Ridge was more than thirty miles from the Manx's home. He wondered how the woman had been able to talk herself into believing such an obvious falsehood.

"How about Friday?"

"Friday was Drake's birthday, and we had cake and ice cream, then watched him open his presents."

"On the days he's been home, has he seemed nervous? On edge? Maybe he even has a shorter fuse than ordinary."

Another pause as she relived the last few weeks of her life. "I suppose he's acted like himself. Whoever that is..."

"Does he treat you well?"

She went straight to examining the house, as if material goods equaled a good spouse. "He does."

"Has he ever hit you or your children? Or acted out in violence in any way?"

That one didn't require thought. "Eighteen years, and he's never so much as raised his voice at one of us. Shit," she said. "After all that time, you think you know someone."

Lester saw no sense in pestering her with more questions. He'd done enough damage already. "All right, then. Thank you. And again, my apologies."

She lingered in the doorway while he left.

MORE THAN A DOZEN men toiled on Andalusian Ridge, where the bones of a lodge were being birthed from the ground up. Lester scanned the group, searching for the white hat, and found it beside a motorhome that was bigger than many houses.

He went to Warren Manx, who was nearly six-and-a-half feet tall and had the build of a linebacker. The man was deep in conversation with an orange-hatted laborer, and Lester could hear his raised voice.

"We need to get this foundation set before the ground freezes. I don't give a fuck what the plant said. Tell 'em we need another ten skid of block by tomorrow, or I'm going to Erkshaw's."

The laborer noticed Lester eavesdropping and tilted his head. Manx turned, his sour expression growing even more tart when he saw the Sheriff.

"If this is about that goddamn water permit bullshit from the DEP, I've already got approval and—"

"It's nothing like that," Lester said. He'd noticed W. Manx embroidered on the man's Carhartt work shirt and didn't bother to inquire as to his identity. "Maybe we can speak in private."

Manx threw a glance at the orange hat, who didn't need to be told to scoot.

"I need to know your whereabouts for Thursday and Friday. Saturday, too, if you're feeling generous."

Manx was in his early fifties, his body roped with a working man's muscle but soft around the middle. His rough skin was the color of old leather, and his eyes were a shade of brown most often associated with mud. Lester didn't know what made him so attractive to a girl barely in her twenties but supposed the answer likely lay in the contents of his wallet.

"Why are you asking?"

"Because I am. And I'm the Sheriff."

Manx pursed his lips and sent a spray of tobacco spit a few inches to the left of Lester's boots. "Not for much longer, the way I hear it."

"You heard correct. But that doesn't have any relevance to the matter at hand. Now, how about you try answering what I asked?"

Manx pulled off his hardhat, revealing a shaved head beaded with sweat. He wiped it away with his palm, and the act drew Lester's attention to two narrow scratches that trailed from the top of his skull to his ear.

"All day Thursday, and Friday until five, I was right here, trying to get these assholes to do what they're paid to do."

"And after that?"

"My boy, Drake, he turned twelve on Friday. When I got home, we had a little party for him."

So far, the stories matched. "And Saturday?"

"My wife took the kids up to Charleston to get Halloween costumes. I went to the Blue Stone and got drunk. That's still legal, right?"

"Last I checked," Lester said. "Did you close the bar down?"

Manx shook his head. "No. Left around supper time. The wife always makes spareribs in the slow cooker on Saturdays. They're my favorite."

Lester considered telling him it might be a long while before Mrs. Manx catered to him again but held back on that.

"I answered your questions. Now tell me why you wanted to know."

"I asked because I was curious about your whereabouts when Jenny Millstrom was murdered."

Some of the color drained from the man's face. "Was she the girl they were talking about on the radio this morning?"

Lester nodded. "Tell me about your relationship with her."

"I knew Jenny from the bar. Bought her drinks now and again. That's all." He was a bad liar, but that didn't necessarily make him a killer.

Lester enjoyed a good back and forth, but this Manx fellow wasn't any fun. He couldn't even come up with a creative fib. Time to move things along.

"The problem with dipping your wick in girls fresh outta high school is that they talk. Miss Millstrom told her coworkers about your affair. Now, how about you start telling me the truth, or I'll give you the rest of the day off and a free ride back to the station, where we can continue this discussion in a less appealing setting?"

Manx moved to an oil tank that was still wrapped in protective plastic. He sat on the edge. "One night, must've been last fall, I had two or three more shots of Jager than I should have, and we got to talking. About casual shit."

His gaze drifted away, remembering. "It was nice to have a break from hearing about Drake failing English class or Cindy's dance routines or my wife's constipation. I liked it. It made me feel normal."

You mean single, Lester thought but didn't say. "But you did more than talk."

Manx only nodded.

"How long did it go on?"

"It never stopped," Manx said. His lips pulled sideways in a lizard-like smile. "Best year of my life."

"How about your wife? She ever catch on?"

"No. She's so wrapped up in her bullshit that I could crawl in bed with two dicks, and she wouldn't notice."

Lester could never understand men who used a mediocre marriage for a reason to screw around. Not when divorces were so easily attained. "When was the last time you saw Miss Millstrom?"

Manx dug into his ear with his pinky finger, then excavated a nail full of wax, which he examined as if checking for flecks of gold. "Wednesday. We had drinks and burgers at the bar. then she came back here and spent the night."

"So, it was actually Thursday when she left you?"

He considered it, longer than it should have taken for such a simple question. Maybe he realized that he'd just admitted to being with the victim on what was possibly the day of her death.

"She gave me a blow job in the morning. Then she fried up some bacon and eggs and had breakfast with me before she left for school. She had a class in the afternoon."

Lester knew a trip to the university was in his future, to find out whether that was true and if Jenny made it to that class, or if her short life had come to an end prior. He looked Manx up and down, trying to get a feel on whether he was capable of killing, but so far, he couldn't decide.

"One more question," Lester said. "For the road."

"What?"

"How did you get those scratches on your noggin?"

Manx's hand went to them, his fingers tracing the minor wounds. He nodded toward the construction going on nearby. "Ain't a day goes by I don't end up with something cut or smashed or scraped up. Hazards of the job."

Lester stared past him at the silver monstrosity that shimmered in the midday sun. "I could take a look through that motorhome of yours. See if Miss Millstrom left anything behind."

Manx stood and emitted another mouthful of spit. "Not without a warrant, you can't."

"We're at that stage now?" Lester shook his head like a teacher scolding an unruly student. "Shame."

"I answered your questions. If you have any more, talk to my attorney."

"We still have those in Dupray?" Lester asked. News to him if there were any.

"Clapper & Sons in Huntington," Manx said. "I'd wager their day rate is more than you make in a month."

Lester shrugged. "That's not saying much." He took a few steps toward his Blazer, then glanced back. "Oh, almost forgot. When you see SueAnn, tell her I enjoyed our chat this morning."

Manx's eyes blazed. "You cocksucker."

Lester wouldn't have been surprised to catch a punch and, from a man Warren Manx's size, it wouldn't be pleasant. It would, however, give him a reason to poke around further, and he wasn't opposed to taking one for the team.

"I'm just doing my job, sir. And trying to get justice for Miss Millstrom. If you cared about her as much as you insinuate, you should appreciate that."

Manx passed on the punch, or a verbal response, stomping in the direction of the construction site.

Before this meeting, Lester had thought of it as nothing more than dotting an "i". Now, he wasn't so sure. He wondered if there was any chance this man knew his Diana. Or any of the earlier victims. It seemed like the remainder of his day would be spent learning more about Warren Manx's past.

CHAPTER FIFTEEN

CAROLINA'S HUFFY BICYCLE GLIDED DOWN THE HILLSIDE, SENDING her hair out behind her like streamers. She'd made a brief stop at home, checking the phone book for the Masons' address, and was almost deterred when she realized it was over eight miles away. But it was May. Nightfall was hours away, and her mother had an evening class. Besides, it wasn't like she had anything better to do with her afternoon.

She was flying by the time she hit the level patch at the bottom of the hill, so fast it was hard to breathe against the wind battering her face. The sweet smell of honeysuckle filled her nose, and a chorus of English sparrows, her ears. It was a perfect day.

Aside from the dead girl, she reminded herself.

Since lunch, she wondered if there was something wrong with her. Why was she so excited about someone dying? She didn't dare speak of it to any of her friends lest they think she was some type of sicko. It was only during the bus ride home that she realized that it wasn't the dying that excited her. It was the why. The how. The who. The thrill of the hunt.

Lester would understand, and she couldn't wait to see him and pester him about it. To share her theories. She didn't have any yet, but even at 15, she had the confidence to believe they would come to her.

As she passed a field lined with a barbed-wire fence, she came to a clearing with houses on each side of the road. They were typical of the area. Big and old and in various states of disrepair. She checked the numbers on mailboxes as she pedaled past.

104. 113. 121. 135.

She was close and felt her heartbeat quicken in anticipation. And then she was there.

147.

Painted with a delicate hand below the number was 'The Mason's' along with a trio of daisies. Carolina wondered if Darlene might have been the artist behind them but knew it would have just as easily been Brittany or their mother. Although, when she thought about it, daisies didn't seem Brittany's style.

Carolina slammed the brakes backward, stopping her progress so fast she lurched forward on her seat. A half-dozen cars littered the long, dirt driveway, which led to a farmhouse with peeling white paint and a freedom blue porch that wrapped around the front and right-hand sides.

Despite the crowding of vehicles, the only life she saw was a boy who looked no older than eight. He sat in the yard and dug dandelions with a plastic spade, dropping each weed into a pail after its exhumation. He looked up from his task and saw her.

His face was dirty but had two clean channels on each cheek where his tears had washed away the filth. He was still crying but stopped, or tried to, when he realized he was being watched.

Carolina raised her right hand and wiggled her fingers. The boy only stared.

She was about to say something when a screen door banged in the distance.

A fencepost of a man in blue jeans and a faded Aerosmith t-shirt launched himself off the porch and dashed to the boy, never taking his eyes off Carolina, who was more than ten yards away on the road. He grabbed the child and slung him half over his shoulder.

"Goddamn nosy kids!" The man shouted in her direction. "Can't you give people some peace?"

Carolina considered riding away as fast as her legs could take her, but she thought that might make things worse. That it would feed into this grieving man's paranoia.

"I'm sorry," she said. "I go to school with Brittany, and I just wanted to tell you I'm sorry."

The man's anger drained, replaced with something worse. Hopelessness.

"She's inside if you want to talk to her," he said. "I reckon she could use a friend."

That she didn't want. She doubted she'd said two words to Brittany Mason in her entire life. "That's okay. I can see you've got company."

The man watched, wary, but the anger didn't return. "Okay. You get yourself home and be careful." His voice broke. "Ain't no place safe anymore."

With that, he turned and trudged back to the house. Carolina didn't wait around, spinning her bike 180 degrees.

The ride home was long. The hill that had been so much fun to descend was anything but when reversed.

It gave her time to think. Think about death and dying. About the people left behind. About whether such people stayed broken for the rest of their lives. And about how to help them.

CHAPTER SIXTEEN

As the van idled, Carolina stared at what used to be Darlene Mason's home. It hadn't been in pristine condition the last time she'd been here, and the passage of time had done it no favors.

The porch, which had been the house's finest feature, was leaning harder than the tower in Pisa and looked apt to tumble over at the first strong breeze. The blue paint, the color of America, was bleached almost gray.

Most of the white paint had weathered away with only slivers of what once had been left behind for memories. Two windows on the upper floor were covered in cardboard and duct tape. And the screen door hung ajar on broken hinges.

The lawn was unmowed, but it was mostly weeds and crabgrass, anyway. If it hadn't been for the early '00s white Ford sedan parked in the driveway, a sticker proudly proclaiming *John Kerry Is An Idiot* on the bumper, she might have thought the property abandoned.

She eased her foot onto the gas and turned into the dirt drive, stopping when she became parallel with the Ford. The odds that any Mason's still lived here were better than not. People in southern

West Virginia tended to stick where they were planted, whether they wanted to or not.

That was even more true when you were poor. While though the state offered no future, it also gave you no resources with which to leave and start anew.

And even if you do, you end up coming home sooner or later, she thought. Just ask me.

Carolina intended to rehearse her icebreaker on the short walk to the front door but had no time as it opened before she halved the distance between her van and the porch.

"If you're selling something, I'm not interested," the man said.

Though he was obscured by the shadow cast from the crooked roof, Carolina could see him well enough to recognize him as the same worried man who'd grabbed the boy off this lawn years earlier. Only now, he was less fencepost and more skeletal. He couldn't weigh a hundred and ten pounds, which looked even less on his lanky frame.

"Mr. Mason?" Carolina asked. "Clifford Mason?"

The man looked Carolina up and down. "Who are you?"

Carolina put on her best fake smile and reassuring voice, which were two of the first skills you learned when you became a cop. "I'm sorry; where are my manners? I'm Carolina McKay. I came to discuss your daughter if you don't mind."

Clifford Mason leaned against the door frame, crossing his scrawny arms and blocking it, or trying to. Behind him, inside the house, Carolina could see a mountain of trash.

"If Brittany owes you money, you've got to find her on your own, and good luck to you. I ain't heard from her in the better part of two months."

Carolina hesitated, trying to decide how to proceed. If he was a stone wall at the mention of his daughter that was still alive, how would he react when confronted about the one who wasn't?

Not that Carolina had a choice in the matter. It was the only reason she was here, after all.

"No, I'm sorry. Not Brittany. I came to talk about Darlene."

The man still held his arms across his chest, but Carolina saw the steely look in his eyes shift to sad recollection.

"What for?" he asked.

She only had a second to decide between the truth and a lie. And she decided on the truth, for once. "I'm working with the sheriff's department. Did you hear about the body that was found yesterday?"

"Saw it in the newspaper."

"We're trying to find out whether her death is related to Darlene's."

The man took a staggering step back. "My God," he said.

"Can we talk?"

Clifford nodded. He glanced inside his home, then back to Carolina. "Is it okay if we sit out here? I'm a little behind on cleaning."

"Of course."

He sat on the porch steps, and Carolina followed his lead, keeping a professional distance.

"You from around here?" he asked.

"I am. I actually went to school with your daughter."

He stared at her. "Hard to believe my Darlene would be your age now. If she hadn't..." his voice trailed off.

Carolina didn't bother to correct him but didn't appreciate that she was assumed to be six years older than her actual age. She made a mental note to visit the spa when this mess was over.

"I didn't know her well. And that's the main reason I'm here. To get a feel for who she was."

"Well," he began. "Growing up, she was a bit of a tomboy. More interested in Hot Wheels than dolls. That suited me just fine."

His eyes drifted toward the poor excuse for a lawn as he continued "Smart as a whip, too. I don't know where she got that from. She was the first person in our family, from both sides, to go to college."

He clasped his boney palms together, perhaps thinking it was that very college that led to her demise.

"What did she want to be?" Carolina asked.

"A teacher. She loved learning. Every weekend she'd come home from college and tell us everything she'd learned that week. Didn't matter if it was about the history of China or something dumb like the Latin names of the finches that eat up the thistle plants every fall. Knowing stuff fascinated her."

The remark about the finches struck Carolina. The only course in which she would have learned that information was Bea's, but her mother had never mentioned knowing Darlene Mason.

"Was she popular?" Carolina asked, moving on.

"She had her share of friends. But she could be shy, too. I think she did better with people one-on-one than in big groups."

"How about boyfriends?"

"No. None of those." Clifford's expression turned stony.

His change in mood seemed odd. She understood that fathers tended to be overprotective, but this seemed like something else.

She had to press on. "You're sure about that?"

He looked, no, glared at her. "I said she didn't."

"I only thought she was such a pretty girl. I figured guys would be fighting over her."

Mason didn't respond to that. She wondered if he was jealous.

"How about your relationship? Were you two close?"

His eyes narrowed, gears turning in his head. "Where'd you go to school with Darlene? High school or college."

"High school," she said.

"What year did you graduate?"

Shit. She tried to do the math in her head but was too slow. Clifford jumped to a standing position so quickly that the wooden floorboards shook.

"I'm sorry, Mr. Mason, I'm just trying to find out what hap—"

"Get off my property!"

Carolina hurried down the steps toward her van. She knew she'd blown it but had to make one last attempt at salvation. When she looked back at Mason, he was back to the crossed-arms pose and breathing so hard his chest heaved.

"Can I just ask you--"

"If you aren't on the road in five seconds, I'm getting my .44, and I won't give you a warning shot."

That time, she kept her mouth closed and obeyed.

CHAPTER SEVENTEEN

Carolina took deep breaths as she sat outside the sheriff's station, still on edge after the incident with Clifford Mason. How had she become so rusty so fast? Why did she still think she could do this job when it was obvious that she was out of her depth? Her people skills were long gone.

The thought of turning the van around and leaving all of this behind gnawed at her. Head west. Someplace where she didn't know anyone. Where no one would try to get her to make a plan or help them banish old demons.

Someplace where she could be a drifter. An anonymous bum. A leech on society. That was all she was good for these days.

Or she could dump the entire bottle of pills into her mouth and wash it down with a Deer Park water chaser. There were days and times, like now, when that option sounded downright delightful. The promise of everlasting nothingness was a siren's song.

Maybe someday. Maybe even soon. But not yet.

She slammed the door to her van and climbed the steps up to the sheriff station, which was unchanged since she'd left town. Almost. The gold badge decal on the door announcing Dupray County

Sheriff's Department—Sheriff Lester Fenech was faded and had begun to peel.

It should be replaced, she thought, then realized that it would be soon enough.

Unlike her station in Baltimore, she didn't need to be buzzed in. The door was unlocked and open to the public.

Stepping inside was like passing through a time warp. From the smells (Pine-sol and generic coffee) to the decor that was unchanged from 20 years prior. The oak furniture, the pictures on the wall, even the carpet looked identical.

She'd spent so much of her childhood here, with Lester, that being back inside the walls overwhelmed her. Between the bad turn at the Mason's and this, she was close to tears when—

"Is that you, Carolina?"

Behind the front desk sat Meredith Mosgrove, the woman who'd been handling the office's paperwork and phones since even before Lester was Sheriff. She sported the same permed hairdo, although it was gray now. Her reading glasses had become bifocals, but most everything else was unchanged.

She smiled at Carolina with the warmth of the sun and was already out of her chair and heading her way. As Meredith wrapped her arms around Carolina, she spoke. "I can't believe how you've grown. But you still look so much like your father."

Carolina wondered if that were true. She'd never known him. Had never even seen a picture. Sometimes she forgot that he was a real man who people had interacted with and had memories about.

"I'm glad to see you're still here," Carolina said, changing the subject.

"Oh, Lester's saddled with me for the long haul. Besides, I don't think any of these men can decipher my filing system. This ship would sink without me at the helm."

Carolina opened her mouth, almost bringing up what Lester told her. That he was done in November but thought better of it. She was already sticking her nose in plenty of places it didn't belong.

"That's the truth." When Elven smiled, his chiseled jaw stuck out, making his face look like it belonged on Mount Rushmore, and Carolina hated herself for realizing how handsome he looked.

"Can I get you a coffee? I can't say it's good, but it's hot, and it'll keep you going all day long." Elven's winning grin was still plastered on his face. "I think Meredith pours shots of espresso in there when we aren't paying attention."

Carolina wanted to hate him, but he was so damned personable. "No, I already had my fill for the day."

"Lester's not in yet, but I'd like a word," he said, motioning for her to follow him down a narrow hallway.

There were four doorways. Through the first, she saw Johnny Moore fingering his phone. He dropped it when they passed by, and on the screen, she could see a card game. He reached for a stack of papers.

"Don't pretend to work on our account, Johnny," Elven said, and they continued on.

Across the hall from Johnny's office was one belonging to Trevor Provost aka Tank, a muscle-bound man in his late forties. She remembered him, somewhat, from her time in Dupray, but he was a new deputy then and still green as midsummer grass. He was on the phone as they passed by and paid them no attention.

At the far end of the hall was Lester's office, but to the right was Elven's. He stepped inside and sat against the desk rather than in the chair behind it.

"Why do I feel like I've been called into the principal's office?"

Elven couldn't keep that cocksure grin off his face. "I don't know. You have something you need to confess?"

She had a sinking feeling he knew but wasn't going to give up without a fight. "That depends on how much you know."

Elven reached to his side and grabbed his mug, following up with a drink. The liquid was sand-colored, matching his hair, and she suspected it was more cream and sugar than actual coffee.

"How about this, then," he said. "What brings you by the Dupray County Sheriff's office today, Miss McKay?"

And then he laughed, a genuine, warm sound that melted more of her frost toward him. She wondered if he was doing it intentionally, trying to win her over. As much as she hated to admit it, it was working.

"I wanted to check with Lester and see if there are any updates."

"Well, Lester's out of the office, chasing the elusive wild goose. I haven't heard from him all day. Have you?"

She wondered how much to tell him but was also aware that cutting up the investigation would only serve to make a further mess of things. "I went to Millstrom's place of employment last night. Spoke with a coworker and found out she was having an affair with a married man, Warren Manx."

He nodded, and she thought there was a spark of appreciation in his eyes.

"I called Lester and told him about it, and he was going to interview the guy," she said.

"I see," Elven said. "My folks are friends of the Manx's. Me, not so much. Warren is known to cut corners at the expense of his clients. Bribe inspectors too. Can't say I'm surprised he added adultery to his resume."

"What about murder?" Carolina asked.

He took a second to consider it. "I imagine any man's capable if he feels his back is against the wall." He took another swallow of coffee. "It's a good lead, Carolina. Not sure if it fits into the *serial killer returned from the grave* narrative you and Lester are pushing, though."

"I'm not pushing anything. Just investigating."

Elven nodded. "Speaking of which, Meredith fielded an interesting call a short while ago. Seems some crazy woman was harassing Clifford Mason at his own home."

Carolina cringed and felt her shoulders droop as she tried to disappear into the wall.

"The worst part is this woman was telling all sorts of fabrications. That she was friends with his daughter. That she was employed by the sheriff's office. You've got to wonder what would possess someone to do that, now, wouldn't you?"

Carolina licked her lips and stared at Elven. "To be fair, I did know his daughter. I went to school with her."

Elven lifted one eyebrow.

"I just lied about which daughter I knew."

The look on his face was worse than anger or judgment. It was disappointment.

"You may think this whole thing is a joke, but this is our town. These are our people, and they trust us. You don't get to come into my county and foul that up."

She nodded. He may be smug, but he was right, even if she didn't want to hear it, especially from him.

"You're getting too involved, Carolina. All this *investigating* you're doing, it's tantamount to tampering."

Carolina stepped into him. She knew she bungled the encounter with Mason, but it was ridiculous to say she was tampering.

"Lester wants me here. I'm consulting, officially and on the record, in case you didn't catch the memo the first time."

"To consult, shouldn't the people you are consulting with be aware of your actions? You don't get to go rogue out there and run roughshod over people who've already endured more than their share of pain."

Elven took a breath, regrouping, and some of the annoyance left his voice. "All I'm saying is, no more solo outings without telling me. I may not be the one that asked you to get involved, but I am willing to work with you. It's a two-way street, though. I'll keep you abreast of anything I find out, and I expect you to do the same."

"What about Lester?" Carolina asked.

Elven shrugged. "You know that saying, 'You can't see the forest for the trees?' That's Lester right now. He'll twist everything to fit his theory. I wouldn't be surprised if he were out there right now looking for a way to pin Diane's murder on Warren Manx."

"You treat him like he's a fool." Carolina was back to not liking the deputy. And she wasn't liking herself much right now because a piece of her, one that she didn't want to acknowledge, realized Elven might be right.

"Listen," Elven said, his voice soft. "Lester's more of a father to me than my own. But I've been around him every day for years now, and this has been a long time coming. He's not capable of handling this case. He's not the man you remember."

He's playing me. He wants me on team Elven, just like everyone else in this shithole town.

But she wasn't going to fall for it. "I think it's best we agree to disagree."

His grin returned. "It's your right to be wrong."

Fucking Elven.

"In the spirit of sharing, I need to run something by you," she said, eager to detour the conversation away from Lester.

"What's that?"

"It goes back to the Mason's."

He sighed, overly dramatic.

"Hear me out. Clifford Mason was fine with me being there and talking about Darlene until I asked about her dating life and boyfriends. Then he lost his shit."

Elven shrugged. "So? Most fathers don't want to envision their pure as snow daughters getting it on in the back of some stoner's shaggin' wagon."

Was that a dig at me? If so, she ignored it. "I feel like there's more to it. Like, maybe he really *loved* his daughter…"

She suspected the reaction would not be good. She was right.

"Christ on a pony, Carolina. You're accusing that man of diddling his dead daughter?"

"Not accusing. But if he did, that would make him a prime suspect. I'd like to check into it. See if it's got legs."

He finished his coffee and set the mug down hard. "And how do you propose to go about that?"

"Well, I'd like to question his other daughter, Brittany. Is she still around Dupray?

Elven nodded. "About five hundred feet away in county lock-up."

That was easier than she'd expected. "Are you okay with me talking to her?"

"If I say no, are you going to listen?"

She paused, and that was all the answer he needed.

"In that case, I'm going with you."

CHAPTER EIGHTEEN

BRITTANY MASON WAS THE POSTER CHILD FOR THE MYRIAD OF ways meth will destroy your life. Oozing sores and scabs covered her face while her lips sunk into her near toothless mouth.

Her jaw constantly shifted side to side as if she were chewing imaginary gum. Her eyes, untamed and confused, darted in every direction as if she were swarmed by invisible flies. Carolina would have presumed her to be in her fifties and thought, with no satisfaction, that she finally looked better than one of her peers.

The conversation hadn't begun well and had gone downhill from there. Brittany's brain was deep-fried, and little of what she said made sense, aside from her repeatedly asking when she would be released from jail.

"I'll tell you what you want to hear if you'll get me out of here. You don't know what this place is like. The women, they're fucked up, man. They'll cut you if you even look at them. And the guards, they don't do nothing to stop it. You gotta get me out of here, man."

"We'll work on that," Carolina said. She could feel Elven's stare and refused to give him the satisfaction of acknowledging it. "But we need to talk about Darlene."

Brittany bounced in her chair. "Darlene was my sister."

"We know."

"She's dead now."

"We know that, too. We're trying to find out more about her, though. Before she was killed."

Brittany's gaze drifted toward the ceiling, where she began enthralled with the fluorescent lights. Carolina was tempted to throw in the towel when Elven spoke.

"What was the relationship like between your father and Darlene?" he asked.

Brittany didn't take her eyes off the lights. "She was daddy's favorite because she did anything he told her to do. Not me, though. I was an... independent thinker!" She broke into a ghoulish smile.

Carolina looked at Elven now that she felt more confident in her theory. "Did your dad ever touch Darlene... In her private place?"

Elven stifled a laugh. "She's not five years old," he whispered.

"Shut up."

"Daddy whooped on us when we were bad. Said the bible told him to do it." She took on a comically low tone. "Spare the rod and spoil the child!" She giggled.

"Other than spankings, though," Carolina said. "Did he ever..." Oh, the hell with it. "Did he ever abuse your sister? Or you?" She added the latter as an afterthought.

"He beat Dar real bad after she got rid of the baby." Her manic glee dissipated, and she looked at the two people across from her. It was the closest she'd come to appearing alert since they arrived. "He said she'd go to Hell for doing that."

"Darlene had an abortion?" Elven asked.

Brittany nodded, bobbing her head over and over and over again When she stopped. she looked dizzy. "We're not supposed to talk about it, though. Daddy said it would shame the family if it got out."

"It's all right," Carolina said. "We won't tell him."

"Do you think Dar's in Hell?" she asked.

Elven leaned forward, now invested in the conversation. "Did Darlene tell you who the father was?"

Brittany's brow furrowed, deep in thought. It took a while but then she spat out, "Harley! The motorcycle!"

"His name was Harley, or he rode a Harley?" Carolina was excited they'd made progress and didn't want to lose momentum."

"I rode a Harley once," Brittany said. "All the way to Cincinnati."

So much for momentum. "Brittany, listen to me, please; then, we can talk about getting you out of here. The father of Darlene's baby, was it your father? If not, what was his name?"

"Ice cream!" Brittany said. "I want ice cream."

"Motherfucker!" Carolina muttered, drawing a scowl from Elven.

"Hey Brittany," Elven said, "Can you—"

"With sprinkles! And hot fudge! Annnnd sprinkles!"

Elven shook his head as he stood. "Remind me why I listened to you," he said to Carolina, then motioned for a guard to retrieve the inmate. When the broad, slow-moving man arrived, Elven whispered, "Make sure she gets some ice cream with dinner."

"Whatever you say, boss." The guard took Brittany's forearm and led her away. All the while, she chanted "Sprinkles!" in an endless loop.

"I'll be damned, Elven. Maybe you're not all bad," Carolina said as they left the cramped visitation room and headed toward the jail's lobby.

"From you, I'll take that as a compliment."

"I don't suppose you know anyone in the county named Harley, do you?" she asked.

"Not that I recollect. But I'll put Meredith on it."

It wasn't much of a lead, but it was something. And after the morning she'd had, Carolina would take any victory, regardless of how small.

CHAPTER NINETEEN

AFTER GETTING HER PERMISSION SLIP SIGNED BY ELVEN, Carolina headed to Phil Driscoll's funeral home, where she let herself inside. When she reached the preparation room, she found the doctor hunched over an old and very dead, woman. His body thrust as he grunted, running out of breath.

She watched for a moment, fascinated. "If you need some privacy, doc, I can wait upstairs."

Driscoll swiveled his head toward her. "Oh, afternoon, Carolina. Didn't know you were stopping by."

He stepped away from the body. "Old Mrs. Halliwell went to see her maker last night. Have to break out the rigor before I can embalm her."

"Want me to come back later?"

He shook his head as he pulled off the blue rubber gloves that covered his hands. "I wasn't planning on cardio today, and I could use the reprieve." He dropped the gloves onto Mrs. Halliwell's corpse. "This is a nice surprise, though. We didn't get to catch up yesterday. How have you been?"

"Better now that I have something to occupy my mind," she said.

87

"Are you here to see the Millstrom girl? I already cleaned her up as much as I could, but—"

"No. I actually had a couple of questions for you."

He took a seat on a round, wheeled stool. "Shoot."

"Now, I'll say upfront that this might violate doctor-patient confidentiality laws, but I hope you'll consider making an exception under the circumstances."

Driscoll's bit his lips, causing them to disappear into his furry face. "Not sure I like the way this is kicking off."

"I wouldn't expect you to."

"Go on. Let's see how this plays out."

"Was Darlene Mason a patient of yours?"

He nodded. "She was, like most everyone in Dupray, including yourself at one time."

She smiled at the memory of Dr. Driscoll giving the five-year-old version of Carolina lime lollipops to reward her for being a brave girl after getting her vaccines.

"To your knowledge, was Darlene pregnant around the time of her death?"

Driscoll exhaled, thinking. "I cannot answer that."

That's a yes. She appreciated Driscoll's willingness to cooperate.

"But if you look at the postmortem, you'll see she was not with child when she was killed," Driscoll said.

"Okay. Then let's say, hypothetically, that a young, unmarried woman wanted to terminate the pregnancy; is that something you'd do?"

He shook his head vehemently. "There are physicians that specialize in such barbarism. I am not one of them."

"Would such physicians need to know the name of the father of the unborn child before performing an abortion?"

"No. There's no law requiring the permission of the father in West Virginia, then or now."

"Shit," she muttered.

Phil rose into a standing position. He crossed toward her. "We're still speaking hypothetically?" he asked.

"Of course."

"All right, then. Let's suppose a young woman would have come to me to verify her pregnancy and inquire about her options. After I shared my opinion, I would have walked her out personally because she would be upset, and I'm an old-fashioned sort of fella. And when she left, I might have seen her get into an AMC Pacer with a young man behind the wheel."

"That's a very specific hypothetical, Doc. You're sure it couldn't have been a Gremlin or Pinto?"

Driscoll grinned. "I'm positive because it was the only time that I ever saw such a vehicle in person."

"I don't suppose you remember anything about the driver?"

He shook his head. "I'm sorry, Carolina. I was more intrigued by that damned ugly car."

"That's okay," she said. "This is more info than I came in with."

He led her toward the stairwell that went to the main floor.

"Can I ask why you never mentioned this to Lester when Mason was killed?" It was a rude question, but one that needed asked.

Driscoll thought a moment before answering. "Back then, I suppose I viewed my ethics as less malleable than I do these days."

"Fair enough." She was halfway through the door when she paused. "You wouldn't happen to still have those lime lollipops, would you?"

He nodded. "Upstairs—I'll give you a few for the road."

CHAPTER TWENTY

Carolina managed to open and slip through the station door without dropping the three large pizzas she'd bought at Hank's, Dupray's lone eatery. Grease had already seeped through the bottom box, slicking her palm, which made the delivery even more precarious.

"Let me," Elven said, coming to her rescue.

But she didn't need rescuing. "I've got it." Carolina continued to an empty, steel desk and dropped the pies onto it.

The smell had brought everyone to attention, and she was pleased to be delivering some good cheer. They all needed it.

"By God," Lester said. "You must've read my mind."

He opened the top box and reached inside, snaring a slice. The others joined in, and within minutes, the first pizza was gone, and the second box was half-way there. She eventually fished out a slice for herself and took a bite. It was as greasy as it looked and tasted damned amazing.

After the first few bites satiated their hunger, Carolina was ready to get back to work. She told the men what she'd learned that day.

About her encounter with Clifford Mason and the subsequent discovery of a pregnancy and abortion.

Johnny and Tank were there, but she shifted her attention between Lester and Elven, trying to get a read on their reactions, and was satisfied when she realized they were impressed.

"Not bad," Elven said as he peeled a slice of pepperoni off his pizza and passed it to Yeti, who gobbled it up, then licked the man's fingers clean.

"You're going to fatten up my dog," Lester said.

"A fat dog's a good dog." Elven slipped Yeti a piece of sausage.

Listening to their banter, feeling this camaraderie, Carolina realized she was something she hadn't been in a long while. Happy.

As soon as she thought that, she felt guilty. Why did it take other people dying to give her a reason to live? But it wasn't that. Not exactly. It was knowing she was still good for something.

"That's a high compliment from you, Elven," Carolina said, chomping down another mouthful of glorious decadence.

"As it should be," he said.

"So, we've got two fair leads." Lester set aside his uneaten crust, ignoring Yeti's pleading gaze. "Your mystery fella," he said to Carolina. "And Warren Manx. I spent the afternoon digging around in Manx's past. He's a Dupray lifer, and he was here during the first killings. Working construction then too, but as one of the grunts and not the big boss."

"He didn't drive an AMC Pacer, did he?" Carolina asked.

"That I don't know. I'll check on it in the morning."

She'd been joking but didn't correct him. It was clear Lester had welded the past and present crimes together, not to be separated. She was about to say something when the office phone rang.

Meredith was gone for the day, and Tank grabbed it. "Dupray County Sheriff's Department." He listened.

As Carolina chewed on her crust, she saw Tank's eyes grow wide. Now what?

91

"Yes, we'll have someone there as soon as possible," he put his hand over the receiver, eyes focused on Lester.

"What is it?" the sheriff asked.

"There's been a shooting at nine eighteen Oisan Lane," Tank said.

Lester set his pizza aside. "That's the Manx's address."

THE SUN HAD SET by the time they arrived. Carolina rode shotgun with Lester at the wheel and Yeti occupying the space between them. Elven followed in his Wrangler.

Lester was first out of a vehicle, seeming sprier than she'd seen him since her return to town. It was amazing the way the job could transform a person. He didn't draw his gun but kept his hand on the grip. Ready if he needed it.

The door to Warren Manx's home hung ajar, light spilling through the passage and painting an irregular rectangle on the hardscape. A pool of blood had turned the concrete black. From it emerged large footprints, those made by a man's work boot.

"Warren? SueAnn? This is Sheriff Fenech," Lester called out.

No response came.

Carolina and Elven followed him into the house. The style of the decor was that of new money and consisted of oversized leather furniture and gaudy decorations. A crystal chandelier hung from the vaulted ceiling.

"If anyone is armed. you'd be best served to come out now," Lester said.

Elven had his pistol drawn, finger on the trigger guard, and ready to fire if needed. Carolina decided to follow suit and pulled her own weapon from its holster.

The bloody footprints led them through the foyer and into the kitchen. That's where they discovered Warren Manx propped against a row of shaker cabinets. He held a blood-soaked tea towel against his abdomen, and a growing pool of the red stuff was spreading around him.

When he became aware of their presence, he looked up with woozy eyes. "I got shot," he said.

"I see," Lester said. "Your wife do that?"

Manx nodded.

"Where is she now?"

Manx paused to think about it. He opened his mouth to answer, but a gunshot beat him to the punch.

Splinters of wood exploded as one of the upper cabinets caught the bullet. Carolina ducked as they rained down on her.

She felt her heartbeat quicken and her pulse thud. She slipped behind the kitchen island (a monstrosity of granite) for cover.

Elven was at her side. Lester and Manx were out of sight.

"Put the rifle down, SueAnn," she heard Lester say.

"That bastard ruined my life!" SueAnn Manx shrieked. Another shot boomed, and Carolina heard glass break.

She slid to the end of the island, peeking around it. Lester still crouched beside Manx, neither the worse for the wear. If SueAnn Manx was trying to kill them, she was doing a piss-poor job of it.

But Carolina knew how fast things could turn. She crept around the corner of the island, scanning the area from where she thought the shots came.

The reflection of SueAnn Manx was visible in a gold-framed mirror. The woman, in her nightgown, held a long-barreled hunting rifle that she aimed into the kitchen.

"Mrs. Manx," Elven said. "I'm going to step out, and we'll have a calm discussion, all right?"

The woman didn't look capable of doing anything calmly. "Let me kill that son of a bitch!"

She aimed, or tried, and shot again. This one took out a ceramic decoration that read *Live, Laugh, Love.*

Carolina turned toward the woman, still safe behind the island. She had a shot, though. But she reminded herself that she wasn't a cop, not in Dupray, not anywhere. She sought out Elven, trying to lock eyes with him to see what to do when—

"Mommy?" A girl's voice called. "Mommy, why are they setting off fireworks?"

"I told you to stay in your room!" SueAnn shouted.

Having a child on the scene changed everything. It made every stake higher and more dangerous. The room for error disappeared.

"Where's daddy?" the girl asked.

Carolina wasn't taking any more chances. She stood, exposing herself, pistol trained on SueAnn Manx. Beyond the woman, she saw a girl clad in pink pajamas and holding a pristine, white stuffed tiger.

"Put down the gun," Carolina ordered.

"Carolina!" she heard Elven say.

Then he was standing too. Both had their guns on SueAnn, but they looked at each other.

"Holster your weapon," Elven told her. "You shouldn't even be here right now."

But she wasn't going to risk another child getting injured in her presence. Once was enough. Her finger was on the trigger, squeezing.

Sue-Ann went down, the rifle clattering to the floor. The daughter screamed and ran to her, and Elven rushed to them. All the while, Carolina stared at her pistol, trying to figure out when she'd fired.

Then she heard Lester's voice in her ear. "It's all right, hon." He put his left hand on her shoulder. She turned and saw wisps of smoking drifting from the barrel of his .357. "I took care of it for you," he said.

CHAPTER TWENTY-ONE

Lester's shot was incapacitating but non-lethal. They waited around for the ambulances to arrive: one for the wife and one for the husband. The two kept sniping at each other as they were put on the stretchers and loaded up.

Happily ever after? Yeah, right.

Once back at Bea's, Carolina retreated to her van, closed the door, and dropped onto the bed. Her hands trembled as she grabbed her pills. She wasn't sure if that was because she was overdue or her nerves. Either way, two oxys would solve the problem. She dry swallowed them.

The image of the Manx's daughter, clutching that stupid stuffed animal, came back every time her eyes closed. It transported her to the standoff that had ended her career.

That shooting that made her question whether life was worth living. She'd have traded her entire future for the chance to go back and change that day.

At least this night had ended better.

But she wanted - needed - to sleep. To forget about everything.

She grabbed another pill and popped it in her mouth. Only

instead of swallowing it, she bit down, her taste buds rebelling against the bitter invasion. She chewed it to a gummy paste, then let it dissolve.

That worked. She felt the stress of the day floating away. The numb nothingness washing over her.

Bliss.

Her phone buzzed. She fumbled for it, but her fingers wouldn't cooperate, and it fell to the floor. Somehow, by dumb luck, randomly swiping at the screen answered the call.

A man's voice wafted from the speakers. She thought she heard her name. And she wanted to answer him, but it was easier to fall on her side and let the opioids carry her away.

CHAPTER TWENTY-TWO

Lester stared at his phone. The screen was illuminated, the timer ticking upwards. Why didn't Carolina say anything? Or maybe she did, and he couldn't hear her. Cell reception was shitty all over the county. He just hoped she'd be there soon.

"Carolina?" he said again. "Did you hear me?"

No response.

He shut off the phone and rubbed the bridge of his nose, trying to make the headache disappear. Everything was too much to handle. He needed a break, but he knew there was no time. Not until they solved this case. Only then would he be able to rest.

He pocketed his phone and turned back to the crime scene. He let out his breath slowly and stepped into the alley, which was poorly illuminated by the streetlights in the distance.

This time, the body was fresh. It had been less than a full day since the girl had been murdered. And he needed to find one thing. Evidence that this was the same monster who murdered his own daughter.

Because Elven could say whatever he wanted about the decade long layoff. About coincidences. But he knew better. This was the same animal, back in Dupray and hunting again. This time, Lester promised himself he'd catch him or die trying.

As he approached, he looked up at Elven's face, catching his eyes. Elven gave him a nod, then returned his gaze to Lauren Jacobs, the woman who'd found the body. In the midst of walking her dog, a cocker spaniel, the animal went crazy and led her into the alleyway.

This murdered girl was found between Shawley's Fine Paper Company, a shuttered mill, and Robison's Plastics, also long closed. And she was posed.

Her lifeless body knelt behind a stack of hardwood pallets and beside a half-dozen rust-slicked metal drums. Placed there, amongst the detritus, like her body was nothing more than trash.

A few people had gathered at the end of the alley, behind hastily strung police tape. Johnny occupied himself with holding them at bay and ignoring their questions. Lester wished he had someone who could inspire more confidence, but you have to make do with what you've got.

Not far away from Elven and Lauren Jacobs, who was animated and crying, Phil Driscoll leaned against the exterior wall of Robison's warehouse and stared at the body.

"What do you say, Doc?" Lester asked.

"Nothing good." Driscoll took a step toward the dead girl. "What you see is what you get. And I doubt any of it'll come as a surprise to you."

Her chestnut hair was pulled into a loose ponytail. Her frame was small but fit. He thought she looked to be about 5'2", under 110 pounds soaking wet. Her skin wasn't wet and rotting like Jenny's, but it had lost its vitality and gone a pale gray, the color of wood left to weather.

The girl's throat has been sliced open, her lifeblood turning her sweatshirt, once sun yellow, crimson. And then there were her eyes.

With the eyelids cut away, they stared in perpetual terror. A small amount of blood ringed the sockets like ghastly eyeshadow. Some had trickled down her face like tears.

Lester sighed; he felt defeated and at a loss. This was history repeating itself, and he had a sickening worry it could end the same way. With more death and a killer on the loose. Uncaught. Unpunished. Justice left unserved.

He couldn't let these girls down twice. He couldn't fail Diana again. He closed his eyes to block it all out.

"You all right, Lester?" Driscoll asked.

Lester took a deep breath. Another. Then he looked at the doc. "I don't know how I'm supposed to answer that."

He motioned to Elven, who was wrapping things up with the distraught woman. Her dog panted at her side, eager to recommence its walk. He beckoned Elven, and the deputy sent her on her way and came to them.

"She gonna be okay," Lester asked.

"Shaken up, to say the least. But yeah."

"That's good."

"Have Johnny get the names and addresses of all those lookie-loos."

"I already took care of that," Elven said, pulling a small notepad from his pocket.

The boy was a fine cop and, as much as Lester resented being pushed out of the job, he felt the county would be in good hands with Elven.

"Any ID on the body?" Elven asked.

Driscoll spoke up. "I know this one. Vanessa Wehner. Known her since she was in her mother's womb." He paused, swallowing his emotions. "Shit, I can't imagine how her folks are gonna take this."

When he said the last part, he seemed to realize that one of the men beside him had lived through that hell. He quickly went on, trying to let facts get in the way of feelings.

"I'd surrender my medical license if this wasn't done by the same man who killed Jenny Millstrom. The throat wound is almost identical. And the eyelids... well, no way to write this off as damage caused by Mother Nature."

He crouched and used a gloved finger to push up the dead girl's eyebrow, revealing a jagged cut where the thin fold of skin which should have been covering her eye was removed. "Killer used a more delicate blade here than on the neck. If you look closely, you can see several small starts and stops."

"Meaning what?" Elven asked.

"My professional opinion, which means all of jack and shit? I'd say they were cut off with scissors. The mini versions women use for sewing tasks, perhaps. Just like the first trio of girls."

Elven chewed his lip for a moment, eyes on the body, then looked to the sheriff. "Seems like you were right, Lester. We either got a copycat or that old boy decided it was time for a second go around. Either way, Dupray's past has come back to haunt us."

The admission that Lester was right didn't provide him with any satisfaction. If anything, it was worse. Because two more girls were dead, and it was his fault for not catching the killer the first time around. His head pounded, and he rubbed the bridge of his nose as he tried to fight off the memories.

"Lester, didn't you hear me? I said you were right," Elven called out to him.

"I heard you, Elven. But I didn't need your approval. I always knew I was right."

CHAPTER TWENTY-THREE

BANG!

The gunshot woke Carolina from a deep sleep. Her instincts had her off the bed before she even knew what was happening. She hit the van floor hard, pain flaring in her shoulder, but she barely gave it a thought.

Who the hell was shooting at her?

She grabbed for her gun as another *Bang* rattled the van.

Her eyes scanned the interior as she tried to determine what direction the gunfire was coming from, but there were no bullet holes.

She listened. Focused. And heard a lawnmower.

Son of a bitch.

She set the gun aside and opened the van door. Her eyes quickly found a middle-aged man on a riding tractor, mowing Bea's spacious lawn. He circled, mower deck gliding across the shale drive, and a pebble soared through the air and bounced off the side of her ride. *Bang.*

Carolina dragged her fingers across the point of impact, feeling the resulting dent. The missing nick of paint. Between being awoken in such a startling manner and the damage to her van, she was ready to rip the guy a new asshole when—

"Well, look who decided to join the land of the living!" Bea called out.

Carolina spotted her mother on her knees, pulling weeds that had the audacity to take up residence with her marigolds and poppies. Bea waved, her hands clad in gloves which had once been white but now looked as if they were dipped in chocolate.

Carolina tucked her gun into her waistband at the small of her back, like some sort of outlaw. Then she gave her mother a return wave, and it was on.

Bea sauntered across the lawn, with a smile much too cheery for the early hour plastered to her face. She didn't even flinch when she saw Carolina's condition. Body unwashed. Hair a crow's nest. Same clothes as the day prior.

"Good morning; good morning!" Bea said in a singsong voice.

"Why are you so… you?" Carolina asked as she tried to smooth her wrinkled shirt.

"Who else would I be?"

"Never mind." Carolina moved onto her pants, which looked and felt screwed on. She pulled at the waistband, straightening them. Then she looked to the man on the tractor. "Is that your lawn boy?"

Bea followed her gaze. The landscaper saw them staring and tipped his head. Bea waved, but Carolina did not. "He's new," Bea said. "I think the last one was Guatemalan."

"That's a little racist."

"Not if it's true."

The man mowing closed in on them. He looked around forty, of average height and build, and his short sleeves revealed a smattering of tattoos: all black ink and little talent. Carolina thought they looked like prison specials.

He cut the mower when he reached them. "Morning, ma'am," he said to Bea, then turned his gaze to Carolina. "Miss."

His eyes were so pale blue as to be almost colorless and looked even lighter against his skin, which, from working outside in the sun for months on end, had turned a shade that made Carolina think of an Irish Setter. A hat declaring Dupray Lawn Care covered his shaved head.

Carolina was still sore over the damage to her van and didn't bother with a verbal response, but she nodded so as not to seem too rude.

"I'll be done mowing in about half an hour," he said. "Want me to trim those lilac bushes back, too, before I head out?"

"If you don't mind," Bea said.

"Not at all." He took an extra-long look at Carolina and gave his winningest smile. "It was real nice to meet you."

He turned the mower back on, engine roaring, shrapnel flying, as he rode off.

Bea gave Carolina a Cheshire-cat grin as he disappeared into the back yard.

"What?"

"He seemed rather smitten with you."

Carolina rubbed her temple. Now that the excitement was over, she could focus on her pain, which was amplified as she hadn't taken any pills since the previous evening. "Please," she said. "He's probably a skinhead."

"Now who's being judgmental?" Bea asked.

As much as her mother's matchmaking annoyed her, Carolina was relieved that Bea wasn't still angry about her carelessness over the victims' photos. Still, she felt the need to do some fence-mending. "How about I brush my teeth, and then we take another stab at breakfast?"

Bea's eyes lit up like a toddler on Christmas morning. "That sounds lovely!"

Her shrill excitement reverberated through Carolina's head. She was ready to tell Bea to get started on the eggs when Elven's white Jeep Wrangler, a Dupray County Sheriff's Department decal residing on the driver's door, sped into the driveway.

He stopped alongside the women and rolled his window down without shutting off the engine.

"Morning, Beatrice," Elven said.

"Good morning to you, Elven Hallie. Did you come to arrest me?"

"Now, why would I do that?"

"For stealing that blue ribbon from your momma at the 4th of July berry-cobbler baking competition, of course."

Elven couldn't stave off a chuckle. "She's still vexed over that. One of these years, she's gonna top you."

"I wouldn't hold your breath," Bea said, full of self-satisfaction. "Carolina and I were just about to have breakfast. Would you care to join us?"

"On any other day, I'd be downright delighted, but I'm actually here regarding some department matters."

Bea lost her smile. "You're gonna steal my daughter away from me, aren't you?"

"I'm afraid I am. I apologize."

Bea sighed. "Men always do." She turned away from him, her face now aligned with Carolina's, and mouthed, *He's single*. With that, she was off.

Carolina glanced at Elven, who wore an amused smirk. "Did she just tell you I'm single?"

"Don't start. It's too early. What do you want?"

"How about we kick things off with a good reason as to why you don't answer your phone."

Carolina considered it. She had vague memories of her phone ringing the night prior but hadn't seen it since. "Battery died, and I forgot to charge it."

Elven looked past her to her van. He pointed to the solar panels on the roof. "Got yourself quite the little set-up there."

"Ah, condescension. My favorite way to start the day."

"I was going to tell you that there's a second body. But if you have better things to do, maybe give that rig a tune-up or—"

"Give me a minute to change." She couldn't care less about the clothes. But she needed a few pills to be able to focus.

"You're not getting judged in the evening-gown competition. Get in," he said. "Lester's been at the station all night long. I need you to help reel him in."

"At least let me get my phone."

"It's dead, remember?" Elven asked, examining her.

If she made another attempt to stall, he'd know something was up. Maybe he did already, but she wasn't going to give him any more ammo. "Fine."

CHAPTER TWENTY-FOUR

"There's something I need to know," Elven started.

She studied his face and tried to push through the fog.

"What?" she asked.

"You've been back in town what, two-and-a-half days?"

"About that."

"How many men has Beatrice tried to set you up with?"

"Jesus," she huffed.

"I'm only curious whether I'm somewhere near the top of the list or—"

"Seeing as how she just tried to trade me to the gardener for a few bags of mulch, I wouldn't be too flattered."

He paused, considering that. "Seems drastically undervalued if you ask me."

Was that a come-on? She felt her cheeks heat up. Time to change the topic. "When was the body found?

"Last night—back alley near the industrial park."

"Why didn't anyone come to get me, then?"

"Lester said he tried calling you. Got no answer. And the sheriff's department is not a chauffeur service."

"Isn't that what you're doing right now?"

Elven nodded. "Touché."

"Same M.O.?" she asked.

"Same as Jenny Millstrom. And posed so darn close to the previous victims that it could be a mirror image."

"You mean?"

Elven blew through a stop sign as he rolled into town. No worries, though. They were the only vehicle on the road. "Yep. This time, it can't be denied."

"Fuck..." No wonder Lester was so worked up. Everyone had been telling him he was being paranoid, and now, he'd been proven right. His daughter's murderer was out there and killing again. Trying to calm him now would require a Herculean effort.

CHAPTER TWENTY-FIVE

Carolina had turned watching Darlene Mason's grave into a habit for nearly a week. She'd read that killers sometimes felt guilty after the fact and went to their victim's gravesites. Even though she doubted that, the guilt part, she thought it was a worthwhile way to pass the time. Besides, a family of tufted titmice had taken residence in an old woodpecker hole, and she enjoyed observing them.

Thus far, she'd seen nothing more than birds and Darlene's family members—mostly the mother, who sat on the still fresh earth and sobbed. Sometimes Carolina felt ashamed for spying on her grief. It was a little like peeking at someone going to the bathroom. A private moment not meant for onlookers.

Today, the grave was empty, save for a withered bouquet of daffodils. She was beginning to think the book was full of crap.

Dusk was fast approaching, and she was ready to call it a day when a cherry-red hatchback pulled into the cemetery. It looked odd, almost unreal. Like a car she'd see in a science-fiction movie set decades in the future.

It eased to a halt at the north-west corner, too far away for Carolina to see anything but a shape behind the wheel in the diminishing light of day. As the engine died, Carolina waited and watched and held her breath.

But whoever was in the car took too long. She sucked in a mouthful of wind, then exhaled disappointment.

Then the driver's door opened.

A leg emerged, dropping to the ground, followed by its mate. But the man - she assumed it was a man because he wore black dress shoes - was hidden by the door.

Come on, already.

The man took a half step away, enough space to close the door. Then he did.

He was anonymous at this distance. No more than ebony slacks and a peacock-blue Polo shirt. The man was unusually tall and stood with a strange, stooped over posture, back hunched, chin jutting forward like a boxer on his last legs and begging for the knockout punch that would send him to the canvas for a ten count.

The man looked to his left, then his right, eyes scanning the cemetery. Carolina pressed herself against the trunk of the silver maple, confident that she couldn't be seen but taking no chances. He repeated his slow observance, then seemed satisfied and began to move.

His path brought him closer to Darlene's grave, and Carolina pushed herself to her feet. The sun was setting behind him, and she couldn't make out his features.

He stopped five graves before Darlene's. That plot was old, featuring a weathered tombstone topped with a Celtic cross. He lingered there, and her heartbeat slowed. False alarm.

Damn it.

But he was on the move again. Coming nearer.

One grave away.

And then he was standing atop the still grassless dirt. He stood, motionless. Eyes cast down as if he could see through the ground and find the dead girl planted under his feet like a tulip bulb, too deep to ever bloom.

But he was still featureless. And unless she could identify him, all of this was for nothing.

Carolina risked a step away from the tree. Then another. Every move was a dance as she made certain not to drop her foot on anything that could make noise.

She circled, taking momentary residence behind a mausoleum with O'Herlihy emblazoned above the door. She could almost make out the man from there. His hair was light brown or dark blonde, she couldn't be certain which because it was cropped close to his head.

She needed to get closer, though, if she would have a chance at painting him in anything other than broad strokes, and she left the safety of the tomb and made it five feet before--

He looked up. His eyes locked on her.

Carolina felt wild excitement, mixed with fear, rip through her body. She saw his face, or a glimpse of it, anyway. He looked young-ish, a man just out of college, maybe. His brow was heavy, casting deep shadows over his eyes. His jaw was long, giving him an almost horse-ish look. And he was angry.

"What're you doing, you little bitch?" He yelled in a thick, guttural voice.

He didn't wait for an answer, instead loping after her with an awkward gait.

She spun in midair and dashed toward her bike, ignoring the man's voice as he called after her.

"You spying on me?"

Carolina grabbed the bicycle from its lazy resting spot against the tree, hopped aboard, and pedaled.

CAROLINA WAS out of breath and a sweaty mess by the time she made it to the sheriff's station, but she was so full of adrenaline and accomplishment that she vaulted up the steps and into the building.

She couldn't wait to tell Lester what she'd seen. What piece of evidence, no matter how scant, she'd obtained all on her own.

When she pushed through the front door, she expected Meredith to be in her usual spot behind the front desk, but she was nowhere to be seen. No problem, though, as Carolina knew exactly where she was going.

She made it a third of the way down the hall when she heard the strangest noise that she'd experienced in her 15 years: a man crying.

She'd never heard a man cry before, and the sound made the fine hair on her forearm raise to attention. It wasn't the soft, almost delicate sound she herself made when upset. Nor the slightly coarser noise that came from her mother after yet another heartbreak.

This was deep, as if the sound began at the man's feet and picked up steam as it rolled up his legs, along his belly, then exploded out of his mouth. It was the worst thing she'd ever heard in her life.

A door opened, and the sobbing grew louder. Johnny the janitor stepped from the room that she knew as Lester's office. His eyes were bloodshot, and snot leaked from his nose, but he was quiet. The wretched bawling went on from an unseen source inside.

"Carolina!" Johnny said. "You shouldn't be here now."

"Why? What's wrong?"

When she made it to him, he reached out, his hand catching her arm. "Just go home. Go home and find your mother."

"No!" Carolina jerked her arm free and slipped past him. She felt a light breeze as he went in for round two, but she was out of his reach.

She slipped through the doorway, ignoring Johnny's commands to stop, and passed into Lester's office. Then all the excitement and self-satisfaction she'd worked up vanished.

Lester was huddled in the corner, knees drawn to his chest as he rocked back and forth. His face was red as a beet, and his mouth hung agape as those God-awful sounds escaped.

Meredith crouched beside him, her hands on his shoulders in a half-embrace. On the other side, his dog, Ghost, laid with his head on his oversized paws. If a dog could join in on the grieving, Ghost was.

She watched them, dumbstruck, for what felt like days. Then she managed to get out words.

"What happened?" Her voice had risen, making her sound like the 10-year-old version of herself. It was only when she heard herself that she realized how scared she was.

Both adults on the floor snapped their attention to her. She'd expected Lester to react first, to tell her everything was okay and not to be worried, to be her strength, but he only covered his face with his hands and hid.

Meredith scrambled to her feet, smoothing her skirt, which had ridden up and exposed the top of her thigh-high hose. She put an arm around Carolina's shoulders and deftly steered her away. "Come with me, hon," she said, and in an instant had her out of the office. She shut the door behind her, trapping Lester in the room with his tears and his dog.

"What's going on?" Carolina repeated. "What's wrong with Lester?"

Meredith led her all the way to the front desk before speaking. Carolina realized then that Meredith had been crying, too, but she managed to pull herself together and be the responsible one. She was quick and to the point. "I hate to be the one to tell you this, but Diana's been murdered."

Carolina knew she'd misheard the woman. Diana couldn't be dead. Nothing that terrible could be true.

For the first, but not the last time, she was shown how unfair life was.

CHAPTER TWENTY-SIX

"Last time, the killer worked quickly," Lester said, his voice firm, unwavering.

Carolina was glad to hear him speak with such confidence. She hadn't known what awaited when she entered the station and half-expected to find him crying or raving. She wouldn't have been able to handle either, especially with the effects of going without her pain medication hitting her like a semi-truck.

"All three girls were murdered within a span of twelve days. Once our boy got a taste of it, it was like he couldn't stop."

"Except for the nineteen-year hiatus," Elven said. He straddled a backward chair just a few feet from Carolina. She shot him a peeved glance, but he ignored her.

Lester did the same. "We've got two dead already. The doc estimates victim one was killed on or about September fourteenth. And we know our girl last night was fresh; so, that would put her demise on the twentieth. If the past holds true, we likely have less than a week before we get hit with another body—unless we catch whoever's doing it first."

He pointed to Elven. "Elven has a thought he wants to share. Go ahead," Lester said to his deputy, offering him the spot at the front of the office.

Elven stood, freeing himself of the chair, and sidled up beside Lester. "The condition of the bodies indicates that the original killer has decided to come out of retirement. Now, I'm no profiler, but I do watch a lot of TV."

Carolina couldn't hold back a smirk. He was winning her over again.

"The question that comes to my mind is, why now?" Elven said. "What's he been doing for the last two decades? I think he's been missing in action, probably not by choice, and now he's home to roost."

"You want us looking at ex-cons?" Carolina asked.

"I knew there was a reason I kept you around," he said with a smile. "Carolina hit the nail on the head. I want to check out convicts with a history of violence. Particularly ones who have been released back into the community within the last six to twelve months."

"Shouldn't we call the FBI about this? Get them to help out." Johnny checked the room and discovered his opinion wasn't valued. "I just mean, I know we're good at helping people, but a serial killer seems a bit above our pay grade, don't it?"

Carolina rolled her eyes. Johnny meant well, and this was certainly out of his depth, but she was confident the rest of them could handle it, if they could work together.

"The last thing we want is a federal agency bulldozing through Dupray," Carolina said.

Elven grabbed his coffee mug and took a drink. "I'll be the first to admit my surprise over what I'm about to say, but Carolina and I are on the same page. We're gonna find the killer, and we're doing it in house."

Carolina threw him a raised eyebrow.

My turn to talk?

Elven nodded.

"I know we like to brag about our small-town values, but

Dupray's a hard place to live, and that can bring out the worst in people. We're going to be dealing with a lot of dangerous men, even if they aren't the killer we're looking for," Carolina said.

"That's right. These aren't your Saturday-night drunk drivers. We're looking for fellows who've been locked away for assault, manslaughter, rape, murder. That's all on the table," Elven said.

"I'm going to the probation department to see what they can tell us, and Meredith's going to do her thing. I expect we'll have our share of possibilities when both of those things are done." Elven clapped his hands as if he were in a huddle. Ever the captain.

Lester turned toward his office, probably to grab his hat, but Carolina caught up with him. When Elven had said *rape,* a memory clicked.

"Heard you pulled an all-nighter," she said.

He had enough baggage under his eyes for a six-month cruise. "Couldn't sleep," he said.

"I had the opposite problem. Sorry I missed your call last night. I was dead to the world." Not the best choice of words, she realized after she said it.

"Don't trouble yourself over it."

"You have any place you want to start on all this?" she asked.

"North to south?" he suggested.

She didn't respond right away, and his eyes grew more alert. Studying. "You know something, don't you?"

"Just a hunch."

"Spill it."

"When I was in school, the girls used to talk about an older guy who hung around the kids and went to all the parties. Paid more attention to the cheerleaders on Friday nights than the football games. Today, they'd call him a creeper, I suppose. But back then, he had a nickname. Raper Roy or Roy Rape. Something like that. It was a play on his real name, but I don't think I ever knew what that name was."

She looked at Lester, his eyes avid. "You remember anything like that?"

Lester leaned into the wall, thinking. Then it came to him. "Ray. Ray Lape."

"I was close."

"Close enough for horseshoes," he said. "We had our eyes on him, but nothing ever came to light. Seemed more the type to look than act."

"Is he still around?"

Lester chewed on his lip. "Moved to North Carolina, last I heard. Had some trouble there with the law."

"When was that?"

He considered it, then his eyes narrowed. "Just shy of twenty years ago."

"Does he still have family in the area?"

"Oh yeah. Out on Coon Branch. Want to go for a ride?" Lester grinned at Carolina, and seeing some semblance of happiness on his face always made her feel better.

"Sure do," she said.

"Just let me get my hat."

"I'll meet you at the Blazer," she said and headed out.

CHAPTER TWENTY-SEVEN

Max Barrasso adjusted his jacket as he approached the steps to the sheriff's department. He wasn't sure if he'd ever been in such a Godforsaken, backwoods shithole, but he wasn't too surprised at the despair that clung to it like cheap cologne.

Places like rural West Virginia had a reputation for a reason, and Dupray was only a few generations removed from Lyndon B. Johnson, mugging for the camera with skinny, filthy, white kids on his lap while he vowed to end poverty.

Note to LBJ - You failed.

As much as small towns like this shocked him with their squalor, he appreciated the wake-up call it gave him. People that lived in cities, like himself, were sheltered in a different kind of way than these people, but they existed in their own tunnel-vision version of America, nonetheless. Sometimes, he needed a reminder that not everyone was spending fifteen bucks a day on gourmet coffee and living in an apartment that cost two large a month.

All that said, he never regretted leaving these kinds of places in the dust after he got what he needed and was finished with them.

He was halfway up the steps when the door opened

outward, allowing a woman to slip through. She was pretty but in an unconventional, unapproachable way. She reminded him of an old-time movie star, with alabaster skin, intense, hazel eyes, and a look on her face that exuded an *I don't take shit off anyone* attitude. Only her disheveled appearance - wrinkled clothing, hair pulled back in a sloppy ponytail - ruined the package.

He tried to make eye contact, but she had tunnel vision to the point where they brushed against each other as she passed him by, only pausing for a beat.

"Sorry about that," she said.

"No problem," he returned, but she was already on the sidewalk and crossing the street where an almost-antique Chevy Blazer was parked.

He lingered, watching her. She seemed so familiar.

"Can I help you?" a man's voice asked.

Max turned toward the station and found the sheriff standing at the top step. He wore a white hat and loomed over him like the hero in a John Ford Western.

"Are you Sheriff Fenech?" Max asked.

"I am."

"My name's Max Barrasso. I'm a reporter covering the serial killings and was wondering if I could ask you a few questions."

Lester's eyes narrowed. Max had low expectations, and the look on the sheriff's face did nothing to raise them. "You from the paper up in Charleston?"

He considered lying, then decided against it. "No, sir. I'm more of a freelance journalist."

"You coming, Lester?" The woman across the street asked.

"One sec, Carolina," he said.

Carolina?

Lester took a step down, still one above Max. "Put a pin in that for a moment, would you, son?"

Max nodded and watched as the sheriff passed him by and went to Carolina. He busied himself by looking at his phone but tuned his ear into their conversation.

"I'm gonna have to stick around here a bit. You can find your way to Coon Ridge and back?" Lester asked.

Carolina nodded. "Not a problem."

"Good. The Lapes' homestead is the only one that far out." He handed her a set of keys. "Be careful. The family's rough."

"I always am." She flashed a winning smile, then seemed to sense Max watching and looked his way. He snapped his face back to his phone and pretended to text.

"You need backup, give me a call on the radio."

"I'm not worried," Carolina said.

"I know. That's why I am." He patted Carolina on the upper arm, then returned to Max.

"You mind if I sit?" Lester asked. "It's been a long night."

Max had been expecting more pushback. Hell, he'd expected the sheriff to escort him out of town and to tell him he didn't want to see him around these parts ever again. So much for stereotypes.

"Not at all. I'll join you."

When Lester sat, joints scattered across his body went off like firecrackers. He gave a little grimace, and Max wondered how old the man was. He'd have guessed mid-seventies, but seeing the wear on his face and hearing the tear in his body, he began to wonder if eighty might be closer to the mark.

"What's your name again?" Lester asked.

"Max Barrasso." He extended his hand, and the sheriff took it. The old man's skin was calloused at the usual spots but felt almost paper-thin on the back of his hand.

"Lester."

"Nice to meet you."

Lester nodded. "Not from around here, huh?"

Max laughed. He'd been in town for a few hours and hadn't seen a single person of color aside from when he caught his own reflection in a mirror or window. "How'd you guess?"

"Good observational skills," Lester said. He looked Max up and down, taking an extra-long look at the chest tattoo that was visible above the V on his shirt; then, his eyes settled on Max's face. "How'd you hear about our predicament?" Lester asked.

"One of my readers contacted me a few days ago. After…" He checked his notes on his phone. "Jennifer Millstrom's body was found. Said it reminded her of a series of murders twenty years ago."

Lester gave a small, almost imperceptible nod.

"Then she wrote me again after the body was found last night; so, I decided to head down here."

"Where'd you travel in from?"

"New York City."

"Long drive," Lester said.

"Even longer in the dark. There were times I wasn't sure if I was on a road or a cow path."

That made the sheriff laugh, and his tired eyes shone. "Could've been both."

Max liked the man, but he wasn't here for chit-chat. He had business to attend to. "Can you tell me anything about the killings?"

Lester waited a long while before answering, and Max wondered if he'd pushed too hard, too fast. Eventually, though, he got around to responding.

"There's not much that's public yet. We have two young women who've met an early end. Had three others some time back. And yes, there are similarities."

Max knew all of that. "Any suspects?"

"We're following up on multiple leads," Lester said, but he glanced away when he spoke.

You're a mediocre liar, Sheriff, Max thought but in a way that endeared the man to him. He seemed like someone who was trying to do his best in the middle of what must be, for a town this size, an unimaginable tragedy.

"Does the killer have a signature?"

Lester put his hands on his knees. "I'm not at liberty to discuss that at the moment." He pushed himself to his feet, stretching out his tired body. "I hate to cut this short, but as you can imagine, we're all a little frazzled."

Max stood. "I understand. Maybe we can talk later. I'll buy you a burger, or whatever's good around here."

Lester looked past him, eyes drifting across the town - his town. "Don't know if there's anything good around here anymore." He turned, climbed the steps, and moved into the building.

While the discussion hadn't yielded anything substantive, Max had a good feeling about this story, even though he had no clue where it would take him.

CHAPTER TWENTY-EIGHT

Carolina stayed on Route 52 for almost half an hour before making a hard right onto Coon Branch. The road was shale for the first quarter-mile, then transitioned to dirt. Or more accurately, mud. Thank God she had Lester's Blazer and not her van as she threw it into four-wheel drive and climbed up the path and into the mountains.

Even while living in Dupray full-time, she rarely ventured this far from town. The people that lived this deep into the mountains were a different breed and fiercely guarded their privacy. To prove that point, she passed a crudely spray-painted sign that read:

Trespassers will be shot. Survivors will be shot again.

She glanced at her pistol, which she'd tucked beside the emergency brake. It was reassuring to know it was there.

This Lape character was a long shot, but his reputation made it a lead worth following up on. Still, though, it wasn't worth getting into a confrontation, especially with people who were likely to shoot first and ask questions later. And when she wasn't even certain she had the power to make an arrest, should it come to that.

She slowed the Blazer as she cruised by a dilapidated mobile home. The roof was caved in, and through it grew a sugar maple, flush with foliage. She was getting close.

Scores of vehicles in various states of disrepair littered the wooded surroundings. Some were tireless and propped on concrete blocks. Others had their hoods up and no engines. A few were little more than axles and wheels.

In a clearing twenty or so yards ahead, she saw two RVs, each once white but now stained green with algae, one double-wide trailer, and one ancient log cabin, the roof of which looked like a carpet of moss. A few four-wheelers were strewn about the grounds, along with a faded maroon Jeep Cherokee with a three-inch lift and 37-inch tires.

It looked like a setting straight out of a horror movie, the kind where the clueless woman wanders onto the property, oblivious to the danger, and ends up inside someone's freezer on the way to becoming Sunday brunch.

No thanks to that.

Carolina reached for the radio, preparing to call into the station and tell them that she was at the Lape homestead. And maybe add that if they didn't hear from her in twenty minutes to send Search and Rescue, but she didn't have a chance

The spring hinges on the double-wide's front door shrieked like a cat in heat as the aluminum egress swung open. Out marched a woman who looked half-wild and who had a shotgun leveled off at the Blazer's windshield before Carolina could so much as blink.

Splendid idea investigating the Lape's alone. Top-notch detective work.

"What the hell are you doin' on my land?" the woman demanded.

She was a twig with unwashed, chopped up blonde hair that looked like a Barbie doll that had just fallen prey to a four-year-old and scissors. She wore a too-big *Slayer* tank top, the sides of which gaped open and revealed her mosquito-bite breasts, and cut-off jean shorts. Her eyes, nose, and mouth seemed pinched together and disproportionately small on her face.

"My name's Carolina McKay," she said. "Is it all right if I get out of the truck?"

The woman didn't lower the gun but nodded. "Do it real slow."

Carolina moved, sloth-like, as she exited the Blazer. She took three steps closer to the hood.

"That's far enough," the woman said. "Now what are you doing up here?"

Carolina was never one for pleasantries and didn't mind skipping them now. "I'm looking for Ray Lape."

"Ray's my daddy," she said. "And he's been dead fourteen years now, so you can scoot on out of here in your fancy po-lice truck."

That didn't make sense. This hill jack woman looked to be in her late thirties. Maybe a half-decade less if you took into account her hardscrabble life. "Maybe I'm mistaken," Carolina said. "The man I'm looking for is in his forties."

"You must want my brother, Ray Junior." The woman let the barrel of the shotgun drift toward the ground. "But ain't no one called him that since he was knee-high to a dog's pecker. He goes by his middle name: Harvey."

"Damn it, Bonnie, you put that shotgun down before you go on and do something stupid," a man said as he emerged from the double-wide. He was half-way through pulling on his shirt as he spoke, revealing a torso covered with tattoos. Familiar tattoos.

"What's this bitch got business with you for anyway?" Bonnie asked. "What've you been up to?"

His head popped through his shirt like the rodent in whack-a-mole, and Carolina recognized him immediately as the man who'd been mowing her mother's lawn a few hours earlier. The one who had dented her van with his carelessness.

"Maybe if you shut that hole in your face and let her talk, you'd find out," Harvey Lape said, strutting toward Carolina.

Bonnie popped her bottom lip in a pout.

"You're looking for me?" Harvey asked, getting closer to Carolina. As he did, he squinted his eyes. "Wait; I know you."

"From Bea's house."

"That's right," he said. "Her daughter."

Harvey looked her up and down lecherously. "I must've made quite the impression on you this morning to bring you all the way up here." He pursed his lips. "Why, I'm downright flattered," he said, getting closer. Close enough to smell the soap he'd used to clean up after work.

He seemed the saner of the siblings, but that was a low bar. And as he drifted closer, Carolina took a subconscious step back. Maybe it was just her gut going off, but her gut had kept her alive this long, and she tended to trust it.

"Yeah, it is a bit of a drive," she said without smiling but trying to keep the mood cordial.

"So, what is it, then?" he asked. "This about Bea's lawn care? If it is, you need to talk to Eddie Degan. He's the boss. I'm just the grass monkey."

Harvey gave his winningest smile, which wasn't saying much. "Though, I tell you, I did a damn fine job on that yard."

He finally stopped, closing in on Carolina, and some of her nerves dissipated. Now if she could just get that skinny bitch of a sister to give that shotgun a rest. She still looked like she was one cross word away from opening fire.

But she had a job to do. Feeling threatened or not.

"No, Bea didn't send me here."

"Then what is it?"

Some of his faux geniality faded, and she could see his true character seeping out from behind the facade. Simultaneously she saw Bonnie Lape tighten her grip on the shotgun.

This was the worst of bad spots to be in. Why the hell hadn't she waited for Lester?

"I have a few questions. Starting off with your whereabouts yesterday evening and last night."

Harvey's eyes turned steely. "Didn't know Bea's daughter was a cop." He spit out the last word like it was a blasphemy.

Carolina glanced at Bonnie, who bounced from left to right, left to right like she was doing some primitive dance.

"No," Carolina said. "I'm not a cop. Lester's an old friend, and I'm doing some legwork for the department while I'm in town."

"If you ain't a cop, then I don't got to answer your questions."

"That's right," Carolina said. "But I only need to—"

"You're lying," Bonnie shouted, her finger twitching against the trigger. "You smell like bacon, girl! Come up here to kill us, but not if I git you first!"

Harvey pointed at his sister. "You put that popper down, Bonnie, or I swear to God, I'll beat you bloody!"

"It's okay," Carolina said, raising her hands, making sure Bonnie could see she meant no harm. "I'm unarmed. I'll show you." Her heart was pounding again. So was her head. Why hadn't she made a detour by her van for some pills before this road trip to Hell?

"Spin around," Bonnie demanded. "Slow."

Although part of her wished she had the gun on her person rather than in the Blazer, she knew she was safer without it, at least for the moment. Carolina did as asked, showing them no gun holstered at the small of her back. Thank God she left it in the truck.

"See, I'm unarmed. Wanna check for a wire while we're at it?" Carolina asked, voice dripping with sarcasm.

"Damn right," Bonnie said. "Let's see them pretty titties of yours."

Carolina shook her head, cursing herself for using sarcasm on a moron. But a woman with a twelve-gauge pointed at your face was not a woman to disobey. She lifted her shirt far enough to reveal her bra, then did a three-sixty. Harvey Lape's eyes never left her breasts.

"Think you could put down the shotgun now?" Carolina asked when she completed the circle and again faced Bonnie Lape.

But Bonnie didn't move. Instead, it was Harvey who stomped to his sister and snatched the gun from her hand so roughly that Carolina half expected it to go off.

"You're too fuckin' stupid for your own good, you know that?" He set the weapon against the trailer's skirting.

There was a moment, a brief one, where Carolina considered using this momentary distraction as an opportunity to jump into the Blazer and get the hell out of Dodge, but then this whole ordeal would have been for naught, and she'd have to tell Lester how she'd screwed the pooch. She wasn't going to give up that easy.

As Harvey passed Bonnie, he grabbed her arm so hard the woman's pink skin turned white. "Don't you fuckin' touch my gun again, you hear me?"

Bonnie stared at him and nodded, swallowing hard. "You're hurtin' me. I was just--"

"You was just being a stupid bitch is what you was just."

He shoved her away from him. The woman caught her foot and stumbled, falling sideways into the metal railing that lined the steps up to the trailer.

And there it was. Gone was the genial lawn boy, and in his place, the hothead convict. But was he a murderer, too?

Carolina looked at the handprint seared onto Bonnie Lape's arm just before the woman covered it with her own hand and shame.

Harvey turned back to Carolina. "Back to where we were," he said. "How exactly were you helping your friend? The sheriff?"

"We're checking in with every county resident who has a conviction for a violent crime." She was bluffing on the last part. She had no idea whether Lape had been arrested, let alone convicted, for a violent act, but the pieces to the puzzle were all there, and she was willing to take the risk.

And Lape didn't flinch. "I did my time. I got a respectable job. I keep to myself. I ain't got nothing to hide." Harvey crossed his arms which flexed and added an aura of power. "But I won't stand for harassment from some lackey."

"If you won't talk to me, then it's just going to be the sheriff or one of the deputies out here asking these same questions. I'm not sure how tolerant they'll be with your sister's chosen form of greeting," Carolina said.

Bonnie bared her crooked teeth like she was rabid.

"This is our land," Harvey said. "And West Virginia has the Castle Doctrine, which gives us the right to defend it."

Carolina wondered what prison law textbook he pulled that from but ignored it.

"That's right; I could blow you away right now," Bonnie said. "Defending myself and my land."

"But I'm unarmed," Carolina said.

"And you're still alive," Harvey offered.

She had no interest in a legal debate, and her patience was wearing thin. "Listen, Harvey, are you going to talk to me or not?"

"Lady, I ain't gotta answer you for nothin'," he said. "But if it gets you outta my life, then fine, I'll tell you where I was." He raised his arms to his side. "Right here, on my own little patch of Heaven."

"You have witnesses that can back that up?" she asked.

"I was here with him," Bonnie said, stepping forward. Manic triumph on her miniature face.

"I'm sure you were, but being his sister, that might be a hard sell."

"There were a bunch of others, too," Harvey said. "We were havin' a bonfire. Drinkin' a little apple pie shine, shootin' the shit with friends."

"Can you give me the names of these friends?"

"Oh, I don't know. There were so many…"

"How about two?"

Harvey's right nostril ticked upward. "Uh, let's see. There was Jeff Hostetler. Marc Bulger. Oh, and Pat White stopped by for a while, too. Good guy, that Pat."

"All right then." Carolina grabbed the Blazer's door handle. "Make sure your *friends* get their stories lined up. And you might want to consider giving one of them that shotgun. If you're caught with that while on probation, you'll get a free ride back to prison."

Bonnie sneered at Carolina. "It's my gun!"

"Okay," Carolina said, managing to stop herself from rolling her eyes. "One other thing, Harvey. Did you ever know a woman by the name of Darlene Mason?"

Harvey shook his head. "Don't think so. But then, it's not their names I'm interested in. It's that little patch of fur between their thighs." He huffed out a low laugh. Heh. Heh. Heh.

What an asshole.

Carolina did a three-point turn in the mud that passed for a lawn, and all the while, Harvey and Bonnie stared. She had no intention of coming back, especially over a petty gun charge, but she didn't appreciate being threatened. As she drove off, she thought she might look up Harvey Lape's probation officer and give him a tip out of spite.

CHAPTER TWENTY-NINE

A WHITE TAURUS HAD BEEN FOLLOWING HER FOR MORE THAN fifteen miles. Carolina kept stealing glances into the rearview mirror, trying to ID the driver, although she wasn't sure why.

It wasn't as if she'd made a half-dozen turns. She'd been on the state route the entire time, and that road was one of just three ways into and out of Dupray. Yet her adrenaline was still pumping after the encounter with the Lape's, and her nerves were on edge.

You're being paranoid.

Maybe, but that didn't mean someone wasn't tailing her.

What if Harvey Lape had sicced one of his drinking buddies on her?

So paranoid.

It didn't help that her head and stomach were both killing her. Nor that the pain in her shoulder felt like a ticking bomb ready to blow at any time.

God, she needed a pill. Or two.

She kept replaying the scene with the Lape's in her head. They were dangerous, no doubt about that, but both were hotheads.

Harvey might do a better job at putting on a facade of normalcy, but he was no different from the type of guy who has one too many beers and beats in someone's skull for looking at him the wrong way. She could see him as a killer, as a rapist, but struggled to view him as someone smart enough and patient enough to kill and mutilate five women in twenty years.

But was she underestimating him? There was the Harvey/Harley connection. And if he turned out to be the man who'd impregnated Darlene Mason, that would certainly be a black mark. Serial killers frequently began their rampages with someone they knew. Nevertheless, her instincts said Harvey wasn't their man.

Another look in the mirror revealed the white Ford still a safe and responsible ten yards behind. As she stared at it, she remembered something.

Clifford Mason had a white Ford. They'd parted on poor terms. Maybe,. he'd lost his mind upon discovering his eldest daughter had an abortion, then went on a killing spree. And now, he wanted to put an end to the woman who was nosing around in his business.

That seemed far fetched. But not impossible. After all the fucked up, horrible things she'd seen in her career, she didn't rule anything out.

When she came to a straightaway, a rarity on West Virginia roads, Carolina eased her foot off the gas and let her speed fall by half. If the person behind her was a typical motorist, they'd take this opportunity to pass. To hurry up and get on with the getting on.

Instead, the Ford slowed, too. This whole scene reminded her of a time when she was fifteen years old and, quite possibly, came within minutes of death.

"Fuck this."

She snagged her pistol, flicking off the safety as she set it on the passenger seat. Then she whipped the Blazer to the right and slammed on the brakes as she hit the cherry light and siren.

The Ford came to an abrupt stop, a little screech of the tires revealing she'd caught the driver off guard. She half-expected it to make a u-turn and flee, but it remained stationary. Waiting.

Carolina jumped from the truck, pistol raised. The weight of it in her hand, in this situation, immediately thrust her back into her life as a cop. How quickly we fall back into old habits.

"Get out of the car!" She shouted.

As she approached the Ford, she held the pistol steady, ready to fire at the first sign this was going bad. Then she remembered that, no matter what title she'd held a year earlier, she wasn't a cop any longer. If she shot whoever was in that car, she couldn't opine that it happened during a violent traffic stop. She wouldn't have a union backing her up.

Why did life have to be so damn complicated?

The door to the sedan opened, and a foot dropped out. She saw an Air Jordan sneaker, the kind that people collected, hit the pavement.

"Keep your hands where I can see them!" She ordered.

A pair of palms rose up from behind the door. "Hey, I'm sorry, I--," the man's unsteady voice was full of rattled nerves.

"Out," she said.

He climbed out of the seat and stood, putting himself in view and the line of fire. And then she recognized him.

This was the man she'd seen outside the police station earlier that morning. His eyes were wide, two shining orbs of white against his dark skin. His hands trembled above his head.

"I'm sorry," he said. "I wasn't trying to—"

"To what? Follow me?" she asked.

He swallowed hard and nodded. "Well, yeah. I was following you. But I didn't mean to scare you. I just wanted to talk."

She hadn't bothered to take a good look at him outside the station, but now, she did. Max Barrasso was a lean 5'10." His black hair was short but casual, and he had a close-cropped beard and mustache. Tattoos, much finer than those sported by Harvey Lape, decorated his forearms, and she could see empty holes in his earlobes where he once wore earrings.

Aside from the color of his skin, what made him stand out even more in Dupray was his attire. He wore designer jeans, faded and torn in all the right spots, and a lightweight, fitted gray sweater that was pushed up to his elbows. A pair of Tom Ford glasses completed the hipster look.

He was the type of handsome guy she'd see walking into a club in the city or ordering a triple mocha jumbo-somethingorother at one of those niche coffee shops that checked your coolness factor before serving you. Here, in southern West Virginia, he wasn't just a fish out of water; he was a fish out of its universe.

"Why are you following me?" she asked.

He tilted his head toward his car. "Can I show you something?" His voice was calming down now and almost sounded... playful.

"Do you really think that would be wise?" she asked.

"All right," Max said, taking a step further away from the vehicle. "Although, I don't believe it's legal to draw a weapon on someone when all they were doing was traveling on the same road as you."

She motioned for him to move further back. He did, and she stepped around his door, standing where he was moments before. She could feel the warmth from the heater drifting into the outside air.

Leaning into his ride, she took a good look around. No weapons. Just an iPad and a pack of cigarettes laying on the passenger seat. In the back were two bags of luggage. Carolina took the keys from the ignition and pocketed them, then returned her attention to the man.

"I'm not sure where you're from, but stalking a law-enforcement official is against the law," she said, hoping her lie came off confident enough. "Now, put your hands on the trunk."

"If you'd just let me—"

"Now!" she shouted.

He shook his head and stepped toward his car, planting his hands on the trunk. Carolina kicked his feet apart and patted him down with her left hand, still pointing the gun at him with her right.

There was no weapon on his person. She patted the back of his pants but found no wallet. She reached around and fished in his front pocket.

"Whoa, careful what you pull on there," he said. His voice sounded like he was smiling.

She ignored his remark and extracted a slim, leather wallet. She pulled the ID out and examined it.

"Max Barrasso," she said. "New York. Twenty-six?" Damn; now she felt lecherous for thinking he was good-looking.

"That's right."

"Okay, now I'm curious," she said. "How do you go from Manhattan or wherever the hell you're from to riding my bumper in Dupray, West Virginia?"

"Can I turn around?" he asked. "Or are you gonna make me stand here like a perp all day?"

Carolina stepped away from him and lowered her pistol. "Go ahead. But don't be stupid."

"Can't make any promises." Max grinned, revealing teeth straight out of a Colgate commercial. "I saw you outside the sheriff's office."

"I remember."

"I should hope so," he said. "I knew you looked familiar. Then, when I heard the sheriff call you Carolina, I knew it was you." He motioned to his car again. "May I?"

"Slowly," she said, then remembered crazy Bonnie Lape saying the same to her. He likely thought her every bit as mad, and she tried to dial it back.

He retrieved the tablet and tapped at the screen. It lit up, and he turned it her way. "Check it."

She looked and found a headline reading: "Baltimore City Hero Detective Retires After Sustaining Life-Threatening Injury."

"A little wordy, don't you think?" Carolina asked, slathering the remark with sarcasm. Then she kept reading and saw the name under the headline: Max Barrasso.

"Oh fuck. You're a reporter? Who do you work for?"

"I freelance," Max said.

She looked further and saw the URL. "Max B. tells all dot com," she read. She looked up at his mugging face. He was quite proud of himself. "You're worse than a reporter. You're a blogger."

She handed the tablet back to Max, shaking her head. After he accepted it, she spun around, making her way back to the Blazer.

"Hey, wait. I didn't get to tell you why--"

"I don't care anymore. I'm not going to give you any information. Call the sheriff's department and ask for Johnny Moore. And please, don't follow me again."

"You were after Harvey Lape, weren't you?" he asked.

She had her hand on the door handle—almost made a clean getaway. But she froze when Max mentioned Lape.

"What do you know about him?" she asked, looking over her shoulder.

"Heard the sheriff tell you to go to Coon Branch. By the way, is that a racist thing?" he asked.

Carolina shook her head. "Raccoons."

"Ah, okay. Anyway, I did a quick property search, and there was only one name listed. Raymond Harvey Lape. Then I did a criminal background search. Fifteen years in Anson Correctional Institute for murder in the second degree. Prior arrests for assault and harassment. Seems a likely enough suspect."

"You found all of that out online?"

He tapped his tablet. "You can find anything if you know where to look."

"I'll be damned." She was impressed. Her own computer skills didn't extend far beyond playing minesweeper and the occasional game of solitaire.

"I bet I know something about him you don't," Max said.

After everything he'd found out already, that didn't surprise her at all. "Oh yeah? What's that?"

"He tried to kill a guy, years back but got off. Happened a county over, some place called Monacan. I even have the dude's address if you're interested."

He was obviously enjoying himself, but she didn't appreciate the slow leaking of information. "This isn't your blog. You're not getting more ad revenue every time I have to click to the next page. Spit it out."

It didn't seem possible, but his smile widened. "Only if I can tag along."

She shook her head. "Not happening. There's no way I'm getting a failed journalist involved in a murder investigation. I can find out whatever you're hiding on my own."

He shrugged. "Go ahead and try." He placed his tablet back into the car, putting on a show of being willing to drive away with his secret intact.

He dropped into the driver's seat, and she was willing to let him go. It was a standoff.

Until he blinked.

"Something does rub me strange, though."

She lifted her eyebrows, waiting for him to finish his thought.

"Why would a retired detective from a different state be running around, asking all sorts of questions about an active investigation? And on top of that, why is she pulling a gun on a random stranger who has committed no crime?"

She gritted her teeth. "If you want to file a complaint with the sheriff's department, I'm sure they'd be happy to fill out the paperwork."

He shook his head. "I don't think that's necessary. But my readers would eat this up with a spoon. Privileged, white ex-cop nearly shoots an innocent African-American man who wasn't doing anything but driving down the road."

She took a deep breath and let it out. "Fuck," she muttered.

"Fine, but none of this investigation gets put on your shitty website. Those five or six armchair dicks who read your drivel don't get to read a word about this until the killer is caught. Got it?"

He looked at the empty road and nodded. "I think I can live with that... Partner."

She rolled her eyes. "Jesus, don't call me that again, or I will shoot you."

He cheesed that perfect smile and pissed her off even more.

CHAPTER THIRTY

Carolina trailed Max's Taurus for the next half hour, passing out of Dupray County and into Monacan, a place she only knew by reputation. And that reputation was not good. This jaunt was foolish at best. In Dupray, at least, she had Lester's badge backing her up. Here she was in the wind, and if something went awry, she was beyond screwed.

That's why you don't let anything go wrong.

Max's brake lights came on as the vehicles approached a rickety mobile home with vaguely white paint and peeling maroon trim. The windows were weather-sealed with plastic, most of it shredded by seasons of wind. In lieu of steps, a rusty ladder connected the entrance to the ground. This place made the Lape's homestead look like a four-star resort.

The Taurus slowed to a stop, and the door opened as Max stepped into the open. The notion that this was some kind of setup flitted through Carolina's mind. But coming all the way from New York City solely to ambush her seemed far-fetched. Besides, all she had to lose was her life, and that wasn't worth much these days.

"You take me to the finest places," she said as she joined him in the patch of weeds and dirt that substituted for a lawn.

"You're the one that's from here. Not me." Max grabbed his tablet and a small microphone from the car, then closed the door.

"Who are we here to see?" Carolina stared at the trailer, which might have been abandoned if not for the pick-up that waited at the far end. It was a Dodge, twenty or more years old. Ragged metal framed the wheels where rust had devoured the fenders. Two washing machines and a row of metal filing cabinets filled the bed.

"His name's Dominic Gale. Self-employed as a scrapper."

She knew the job, such that it was. Scrappers collected appliances, car parts, tools, anything from which they could scavenge metal and sell to the junkyard where it would be crushed and melted down as it awaited a new life as a bed frame or rebar or railroad tracks.

"Some career," she said.

"What's your job again?" Max asked.

"Retired," Carolina said. "So, what happened between this Gale person and Harvey Lape?"

"I'm not entirely sure. All I could find was an old newspaper article about an assault with a deadly weapon. Then, when it came time to go to trial, Gale refused to testify, and the charges were dropped."

"So, this might be nothing at all?" she asked, wishing she wouldn't have followed Max Barrasso on this hunt for the wild goose.

"Maybe." Max knocked on the side of the trailer. "Or maybe he doesn't trust cops. And who could blame him?"

She was about to protest when the door swung open. This time there was no shotgun greeting, just a pot-bellied, shirtless man with tired eyes, a scruff of a beard, and thinning, brown hair. A faded, vaguely green tattoo of an anchor decorated his sternum, and in his right hand, he clutched a half-empty, two-liter bottle of Mountain Dew.

But it was hard to pay attention to those details because the first thing Carolina noticed - the only thing she could take in - was that Dominic Gale was missing his nose.

It wasn't the clean, surgical disfigurement that he might have displayed if he'd been in an accident or suffered from an aggressive skin cancer. And it wasn't the unnatural absence left from a birth defect.

This was the result of a crude, violent mauling that left ragged, purple flesh in its wake. That skin did little to conceal the pair of oblong holes that looked like the roman numeral II on the center of his face. Through them, she could see the moist, pink tissue that wasn't meant to be viewed. That was usually covered by nostrils and cartilage and flesh. It was like looking at a cadaver in a morgue after a horrendous accident, but this cadaver was upright.

She realized she was gawking like a teenager who'd just dropped a quarter in the slot at the peep show.

"Getting a real good look, are ya?" Dom asked.

He made no effort to cover his injury, and Carolina forced herself to look away. "I-- Uh, I'm sorry."

Dom smirked, an expression of good cheer that did nothing to lessen the impact of his injury. "Don't waste your time with sorrys. I like to give folks shit for staring, but I'd do the same if the situation was reversed."

Dom's grin faded as he looked at Max, then back at Carolina.

Carolina took a step closer and extended her hand. Dom didn't accept. She supposed she deserved that. "I'm Carolina McKay. I'm assisting with an investigation for the sheriff's department."

"Sheriff Bando?" Dom asked.

"Sure," Carolina said, seeing no need for honesty.

"And him?" he motioned to Max with his chin.

"I'm in research," Max said. "Is it all right if I record this interview?" He tilted the microphone, which was now connected to his tablet.

"What's all this about?" Dom set the bottle of Dew on the trailer floor.

"We're investigating a murder. And we think you might be able to help out," Carolina said. "We want to talk to you about Harvey Lape." She kept her eyes locked on his to ensure she got a good read. His caution was replaced with surprise.

Dominic Gale kept a hand on the door jamb as he descended the ladder that served as stairs. When he reached the ground, he sat back on it and pushed his fingers through the remnants of his hair. "I didn't do it," he said. "But if you find out who killed that rat bastard, let me know, and I'll buy him a pitcher."

"I'm sorry; I wasn't clear," Carolina said. "Lape's not dead."

Dom sneered. "Well, fuck. You got my hopes up." He hocked a loogie and launched it forward. It landed with a wet splat next to Max. "Tell me again what you want from me. And get it all out this time, not this piecemeal bullshit."

"Harvey Lape is a suspect in some murders. He has an alibi, but we don't know if that holds water yet. Until we find out, we wanted to talk to you and see what you can tell us about him."

"Meanest cocksucker in West Virginia," Dom said. "Got himself a one-pound trigger, too. And that's a bad combo."

"And you pulled that trigger?" Carolina asked.

He shrugged. "I was at the bar, playing darts. He was watching, making comments about how I couldn't throw worth shit; so, I bet him twenty bucks I could get closer the black hat than he could. He took me up on it.

"Lape demanded to go first. Guess he thought he'd intimidate me with his skill." Dom chuckled. "Dipshit didn't even get it in the center ring. Then I went and almost hit it dead on. I turned to him and told him his friend Andrew Jackson wanted to come live with me. I thought it was funny." His gaze drifted to the dirt. "Fucker lost his mind."

"He cut off your nose because of a game of darts?" Max asked.

Dom shrugged. "Lape don't need an excuse. He wears violence like a winter coat."

"How did he do it? Your nose, I mean," Carolina asked. She

wondered if he used scissors. Scissors like the killer used to excise the eyelids from the dead girls.

"He popped me in the jaw to start. I was seeing birdies like in one of those cartoons, flying all around my head." He mimed the birds soaring around him.

"Next thing I knew, I was on the floor, and Lape was on top of me. Just hitting and kicking me at first. He got right in my face and was screaming at me about how I thought I was a comedian. He was so close I could smell the onion rings on his breath." Dom shuddered. "I still can't eat those goddamn things.

"I figured I was in line for an old-fashioned beating. Wouldn't of been my first. And I laid there, taking it. Because a guy like that, you try to fight back, it just gets worse. That went on for a bit, and I thought he was winding down. Instead, he pulls out one of those red Boy Scout knives and goes to work." His hand drifted across his face. "Few minutes later, I looked like this, and I'm gagging on my own blood."

"This happened in public? And no one stopped him?" Max asked.

Carolina didn't appreciate his interjections and shot a scowl his way. He either missed it or ignored her.

"If you saw a bear attacking someone in the woods, are you gonna jump in and try to fight it off? Cause that's what Lape was like. A wild fucking animal."

It was a horrible tale, but Dom seemed unfazed at reciting it. Carolina had a feeling he had a lot of experience. "Why do you think he didn't go any further?"

"Further? Like what? Like why didn't he kill me?"

Carolina nodded. "Yeah."

He gave a rueful laugh. "Beats the shit out of me. Maybe he figured me walking around all my life looking like some Quasimodo motherfucker was a worse punishment." He caught his own reflection in his truck's chrome bumper and stood. "You two need anything else? It's almost time for *Days of Our Lives*."

"That's all. Thanks for your help," Carolina said.

He climbed two rungs on the ladder, then paused. "So, who do you think Lape killed?"

"Some girls. A series of them."

His eyes narrowed, making his unfortunate face even more unsightly. "Huh?"

"Huh, what?" Carolina asked.

"I don't know," Dom said. "Just don't seem his type."

"Why do you think that?" Carolina stepped closer to him, reading him.

"I could see him killing a wife or girlfriend if she sassed him. Like I said, one-pound trigger. But serial killer shit. That seems above his weight class."

"I appreciate your insight," Carolina said as he continued up the ladder.

"Sure. Thanks for the memories, doll." He moved into the trailer, closing the door behind him.

As Max and Carolina returned to their vehicles, he asked, "So, what'd you think?"

She leaned into the Blazer, hoping Max couldn't hear her stomach rumbling. She was hungry and nauseous at the same time. "I think someone should go into the business of making prosthetic noses."

Max chuckled. "I agree. But I meant about his read on Lape."

"I think he's right. Harvey Lape's not our guy."

"Really? Even after the nose thing? That shit's fucked up. I'd think a man who could cut off someone's nose would be capable of taking some eyelids for keepsakes, don't you think?"

Carolina opened the driver's door and hoisted one foot inside. What Max said seemed true on the surface, but she wasn't buying it. "That was done in rage. Lape is impulsive—out of control. *Wild*, as Gale put it."

"And?" Max asked.

"The killings of the girls were planned. The way the eyelids were removed took time and skill. Lape, with his Swiss Army knife, isn't being careful. Our guy... he's almost surgical."

She dropped into the driver's seat and started the engine. She reached to close the door, but Max's hand closed over hers.

"You're running off on me, just like that?" he asked.

Carolina nodded. "That was the plan."

"No, the plan was for the two of us to Scooby-Doo this bitch."

"Sorry, Max." Carolina slipped her hand free. "I work better alone."

He stared at her as she shut the door and drove off, but she didn't look back. Instead, she focused on the horizon, where a smattering of clouds dotted the cobalt sky. She didn't plan on reneging on the deal, not entirely anyway, but she had a killer to catch.

And now, she was back to square one without a single lead.

CHAPTER THIRTY-ONE

Two pills, down the hatch.

Carolina sat on her mattress, eyes closed. It would take a while before they kicked in. Before they pushed away the throbbing that began in her shoulder and radiated into her arm and chest. Before her stomach settled. Before her head cleared.

Ti-i-i-ime, ain't on my side, she thought.

Another girl would be dead soon. She was sure of it. And here she was with the headache from hell and no idea what stones to overturn next.

She felt like she was letting these girls down. And letting Lester down. She wasn't sure which was worse.

As much as she wanted to get back to the office and fill everyone in on the day's events, what she needed was a few minutes to close her eyes and push aside the craziness around her. She kicked her shoes off and swung her feet onto the bed.

CHAPTER THIRTY-TWO

COOL RAIN FELL, SATURATING CAROLINA'S CLOTHES AND CHILLING her to her marrow. She tried to squeeze tighter against Bea to gain some of the benefits of her mother's umbrella but only caught the periphery. One arm dry. The rest of her soaked.

A crowd of nearly fifty people circled the open grave, and all of them seemed shrunken and huddled, as if they were contracting into themselves, Withering in the wetness. It was fitting, considering the prevailing melancholy.

Pastor Luke Magner droned on at the head of the grave, his thin arms occasionally gesticulating. Sometimes he motioned to the sky, where presumably God joined in their grief. Other times, he pointed to the crowd, toward Lester, who sat stone-faced and numb.

The sermon was background noise to Carolina, who was more focused on surveying the mourners and trying to discern whether the killer sat amongst them.

It seemed more likely than not. In a town the size of Dupray, everyone knew everyone, and whoever was cruel enough to murder Diana would be able to get a nearly front-row seat to observe the pain he had wrought.

She scanned the crowd, taking in their expressions, trying to determine whether their sadness was real or an act. So far, she'd come up empty.

As she watched them, she also tried to match them with the man she'd seen at this same cemetery. But all she could look for was a general age, face shape, and posture. Nothing distinctive. If only she'd got a better look at him. Because she was sure that man was the murderer.

Why did I run? she thought. *Why didn't I stick around another five seconds and get a good look at his face?*

Then her gaze drifted to the closed casket, and she realized that had she not fled when she did, this could be her funeral.

She felt her mother take her hand and squeeze. Hard enough to make Carolina draw back in pain. When she looked at Bea, she saw her mother's lips pursed, and eyes narrowed.

"Quit gawking around and pay attention to the pastor," Bea whispered, her voice low enough to remain unheard by anyone other than its intended recipient.

Carolina tried to obey, but it was a chore. Pastor Luke's talk about eternal life, about a place in the sky where deceased loved ones awaited, was hard to reconcile against the weeping, broken version of Lester she'd found a few days earlier. If he were reunited with Diana forty years from now, that was well and good. But what about all those decades in between?

"The Scriptures are clear and forceful that in times of crisis, people may feel the absence of God," Pastor Luke said. "There is pain, loss, brokenness, and death in all of our lives. Human beings get hurt and struggle to make sense of life in a death-filled world. During life's challenges, God doesn't always have time to drop by and rub our shoulders and promise us everything is okay."

Jesus, Carolina thought. *Is this supposed to be uplifting? If this were the best that he could offer, she'd get back to looking for the killer.*

THE RITUAL OF the meal in the church basement after the funeral struck Carolina as odd. How were people supposed to enjoy the roast beef and turkey after watching the casket containing someone they loved lowered into the ground? And why did everyone feel the need to offer up a trite platitude?

"I know how you feel."

"She's in a better place now."

"There's a reason for everything."

Yech.

She'd set aside her plate of meat and potatoes, allowing her easier access to drift through the crowd. To study their faces and listen to their voices. If only she could find the man that she saw at the cemetery.

So far, though, no luck. She spotted her mother holding court at the end of the buffet. That morning, she'd told Carolina, "Put on a happy face. No one needs to see you bawling and pouting. Especially not Lester."

But Bea took it beyond stoicism. She seemed to be enjoying herself as she greeted and thanked everyone and carried on like she was the maître d' at a fine restaurant. Sometimes, most of the time, Carolina wondered if she would ever understand her mother.

She found Lester sitting at a table surrounded by old people who showered him with sympathy. For a moment, their eyes met, and Lester gave a sad smile and nod.

God, how she wanted to help him, but she knew she couldn't do that with words or an embrace. The only thing that might help Lester move on was catching Diana's killer.

But right now, she had to pee. She slipped through the mourners, down a cramped hall, and toward the door with its outline of a girl. It was ajar, and she slipped inside, grateful that she didn't need to wait.

She'd just sat on the toilet and begun to relieve herself when the handle jiggled. She'd locked it upon entering though so no one could barge in.

Another jiggle.

Use your brain, jerk, she thought.

"Someone's in here," she said.

Silence.

She let out the breath she'd been holding, and the steam of urine she'd clamped off at the sound. She finished, wiped, and had her slacks half-way up her legs when the doorknob turned left, then right, then left again.

"I said someone's in here." She jerked up her pants, zipping them closed. "Asshole," she muttered.

Carolina reached for the lock, wanting to curse out whoever was being so rude, but she was in a church, so she resigned herself to issuing a peeved glare. But as her hand fell against the porcelain knob, she paused. She could hear a sound coming through the closed door.

Breathing.

Whoever was trying to get in hadn't taken a few steps away to give her privacy. They were waiting just on the other side.

"Who's there?" she asked.

And then she heard the voice. "I know you, girly," it said.

She recognized it straight off. Its course tone. Like he was speaking through a throat filled with rocks. It was the man from the cemetery.

"Your name's Carolina. I know where you live, too."

She felt the knob move in her hand. Not much, only the slightest rotation. Like the man outside of the bathroom wanted to connect with her through the doorknob assembly.

"Maybe I'll come visit..." he said.

She considered screaming, That would draw a crowd, and then she'd have the safety of numbers on her side.

But what if she were wrong? What if it was just some weirdo, maybe one of the losers from school trying - and succeeding - to scare her? Then she'd have caused a scene at a funeral for nothing, and the shame alone would be enough to make her run away from Dupray and never return.

Yet she couldn't hide in the bathroom all afternoon, could she?

Carolina steeled herself. She gave the knob a hard turn, then pulled the door open, hoping to have surprise on her side.

But the doorway was empty.

She poked her head into the hall. There was no one. Only the incoming tide of voices from the dining area, which doubled as the children's Sunday school room when it wasn't used to feed mourners.

Rushing up the hall at a quick trot, she was sure she'd find the man there and catch him trying to fade back into the crowd, or maybe even making a hasty retreat to the exit, but instead, everything seemed the same as when she'd left. People eating and talking. No one there looked like they'd just been in the hallway threatening her.

Carolina wanted to tell Lester what had happened, but when she looked to him and saw him sitting before an uneaten plate of food and looking like the saddest man who'd ever lived, she knew this wasn't the time.

She had to keep this to herself. For now.

CHAPTER THIRTY-THREE

LESTER STARED AT THE STACKS OF PAPERWORK THAT LITTERED his deck and tried to figure out where to begin. That was the worst part of the job these days: the minutia. It seemed to grow every day, like some out of control weed. Every time you clipped one stem, four more sprouted in its wake. It was an unending battle.

A light tap at his office door provided a reprieve.

"Lester?" Meredith asked.

"Come in."

She entered, holding a piece of paper in her hand, and his heart sank. Another form to complete.

"What do you got there, Mere?"

"I've been pulling old assault cases, like you asked me to."

"And?"

"I found a few." She glanced from the paper to his face, eyes tentative. He knew the woman didn't like to be involved with the investigative part of the job.

"Go on."

"One, in particular, seemed to stand out." She turned the paper toward him—not that he had a chance of reading it as a distance. She must have known that and went on. "Charles Weaver. Was arrested for—" her voice dropped. "Rape. But before he could go to trial, the woman who accused him was killed in a car wreck. After that, he left town, but he came back last summer. Elven wrote him up for drunk and disorderly at the fourth of July parade."

Lester motioned for her to hand over the paper. Meredith did. He skimmed it and liked what he saw.

"Did I ever tell you I love you?" Lester asked her.

Meredith beamed. "Once or twice."

He rose from his chair and reached into the cup where he typically kept his keys. But it was empty.

"Shit," he muttered.

"What's the matter?"

"Carolina has my Blazer."

Meredith didn't miss a beat. "Why don't you take the sneaker?"

There was a multitude of reasons why he considered her the office's most important employee. This was yet another.

THE SNEAKER CAR was a mid-nineties Crown Vic in a shade of blue that screamed *Police*. Lester knew every man, woman, and child in the country saw such vehicles and associated them with cops, nullifying their undercover purposes, but it had four wheels and an engine, and that was all he required. Discretion was secondary.

He rolled into Rat's Transmission Shop, where a dozen or so ancient cars surrounded the building like the rocks at Stonehenge. The bay door to the garage was open, and inside, a pick-up sat on jack stands while a pair of legs protruded from underneath it.

Lester stepped into the building, which smelled of diesel and used motor oil. AC/DC blared on a boombox, the kind that had gone out of fashion decades earlier. Lester rolled back the volume on the radio, his fingers coming away black when he finished.

He looked to the truck, to the legs, and saw them twitch.

"Man who can't keep his hands to himself is liable to have them broken," the man under the truck said.

"Couldn't hear myself think," Lester said.

"Don't see how that's my problem." The man rolled out from his place beneath the pickup and glared at Lester. His expression, which had been anything but pleasant, darkened further when he saw the uniform and badge.

"I thought I smelled bacon," he said, then spat a mouthful of brown fluid onto the floor.

He was in his forties and balding with a walrus mustache that swallowed up his mouth. Tobacco juice dripped from the fur. His overalls had once been blue but were now stained black with dirt and garage grime.

"I'm looking for Charles Weaver," Lester said. He already recognized the man from his mugshot but figured he deserved a chance to lie.

And Weaver didn't disappoint. "Don't work here no more."

"Why's that?"

The man shrugged. "Stopped showing up for work. Wasn't a good enough mechanic to waste my time begging him to come back."

"I see," Lester said as he stepped closer to the truck. A variety of tools were laid across the hood. He dragged his fingers over them.

"You really do got a problem with keeping your hands to yourself; don't you, old man?"

Lester closed his hand over a wrench, the heavy kind molded from cast iron. He didn't hesitate as he swung the tool, the fat end catching Weaver in the sternum and knocking him backward.

He tossed the wrench to the side, freeing up his hands to allow him to grab Weaver by his filthy shirt. "And you've got a problem with the truth."

Weaver sucked in pained mouthfuls of air as he tried to catch his breath. "The... fuck..." He managed.

"I know you're Charles Weaver, dumbass. I've got your mugshot in my ride."

Weaver rubbed his chest, his face twisted in a grimace of pain. "Ya shoulda said so."

"I thought I'd give you the opportunity to be truthful. Then I'd know whether I could believe anything that comes out of your mouth. Now you've proven yourself a liar and made my job easier."

Weaver was mostly recovered from the hard knock. "Shit, man. Lies come easier, that's all. Didn't have to hit me for it."

When Lester released him, Weaver backed away, taking a seat on a spare tire.

"Apparently, I did," Lester said. He crouched down, an act that caused his knees to pop, to get at face level. "I'm going to need proof of your whereabouts every night for the last ten or so days."

"What for?" Weaver asked.

"Son, can't you do anything the easy way?" Lester reached to the hood, this time finding a ratchet with a three-quarter inch socket on the end that would work just fine if needed.

Weaver scooted back, pressing himself against the truck. "I'm at Erma Glick's boarding house every night. I have to be in by eight. Part of my parole." He held up his hands, pointing to his shirt pocket. "Can I?" he asked.

Lester nodded.

Weaver reached into the pocket and pulled out a business card. He passed it over, leaving a black smudge on the white paper. Lester read it and saw it was the contact information for his probation officer. He turned it over and found the address and phone number for Glick's Boarding House.

Lester folded the card in half and put it in his own pocket. "I'm gonna follow up on this," he said.

"Go right ahead."

"Might tell your p.o. that you're obstructing an investigation while I'm at it."

"That's how you roll, huh?" Weaver said.

"It is."

Some of the disdain returned to Charles Weaver. "Do whatever the fuck you want. What've I got to lose? Busting my knuckles here all day. Going home to a place full of retirees and retards that can't take care of themselves. All so I can eat ten for ten dollars TV dinners and watch *M*A*S*H* reruns on the community TV. Big fucking loss."

"That's one sorry attitude you've got yourself," Lester said. "You have any idea how many people don't get the kind of second chance you're pissing away?"

Weaver didn't respond.

"I didn't think so." Lester stood, an act that made his back feel like it was going to snap in half. He was long overdue for having the chiropractor snap his spine.

He took two steps toward the open garage door, then stopped and turned back to Charles Weaver "One other thing," he said.

Weaver only stared.

"How good's your memory?"

"Why?"

Lester watched his face. "Darlene Mason. Rhonda Seese. Diana Fenech." His voice cracked when he said his daughter's name, but he recovered without missing a beat. "Those names mean anything to you?"

Weaver thought a moment, then answered. "The last two don't. But the other, that Darlene girl. Someone killed her just a couple days before I got nailed for running coke over in Harlan County. I remember 'cause it was all over the news."

"You're a regular jack of all trades," Lester said. "What'd that get you?"

"Eighteen years," Weaver said, then spat on the floor again.

That was close to half the man's life. He'd spent almost as many years in prison as Diana had lived. What a waste.

"You never told me why you was here for me?"

Lester considered holding back but saw no reason to. "Two new dead girls. That's why."

Weaver's drab, brown eyes narrowed. "You thought I killed 'em?"

"Had you for that rape some years back. That's enough to draw a few questions."

"I ain't never hurt a woman. That was statch rape bullshit. I loved that girl. We was gonna get married before her daddy found out and lost his shit."

That sounded like the most truthful thing Charles Weaver had said. And his alibis would be easy enough to verify.

It was time to move on.

CHAPTER THIRTY-FOUR

Carolina awoke from her nap, refreshed, pain-free, and inspired.

She drove Lester's Blazer to an austere, clapboard sided building. The structure looked little like a church: no steeple, no arched windows. All that belied its contents was a simple placard beside the oak double doors at the entrance.

Dupray Methodist Church
Founded 1913
Pastor L. Magner

She found the pastor to the right of the building, pulling weeds in a flower bed that had been overtaken by hostas and English ivy. He looked up as she approached, revealing a sallow complexion and a large dirt stain on one cheek, making him look like he was halfway through applying war paint when she interrupted.

"Hello there," he said.

"Afternoon, Pastor. I doubt you remember me, but I'm Bea Boothe's daughter, Carolina."

Luke Magner was now in his late sixties. Tall and lanky, he seemed fit at a glance, but his vaguely yellow skin and bloodshot eyes revealed a less appealing picture. Still, though, when he smiled, there was genuine kindness.

"You once set off a stink bomb during communion. Of course I remember you."

It was Carolina's turn to grin. "I expect an extra month in purgatory over that."

"Purgatory's Roman Catholic nonsense," Luke said. "All you need to do is ask God to forgive you, and he will."

"I'll remember that," Carolina said. But on her list of grievances that begged forgiveness, her church prank barely registered.

She told the pastor about her temporary duties with the Sheriff's office and the murders, then got down to business.

"The first three girls to be killed were all members here. What about our most recent victims?"

Pastor Luke stood, wiping his dirt-stained hands on his pants as he shook his head. "No. I believe the Millstrom's are Baptist. I'm not familiar with the Wehner's"

That wasn't a huge surprise. Looking at the deteriorating condition of the church, she suspected membership had fallen dramatically since she was a girl.

"Do you recall any members of the church leaving town after the murders?" Carolina asked.

Luke thought for a long moment, then shook his head. "I can't say for certain. We used to bring in over one hundred souls every Sunday. Closer to one fifty around Christmas and Easter. Not all of them made as much of an impression on me as you did."

He meant it as humorous, but Carolina thought that sounded forced.

"Does the church keep records of members? A roster, of sorts?"

"We do, going back over one hundred years."

"I'm mainly interested in twenty years ago."

He stepped toward the church and motioned for her to follow.

AN EXPLOSION of dust formed a miniature mushroom cloud as Luke dropped a large filing box onto a table. He coughed, waving at the air, which was full of particles that sparkled in the light that spilled through the windows.

"Sorry about that," he said. "We don't have a budget for a cleaning service anymore, and well, I've been lax in keeping up."

"You should see my van. Don't worry about it," Carolina said.

She peeled off the lid and peered inside. Stacks of ringed tablets filled it from top to bottom. On the covers, in small, neat handwriting, were years. They began in the 1950s, and she sorted through the contents for the relevant time period.

"I try to avoid the news," Luke said. "But it's been impossible to block out what's been going on of late. How's Lester handling it?"

Carolina glanced at him. "He doesn't go to church here anymore?"

Luke shook his head. "He came in fits and starts after Diana's death. Sometimes, I'd see him a few Sundays in a row. Then not at all for months. Then he'd reappear. Eventually, he stopped altogether." He looked to the pulpit at the front of the church. "I tried to find the right words for him but never quite succeeded."

Carolina remembered Pastor Luke's sermons and wasn't surprised by that. The man was a biblical scholar, but far from a motivational speaker. Not that there were words to get Lester through the worst thing that could happen to a father.

She came to three notebooks: the year before the murders, the year of, and the year after. "Mind if I take these to the office?" she asked.

Luke considered it, and she could see the worry on his tired face.

"You'll get them back, I promise. And if I lie in church, that's like a direct flight to hell, right?"

He gave a pinched, humorless smile. Better work on your comedy act, girl.

"All right," he said.

"Thank you, Pastor; this might help."

"Do you really believe the person responsible for those... awful things sat amongst us?" He looked around the room as if the mere thought sullied the church.

"I don't know. But we're trying not to leave any stone unturned this time around."

Carolina grabbed the tablets, holding them tight to her body as she stood. She was a few steps from the door when the pastor spoke again.

"There's something which always nagged at me."

"What's that?" she asked.

"What the killer did to their eyes. Do you think that has any biblical connection? An eye for an eye?"

Carolina thought motives like that were more fitting in a Hollywood blockbuster. In real life, serial killers rarely had deeper meanings. They only wanted to hurt people.

"I'd be very surprised if that were the case," she said. "I don't think this had anything to do with the bible or revenge."

"Then, why?"

Why indeed? She had her theories, but they weren't fit to be shared within these walls.

CHAPTER THIRTY-FIVE

She'd hoped to give Lester the details of the day in private, but Elven shoehorned his way in and listened to the entirety of the conversation. He'd kept silent until she got to the point of sharing the names of Harvey Lape's friends. The men who, Lape had assured, would provide him with an alibi.

"We need to contact Jeff Hostetler, Pat White, and Marc Bulger," she said.

A broad grin, the type often described as shit-eating, spread across Elven's face. Even Lester couldn't hold back a smirk.

"What?" She said, feeling like the punchline of a joke had soared over her head.

"Harvey Lape was drinking moonshine with Jeff Hostetler, Pat White, and Marc Bulger?" Elven asked.

"That's what he told me."

The men looked at each other, and her exclusion from whatever was happening began to piss her off. "Spit it out already. What am I missing?"

"Those are football players, Carolina," Lester said.

"What?" she asked again.

"Three of the finest quarterbacks ever to suit up for the Mountaineers," Elven said. "How in the world are you from this state and not aware of that?"

Carolina wanted to melt into the chair in which she was sitting. "Am I supposed to know every asshole who spent his Friday nights giving himself brain damage?"

Elven laughed that time. "College football is played on Saturdays."

"Oh, ha, ha, fucking ha," Carolina said. "I spent my morning almost getting my ass blasted off by Harvey Lape's hill jack sister, and all you can do is point out that I have better things to fill my mind with than sports trivia."

As annoyed as she was with Elven, she was more upset with herself for accepting Lape's word without more scrutiny. That she hadn't run the names herself before sharing them. At least Johnny and Tank weren't sitting in on this sorry show. Having Johnny Moore feel intellectually superior to her would be a fine reason for suicide.

"Enough with the bickering," Lester said, playing the role of the father keeping his kids in line. "We now know Harvey Lape lied about who he was with. And if he did that, maybe he's lying about even more."

Carolina still had her doubts that Lape was their killer, but Lester wasn't wrong. He was hiding something, and they needed to find out what.

"We still need more on him, though, more than a hunch and a lie." She tapped Pastor Luke's notebooks, which lay on Lester's desk. "Why not have Tank scour these? See if Lape ever attended services at the church."

Elven grabbed one and flipped through the pages. "Are you too good for the minutiae of the job, Detective McKay?"

She was still annoyed by the razzing over the false names. "I'm in yesterday's clothes. I almost got shot, and I'm not collecting a county paycheck like you. I believe I've earned an evening off."

He held up his hands in mock surrender. She didn't find that humorous either.

"My, you're uptight," he said. "The city did you no favors, Carolina."

Elven scooped up the other notebooks and exited the office.

Carolina turned to Lester. "I can't believe he's going to be your replacement."

All Lester could do was smile.

CHAPTER THIRTY-SIX

Bea filled Carolina's mug with tea so sweet that it would have sent a diabetic into a coma. Dinner had been pleasant, a welcome change, but some questions needed answering.

She knew that bringing up the murders was likely to ruin the evening, but the cop part of her overruled the daughter part.

"I've been trying to find more out about the original victims. Maybe if I can get into their lives, their heads, I can figure out who could have done that to them."

"Mmm hmm," was all she got in response.

"What can you tell me about Darlene Mason?" Carolina asked.

Bea cocked her head. "I knew nothing of the girl. Her family didn't exactly run in our circles."

What a snob. "But she was one of your students."

"Was she?" Bea asked.

"According to her father. I met with him this morning, and she mentioned ornithology was one of her favorite classes."

That made Bea smile. "Well, then; we know she had good taste."

Her cavalier attitude was driving Carolina crazy. How could she be so flippant about murder?

"I'm serious," Carolina said.

"I know you are, darling. But I don't know how many times I have to tell you I don't want to hear about this anymore. I don't want to live my life surrounded by such negativity."

"We're trying to catch a murderer. Someone who is killing again, in case you haven't been paying attention."

Bea sipped her tea. "Yes, it's all anyone talks about now. Murder this. Death that. Sad. Tragic. Terrible. At some point it becomes background noise."

"Was Jenny Millstrom background noise? Because she also took your class."

Bea set down her cup, her expression tired but serious. "She was a mediocre student. Seemed to have little interest in birds. Most of the students are under the impression that ornithology will be what they refer to as a *blow-off class*. They believe all they'll be required to do is look at pictures of pretty birds all semester and get rewarded with a passing grade. They don't take it seriously. She didn't."

Bea's dismay over students not respecting her class seemed far greater than the grief she felt about the loss of their lives, but Carolina wasn't surprised. Her mother had always been emotionally distant. She was never the stereotypical doting, loving mother to her or Scarlet and seemed to care little when both left her nest. Husbands drifted in and out of her life like ships at a port. And through it all, she was aloof, at best.

Once upon a time, Carolina had admired her mother's ability to turn off her emotions like a light switch, but the passage of time made her realize it wasn't a skill of which to be jealous. It was a flaw.

"What about Vanessa Wehner? Did she take your class, too?" Carolina asked.

"As a matter of fact, she did. I never heard the girl speak a word. Always had her nose glued to her phone."

"Did you ever see men around either of them? Other students, or maybe even faculty? Maybe someone giving them unwanted attention?"

With a sigh, Bea rose from her chair. "Carolina, girls these days want all the attention they can get. They might protest and assert otherwise for appearance's sake, but trust me, they lap up the fawning from their male counterparts like it's nectar from the gods."

She gathered the dishes, this time knowing enough not to touch Carolina's cup. Carolina stood and went to help, but Bea stopped her.

"No need to bother yourself," she said. "Your after-dinner conversation topic has spoiled my previously good mood. I think it's best if you let me be for the night."

That was fine with Carolina, who slunk out of the house hoping that, by some miracle, there'd been a baby switch in the hospital and that Bea Boothe was not her real mother. Before she closed the door, she called back. "You'll probably want to hire a new lawn service."

Bea's face twisted in confusion. "Why?"

On second thought, Carolina didn't want to get into that. "Never mind."

CHAPTER THIRTY-SEVEN

The next week brought with it no new leads, but also no dead bodies either. All things considered, Carolina considered that a win.

Only it didn't feel like one. Lape's name was nowhere to be found in the church registries, and they had nothing more than speculation to tie him to any of the crimes.

Johnny had been put in charge of surveilling the man, and although Carolina was certain Johnny Moore lacked the skills to remain undetected, she thought that might work in their favor. If Lape knew he was being followed, he might stay out of trouble while they continued to dig into his past.

Tank and Meredith were gone for the day, leaving just Lester, Elven, and her in the office. After discussing the day's developments, which were somewhere south of slim and none, the prevailing mood was that of defeat, but none of them would admit it.

"We still have the second tier of parolees to follow up on," Elven said. "I can divvy them up."

Carolina had no faith in that. The first third, the ones they deemed most likely suspects, had all been cleared. These others didn't fit the profile she'd created in her mind. They were thugs, pedophiles, men who beat their wives. The odds of any of them having the mental capacity to pull off these crimes were infinitesimal.

She didn't say that out loud, though, because she had no better ideas.

"We'll handle that later," Lester said, his voice not only tired but weak. Like saying four words was a chore.

"You sure?" Elven asked. "I can run over to Hank's and get an assortment of grub, and we can burn the midnight oil."

At the thought of food, Carolina's stomach growled, a noise that sounded like a feral animal inside her. Both men stared.

"What?" She said. "I can't control my gastrointestinal system. Besides, I haven't had a bite to eat since yesterday."

Lester bit back a yawn. "No," he said. "Everyone heads home now. Sheriff's orders."

As much as Carolina wanted - needed - to work this case, that sounded appealing. She'd been in near-constant misery lately, upping her pain pills from two at a time to three, and even that seemed to have little effect.

She'd nearly exhausted her prescription, which made her nervous because it was supposed to last another two-and-a-half weeks. She dreaded the judgmental look she was bound to get from the pharmacist.

"I'm not one to disobey the sheriff." Elven left the office and, when he closed the door, Lester motioned for Carolina to sit.

"Are you all right?" he asked her.

He's concerned about me? The poor man looked like he hadn't enjoyed an hour of cumulative rest in weeks. The bags below his eyes hung so low they dragged down the lower lid and exposed the pink membrane underneath. And he somehow looked even thinner than he had only a week earlier.

"I'm fine. Why?"

"You seem on edge," he said.

"Under the circumstances, that's to be expected; isn't it?"

He paused to consider it, then nodded. "I just don't want you pushing yourself too hard. I know what you've been through, Carolina. And if this gets to be too much, I understand."

His compassion stabbed her in the heart like a knife, his words twisting the blade. Solving this case was Lester's life, but here he was, concerned about her.

"I'm not stopping until we solve this," she said, and she meant that.

"I appreciate that," he said. "But promise me you won't push yourself too hard."

"I promise," she lied.

He gave a small nod. "Good. Now, why don't you go get yourself some breakfast? It's been a long night."

Carolina opened her mouth, then closed it. She glanced at the clock on the wall; it was 5:40 p.m. Surely, he had misspoken.

"You mean dinner," she said, trying to put on a smile but failing.

"What?" He squinted his eyes, and she saw confusion overrun his face.

"It's almost time for dinner, Lester."

Lester waved his hand, then grabbed some papers from the desk to distract himself, or her, or maybe the both of them.

"Of course," he said. I must've been thinking about having breakfast with that beautiful mother of yours tomorrow and gotten ahead of myself. You know I don't miss my Wednesday morning breakfasts with Beatrice."

She couldn't bring herself to tell him that Wednesday had passed. "I know," she muttered. "Maybe you should head over to Bea's now. Take your mind off the case for a little while."

Lester looked up and smiled. "You know, that's not a bad idea. I'll do that as soon as I get these forms filled out."

Part of her thought she should stay with him, to make sure *he* was okay, but she felt fire in her throat and knew she'd start crying if she tried to say anything else. And Carolina McKay didn't cry. So, she spun toward the door and, as usual, ran away from her problems.

In her hurry to open and push through the office door, she almost ran into Elven, who was standing just outside. She froze, trying to push aside the emotions that were welling up. The easiest way to do that was through anger.

"What are you doing? Spying?" she asked.

Elven studied her, which made her uneasy; she felt like he could read her mind. She expected him to say something about Lester, something bad, but he surprised her.

"Come with me, and let's get some food."

"What?"

"You were complaining about not having eaten all day. Let's remedy that and talk."

As wary as she was of trusting him, the invitation had a certain appeal. "About what?" she asked.

He shrugged. "Whatever you want. I'll let you take the lead."

CHAPTER THIRTY-EIGHT

Carolina sat in the corner booth at Hank's. The restaurant was the kind with sticky floors and thirty-year-old posters on the walls. The tables wobbled, and the seats were plastic. You wouldn't have been surprised to find roaches having a gangbang in the bathroom. But you ignored all of that because the food was good, and it was the only option in town.

The other diners had left almost an hour earlier, when Carolina was only half-way through her calzone. Now, the restaurant was as empty as her plate.

She stared out the window, eyeing the vacant street and feeling like the only person in the world.

Until Elven returned.

She'd been in the middle of dumping two pills into her palm when he arrived and, in her haste to conceal the bottle, it slipped from her hand, rolling across the floor until coming to a halt beside a half-eaten tater tot. Carolina reached for it, but Elven was quicker.

He picked it up, eyes scanning the label before he handed it back. Without a word, he passed it over and slid into the booth across from her, taking hold of the pitcher of soda and refilling his cup. "Top you off?" he asked.

She nodded, and he filled her glass, then used the soda to swallow the oxys. Although he hadn't addressed it, she couldn't keep her mouth shut. "I have chronic pain in my shoulder," she said. "Lots of nerve damage and arthritis from the shooting."

He sipped his soda.

"I have a prescription," she went on. She knew that talking too much was the sign of a liar, but she couldn't help herself.

"So do two out of every three men, women, and children in the state," Elven said. "Just be careful with those. I've seen more lives ended over what's in that bottle than violence."

She nodded, her eyes directed at the street, ready to change the subject. "They really do roll up the sidewalks at dusk, don't they?"

"I like it that way. Keeps things quiet."

She looked to him, raising an eyebrow in skepticism.

"Most of the time," he added, then motioned to the menu, which was propped behind the napkin dispenser.

"You decide on dessert yet?"

She hadn't even considered it. "What do you recommend?"

"Well, if you aren't averse to the calories, I'd highly recommend the pie. It's the best you'll ever have."

Carolina smirked. "Way to be such a cliché."

"How so?"

"Small town eatery?" She put on an exaggerated drawl. "*Best apple pie ever made.* Sounds a little corny, don't you think?"

"It's peach, actually."

He smirked, but his eyes lacked cheer, and she realized that she was being more rude than she intended. It appeared that the former golden boy running back had gotten his feelings hurt, and all he'd done to deserve it was be kind to her.

She wondered why she continued to be such a bitch.

Rhea, a broad, cheerful woman, stepped to the table with a pen and pad in her hands. "All right now, you've finished the main course. So, it's time to fix up that sweet tooth."

"I think we'll just take the check, Rhea," Elven said, his voice monotone.

"You sure, doll?" The waitress looked from Elven to Carolina, then back to Elven.

"Yeah, I'm—"

"You know, I think I'll have a slice of pie," Carolina interrupted.

"I can do that," Rhea said. "Best you'll ever have."

Out of the corner of her eye, Carolina saw a smile creep onto Elven's face.

"Make that two," he said.

"Easy peasy." With that, the waitress was gone.

"Okay, I get your cliché comment, but you just wait," he said. "If you don't think it's delicious, I'll pay for dinner."

"I already thought you were paying," she said.

"What gave you that idea?"

"You asked me here."

His eyes narrowed. "I assumed this was a friendly meal between colleagues. Did you think this was a date?"

She felt her cheeks simmer and downed a swallow of soda to cool them off, but it was lukewarm and didn't do much to help. Instead, she distracted herself with the pile of mugshots that Elven had brought along that lay open on the table. "Anyone else in here trip your trigger?" she asked.

"A few interesting fellows." Elven sorted through the photos and extracted one. "I stopped by this guy's place of employment today, but he was up in Charlestown at a doctor's appointment with his wife."

He passed the papers to her, and she gave them a quick read—Morton Zimmerman: priors for the rape of two minors, complete with homemade videos recording the acts. But he was only 37 years old. And he was a short, fire hydrant of a man. Nothing like the person she'd seen at the cemetery that day so many summers ago.

173

Not that she wanted to share details of her teenage sleuthing with Elven Hallie.

"Doesn't seem to fit," Carolina said as she set the papers aside.

The two of them had already argued about how they should narrow down the suspects. Elven wanted to use basic facts and criminal histories. But Carolina preferred to trust her gut.

"Why not?" he asked.

"His victims were kids. Besides, he would have been, what, seventeen during the first murders."

Elven opened his mouth, but Carolina knew she was right. He would not win the argument. She figured he could waste his time following up on Morton Zimmerman if he so desired, but she had no interest in that creep. Not when they were clearly looking for someone else.

"It's not him," she reasserted.

"Then who are you hot on?" he asked. "I want to stay ahead of this. To stop this guy before another victim comes along." He hesitated a moment. "Not just for the peace of mind for the town. For Lester, too."

She rolled her eyes, ever her snarky self. "The sooner this is done, the sooner you get to be the boss, right?" The words spilled out. She couldn't help it and was too tired to try.

Elven grabbed her hand. It was so sudden that she jolted upright in her booth, caught off-guard. He looked her directly in the eyes, unblinking, making her feel uncomfortable.

"If that were true, I wouldn't cover for him all the time," he said.

"You? Cover for *him*?" She scoffed, but he squeezed harder. It wasn't an aggressive action but enough to keep her attention on him.

"Did you ever notice that stack of forms on Lester's desk? The stack he ignores? I fill out the bulk of the paperwork and have him rubber-stamp it when I'm done. I handle the interviews, and I coordinate the court schedules with the prosecutor's office." He released her hand.

"If I left it up to him to do the duties of his job, the whole county would know he isn't fit for it anymore."

She could see he was serious.

"Why do you do all of that if you want to be Sheriff so bad?"

"You may find this hard to believe, but I love Lester. He taught me so much about this job. He made me the cop I am today. Heck, the man I am today, too." He smiled and looked up to the right, as if remembering something, then went on.

"I've been encouraging him to retire, for his sake, not mine. But he wouldn't listen. And then this case came along, and you and I both know that he won't walk away until this is over."

She stared at Elven, unsure of what to say. What to think. Had she really misread him so dramatically?

Still unable to find the right words, she simply said, "Thank you."

He smiled. "You look tired, Carolina."

"Screw off," she muttered.

"I only mean that you have a lot to deal with—the man you've looked up to all your life is withering away. And I understand how that feels. I had a couple of years to come to grips with this. I can't imagine being in your position. I'm sorry."

"You have nothing to be sorry about. I should be the one apologizing to you. I've been a real shit, and I should have given you the benefit of the doubt." She wasn't comfortable being this raw with him and turned her gaze back to the rap sheets. "So, let's take a deeper dive into those ex-cons."

She reached for the files, leaning closer to him as she did, but he put his hand on top of papers, preventing her from opening them. As she looked up at him, he leaned in, putting his face inches away from hers.

He was smiling, the skin wrinkling around his mouth The overhead fluorescents highlighted his five o'clock shadow. And although his eyes were tired, too, with small blood vessels crisscrossing the sclera, he still managed to look handsome.

She bit her bottom lip. "What?" she finally asked in barely a whisper.

"You said that you should be the one apologizing to me. So, where's my apology?"

She sagged back in her seat. He was that same cocky prick that she knew from high school. And she'd fallen for it.

"Just give me the files," she said, pulling them her way.

CHAPTER THIRTY-NINE

Rita Prescott tiptoed over the still, damp floors and punched the code into the alarm system on the back wall. She'd just finished mopping, then dumped the change from the washers and dryers into the safe by the desk. It was time to make a clean break.

The only good thing about her job at the laundromat was that it closed at eight. If she hurried, she still had time to make it to the bonfire before everyone was too drunk to carry on a conversation.

The box on the wall started beeping, letting her know she had sixty seconds to get out of the building before she would trip the alarm. Once she was outside, she spun around and locked the door, giving it a yank for peace of mind.

The night air was colder than she had anticipated, and she wished she had brought her heavy coat, not just the blue and silver McDowell University windbreaker she had on. But she gave that little thought as she passed through the almost pitch-black parking lot.

Art Glessner, the laundromat's owner, refused to shell out the money to replace the bulbs in the motion detector lights, and although she closed four nights a week, Rita still hadn't become comfortable with the darkness. Plus, Art made her park at the far end of the lot, proclaiming that the closer spots were for customers only.

It was just twenty yards, but it felt like a mile.

As she scurried across the blacktop, Rita pulled out her phone and unlocked it, illuminating the screen. She began to text Leah, her best friend, to let her know she was on her way. But halfway between the business and her father's old pickup, she had the strangest feeling.

She wasn't alone.

Rita paused the text, instead fishing her keys out of her jacket pocket. She felt for the fob, pressing the unlock button. The headlights blinked, momentarily blinding her, and she trudged forward, quickening her pace.

As she walked, she tried to ignore the sound of her own footsteps, listening for noise caused by another. She held her breath, trying to hear beyond the usual sounds of the night.

Then she heard the second set of footsteps.

Behind her. Moving toward her.

Rita gave up walking, breaking into a full-on run. She dodged the pothole halfway between the business and the truck, one she'd always thought of as an ankle breaker, and kept sprinting.

Whoever shared the night with her ran, too.

She wanted to scream, but her throat had tightened like a vise, and there was barely room for air. No sound emerged, other than high panicked breathing.

This isn't real, she thought. This doesn't happen to someone like me. This is the kind of thing you see on TV. It doesn't happen in real life.

She was at the truck, hand on the handle, when she saw the reflections in the driver's side window.

Her own.

And the silhouette of someone else. Behind her.

She gasped and spun around just in time to see the person's arm arc downward. Rita took a quick step to the side, avoiding the worst of the blow, but something, a fist or tool, thudded against her skull.

It was enough to knock her off-balance, and she ricocheted into the truck, sliding down the metal and hitting the ground. Her keys skittered across the pavement, but she kept hold of the phone as she rolled under the vehicle.

She kept rolling, completing four rotations before she was on the other side. Then Rita scrambled to her feet faster than she had ever done anything before and ran again.

Hot blood trickled down the side of her head, filling her ear canal and giving a hollow, underwater effect to the sounds of the night. She didn't want to risk a glance behind, instead using everything she had to put one foot in front of the other. She was panting, pulling in air greedily as she did, and her vision started to blur.

She was only a few yards from the laundromat. She knew she needed to get inside, to lock herself inside, and she'd be safe. Or safer than she was here, exposed in the dark.

It was only when she made it to the door that she remembered her fallen keys. Now she did look back, toward the truck, toward her attacker.

But she saw no one.

That didn't make her feel any better. And Rita ran yet again—this time, for the thicket of evergreen bushes that backed the building. Ten yards.

Five.

And she made it.

As she dove into the cover, she looked down at her phone, trying to focus, but her vision still wasn't clear. Then small, dark droplets splattered against the screen. She squinted and wiped them away, her fingers coming back crimson.

That's when her head began to pound, overwhelmed with fear and panic. She ran her hand through her hair, over her forehead, feeling the sticky heat of her own blood.

"Oh my God," she whispered. As the blood came quicker,

coating her face and raining down her neck, she began to panic. "Help me, Jesus."

She wiped at her eyes, smearing the blood around her face as she dialed 9-1-1.

Rita held the phone to her ear, waiting, listening to it ring while also trying to focus and hear if someone was coming for her.

And then she heard them. Footsteps on the asphalt. Coming closer.

She believed she was hidden, that she could stay that way until help arrived. Now, all she could do was wait.

CHAPTER FORTY

Cliché or not, the pie was damned good. Maybe not the best she'd ever had, but good enough that her annoyance with Elven had faded from a seven to a three.

They were going over the file of a man named Joseph Johns (thrice convinced of stalking and harassment) when Elven's phone rang; he pulled it from his pants pocket and examined it.

"Nine, one, one," he said. "The calls get routed to me after Meredith goes home for the day."

"Shit," Carolina said. "That's dedication."

He smirked as he took the call. "This is Sheriff's Deputy Elven Hallie. Please state the address of your emergency." His voice was smooth and professional, giving Carolina another twinge of guilt upon seeing how seriously he took the job.

She watched his calm expression fade, and his eyes widen. She leaned across the table, trying to listen in, but could hear only muffled noises.

"Yes, Miss, I understand. Please give me your address, and I'll be there as soon as possible."

Carolina grabbed the phone from him and pushed the speaker

button. Immediately, she could hear the panicked breathing on the other end. Whoever was calling had the phone tight to their mouth, every terrified huff and puff coming through extra loudly.

Carolina set the phone on the table. As she did, her hand shook. She wasn't sure if it was exhaustion or nerves or the fact that she hadn't taken pills in almost three hours. Regardless, Elven noticed but didn't say anything.

"Someone hit me. I'm bleeding bad!" Her voice was a whisper and a scream at the same time. "I'm hiding behind—"

A sharp inhalation made the speaker crackle.

"Oh my heck! I think I see 'em," she said, and Carolina could hear in her voice that she was on the precipice of crying.

"Where are you, Miss?" Elven repeated, his voice stern but his face full of worry.

"Spot-On Laundry," Rita finally said.

Elven slid out of the booth. "Can you describe the man who attacked you?" he asked as he pulled on his coat.

"No, I don't know. I just got hit, and now everything's blurry."

"How badly are you injured?" Carolina asked.

Rita didn't seem to mind that she was now speaking to a new person. "My head—I'm real woozy. I don't—"

The phone went silent. Carolina looked up at Elven. "Where is that pla—"

He shook his finger, cutting her off. "Are you still there?" he asked.

"I'm here," she said. "Please, I'm so scared."

"I'm on my way. You stay where you are and stay—"

A scream so loud it turned the speaker to pure static stopped him. Elven snatched the phone and raced toward the exit. Carolina stayed on his heels. They both ignored Rhea, who stared with wide-eyed confusion

"Oh, Jesus, please," Rita begged. There was a rough, clattering noise, and then her voice grew quieter, more distant. "Please! I'll do any—" but then her words cut off, replaced with wet and thick sounds, like she had swallowed her tongue and was choking on it.

Then, there was grunting, struggling, and then a loud, hollow, thud, like a watermelon landing in a puddle of honey.

Realizing that sound was almost certainly the girl's head splashing in a puddle of her own blood on the asphalt beneath her made Carolina half-sick.

"Miss? Miss? Are you there?" Elven asked, dashing across the street and climbing into the Jeep.

The only sound now coming from the phone was breathing. Heavy, quick, tired breathing. Then came footsteps crunching on the ground. They grew louder and were interrupted by a scraping noise as the phone was picked up. The breaths were louder now.

"Who is this?" Elven asked.

The call went dead.

Less than a minute had passed. A minute that felt like an hour to Carolina, who was standing beside the driver's side door of Elven's Wrangler. He pulled it shut and slipped the key into the ignition.

"Wait," she said. "I'm coming with."

"No, you're not."

He gunned the engine, and Carolina grabbed the door frame as if she could hold him back.

"Come on." She hated the whine in her voice.

"This is not a debate. I'm the only actual cop here, and you're under the influence. Now let go and back off, or I'll run you over."

She did both, and he didn't pause, flooring the gas pedal and making the tires scream as he sped away.

As his taillights faded in the distance, Carolina turned back to Hank's, realizing he'd left her with the bill. If she hadn't been so on edge and pissed off, she might have laughed.

CHAPTER FORTY-ONE

When Carolina returned to her mother's house, she was surprised to find all the lights off. In addition to being a morning person, Bea was a night owl. Sometimes, Carolina wondered if she ever slept or if she had a secret stash of speed that she used to stay alert and chipper day and night.

Not that she was in a position to judge.

She'd just stripped out of her clothes and put on a tank top and jeans when headlights blasted through the windshield of her van.

Carolina watched until they shut off. As her eyes adjusted, she realized it was Bea's Mercedes. She considered hiding, but the lights inside the van were on, and she knew it was no use. So, she stepped into the night.

"You're out late," Carolina said.

To her surprise, Bea jumped, startled.

"You about scared the life out of me," Bea said.

Her mother wasn't the jumpy type. She was usually as mellow as a north California hippy and didn't even need the weed to keep herself even-keeled. When Carolina looked closer, she realized it wasn't just her mother's nerves that were out of the ordinary; her appearance matched.

Bea's outfit was almost utilitarian. Tan slacks, plain, gray sweatshirt. Her hair was wet and pulled up in a sloppy bun. Her make-up, usually on point, was absent.

"What are you staring at?" Bea asked.

"You, obviously."

Her mother rolled her eyes, tossing her head side to side in the process. Always so dramatic. "I meant why? You act like you've never seen me before."

"I'm not sure that I have. Not like this, anyway."

Bea sighed and started toward the house. She was out of breath. "I was jogging."

Carolina followed her. "Since when do you exercise?"

"Really, Carolina, after the evening I've had, I don't need to be subjected to your version of the Spanish inquisition."

When they entered the house, Bea flipped on the light, and Carolina saw it wasn't only her mother's hair that was wet; her clothes were, too. It was like she'd stood under a waterfall. Even her sneakers squished out liquid as she walked.

"Okay," Carolina said. "I know you don't appreciate the questions, but really, Bea..." She waved her hand at Bea's wretched condition.

Her mother poured cold coffee from the pitcher into her mug and took a drink. "Promise you won't laugh," she said.

"I'm not really in the laughing mood, So, I think you're safe there."

Bea sat at the kitchen table. "I was jogging off Canberra, that little tree-lined road that runs parallel with Dutchman's Creek?"

Carolina nodded. She knew the place.

"I saw a barred owl hopping along the embankment. It couldn't have been more than a month old, just a ball of down. Then I lost track of it and heard a... *yowl*."

"A yowl?"

"Yes, a yowl. I thought maybe something was after the poor thing. A fisher or a coyote most likely. So I took a few steps, trying to see if it was okay. And I slipped." She threw her hand out. "Right into the water. Thank Heavens it wasn't spring, with the runoff, or I'd have been liable to drown."

Carolina watched as her mother finished her coffee in a long, desperate swallow. She wasn't buying any of this but saw little sense in calling her on it. All her life, Bea had kept secrets from her. They usually involved men and, if her mother had become involved in some sort of deviant watersport, she didn't want to know.

"Did you find the owl?" Carolina asked.

"Strix varia," Bea said, showing off and using its scientific name. "And no, I did not."

Bea moved to the refrigerator, and Carolina noticed that the woman was limping. Maybe the story about falling into the creek wasn't a fabrication, after all.

"Have you eaten anything yet? I have leftover roast beef. I can make you a sandwich."

"No, I'm fine. I had a calzone at Hank's."

"Alone?" Bea asked, her tone insinuating that dining alone was something to be ashamed of.

"No, with Elven."

A too-happy smile pulled at Bea's lips.

"Don't start. He's a son of a bitch. It was a work thing."

"If you say so..."

Bea took a tray of beef from the fridge and grabbed a knife, carving two perfect, razor-thin slices from the roast. An automated deli slicer couldn't have done a better job. She transferred them to a plate, grabbed a small jar of horseradish sauce, and returned to the table.

"How was your day?" Bea asked.

Carolina let out a low groan.

"That good?"

"Worse," Carolina said. She pulled out a chair and sat across from her mother. She didn't want to talk about what came next, either—but she had to know.

"Tell me about Lester," Carolina said. "Have you noticed him slipping?" She paused. "Mentally?"

Bea frowned. She cut off a piece of the beef and dipped it into the sauce, then took a bite, chewed, and swallowed, all before answering. "I don't believe it's proper to speak of such matters."

"That's a yes," Carolina said. "You realize that's a yes, right?"

"Would you fetch me a glass of water?" Bea asked.

Carolina did, filling it from the tap and handing it over.

"You don't know what it's like to age, Carolina. The effect it has not only on our bodies but our minds. That's normal."

"He didn't know what day of the week it was. Again." Carolina said. "And he thought it was time for breakfast in the middle of the afternoon. Do you really think that's normal?"

Bea's calm front vanished. "What do you expect of him? she asked. "You march back here, playing the fallen hero, and lead him on this wild goose chase. Get him all fired up about a serial murderer when you know the toll this has taken on him. I doubt the poor man has had a good night's sleep since you've come home. Of course that's going to affect his thinking."

Carolina waited to see if she was done. She wasn't.

"I'm so tired of everything in this town revolving around a few girls who got themselves in trouble and paid the price. There are people trying to move on and make a life here, but all anyone wants to talk about is death. I'm sick of it!"

Bea pushed her plate to the side so hard it teetered on the edge of the table but didn't tip over. Carolina was disappointed because watching a piece of her mother's fine china shatter would have been a satisfying climax to the rant.

Carolina stood and took a step away from the table. She knew

Bea wanted her to fight back, to send this mouth battle into round two, but she had no intention of giving her the satisfaction.

"Goodnight, Bea."

She could hear her mother seething with ungranted anger as she left the kitchen, and that was the only part that made her feel better.

CHAPTER FORTY-TWO

Carolina needed to sleep, but Bea's raving had her too worked up. Besides, if she stayed in the van, in her mother's driveway, the woman was liable to arrive halfway through the night, pounding on her windows, eager to carry on.

There were better things to do. Like get a buzz on.

The crowd at the Blue Stone was sedate and solitary, and Carolina had managed to down three shots of whiskey without speaking to anyone other than the bartender, an elderly man who shook so badly with the palsy that he spilled twice as much as he managed to get into each glass.

She was about to order a fourth when a familiar voice announced its presence at her side.

"Looks like I have some catching up to do."

When she looked to her right, she found Max Barrasso wearing his trademark grin. He motioned to the bartender, who tottered their way.

Carolina didn't return his smile and decided to pass on drink number four. "I don't want any company."

"Maybe you don't want it, but you sure as hell look like you need it. Those dogs in the ASPCA commercials don't look as miserable and lonely as you do right now."

The bartender arrived. "I'll have four shots of whatever she's drinking, hoss. Plus, one more for her."

The old man half-sneered before grabbing the bottle of Tennessee whiskey and filling four glasses. He shot Max an annoyed glance before leaving.

"You make friends everywhere you go," Carolina said.

"At least they like the color of my money." Max slapped a twenty on the bar, then downed two shots back to back.

"Are you gonna clink the damn glass with me or not?"

It was bad luck to waste free booze; at least, Carolina thought that was a thing, so she tapped her glass against his and threw the liquor down the hatch.

"It's been a week now. Every day. I keep waiting for you to text me and tell me how you Sherlock Holmes'ed this motherfucker."

"Sorry to disappoint you," Carolina said. "I seem to make a habit of that."

"Naw. Good things take time is all."

"Time is what we don't have."

"Are you getting close?"

She flirted with telling him about the 9-1-1 call but stopped herself. There was no way of knowing if it had anything to do with the serial murders—not yet, anyway. And the last thing she needed was to give Max a lead to publish on his website and have it blow up in her face.

So instead, she said, "Not really."

"Well, maybe I can change that," he replied.

She had hoped to avoid any talk of the case, knowing it would just pull her further down the rabbit hole. But her ears perked up at Max's tease. He might be a scum-sucking blogger, but he knew how to bait a hook.

"I'm listening."

"I've been digging through the newspaper archives, back from when this shithole town actually had a newspaper, and I found a story that might lead somewhere. An unsolved assault on a college student."

It was intriguing but vague, and she knew he was drawing it out on purpose. "When did this take place?"

"About six months before the first murder."

He had her on the line now. But something about this seemed too perfect and, as was her nature, she didn't trust anyone who seemed helpful for no reason.

"Why do you keep feeding me this info? Why not give it to Lester or, hell, just post it all on that blog of yours and brag to the world about how you're smarter than the police?" As she stared at his face, it transitioned from jovial to pensive.

He stared at her for a long moment before answering. "I knew about you even before your big hero case in Baltimore. Your old department's notorious for asshole cops. Racist sons of a bitches who get their rocks off tormenting the people they are supposed to protect and serve."

She puts her hand on the bar, beginning to stand up. "All right, I'm don--"

"No, it's not like that. Damn, you're touchy. I was gonna say that you were one of the decent ones. You didn't take shit, but you were fair. That's rare. And I admire that."

Carolina had trouble believing he was being truthful and didn't say anything.

"They did you wrong after the shooting. You deserved better."

Of course, she felt the same way, but she was pretty much the only one. So why was this virtual stranger standing up for her when none of her colleagues had offered the same commiseration? His assertion that she was right made her feel good but confused, and she fell back on her sarcasm.

"Don't know what you heard, but I'm a hero. It was in all the papers."

He smirked. "I'm not just some guy living in his mom's basement typing on a computer. You don't have respect for bloggers, but I'm damn good at what I do. I know how that shit went down. They forced you out because you knew the truth, and they wanted your white ass as far away Charm City as possible. They did you dirty."

"Thanks." It came out in barely a whisper, but it still came out.

He looked down at her again and pushed her hair behind her ear. "There's something cool about you, Carolina."

She smiled at him. Maybe having company wasn't the worst thing in the world.

Max downed another shot, keeping his word on catching up.

HE PROMISED to show her the article on the old assault, but it was in his room. Fortunately, as they were both too drunk to drive, Max was staying at the Starlight Motel, which was across the street and down a block. They walked, or stumbled, until they reached the door to Room 17, upon which someone had scratched *Jimmy is a dead fuck* with a key.

And the room used an actual key, not a keycard. A key which Max dropped as he tried to unlock the door. Carolina bent down to grab it for him as he simultaneously did the same. Their heads collided at low speed, causing them both to break into giggles.

The laughter slowed, then stopped completely as their eyes met. Without thinking, Carolina leaned in and kissed him. He tasted like booze and cigarettes, but his hot mouth felt good against her own.

She pulled away with a smile, took a breath, and went back in for seconds.

They stood outside the shitty motel, making out like horny high schoolers, her hand creeping up his chest, and his sliding down her back and cupping her ass. With his free hand, he unlocked the door and pushed it open. Then he pulled away from her.

"Maybe we're a little too drunk. Maybe I should show you that article in the morning instead," he said, earnest.

She slid her thumbs into the pockets of his jeans. "Yes, we are. And yes, you can."

Carolina pushed him through the doorway and followed him inside.

CHAPTER FORTY-THREE

Carolina's head swam, and her stomach roiled.

I'm gonna barf.

She bolted upright in bed, eyes coming open. Piercing, garish rays of sunlight blinded her, complicating matters.

As she reached for the trash can that she kept beside the bed, she felt nothing but air. She stretched further, harder, feeling the molten vomit rushing toward the exit. All her fingers found was carpet.

She had a moment to wonder how that was possible - carpet in her van - when the booze she'd drank the night before, but hadn't had the time to digest, burst from her like high tide.

Immediately, her nausea began to pass. That wasn't so bad.

Then came round two. That one was bad. The hot acidity scalded the back of her throat, and when she finally finished retching, she needed to cool it down.

When Carolina risked opening her eyes again, they adjusted to reveal she wasn't in her van. She was in a cramped, grimy motel room. The floral print bedspread smelled like cigarette smoke and stale ass and, from the looks of it, hadn't been washed since the previous decade. The yellowed wallpaper was riddled with scrapes and scuffs. A 19-inch tube TV sat atop the particle-board dresser. And a mirror above it revealed her sorry reflection.

She wiped a dribble of barf off her chin, then wiped her hand on the sheets. They were already covered with the stuff. So, in her mind, a little more wouldn't hurt.

As she rolled out of bed, surprised to find herself naked, the events of the day prior rushed back: Lester's failing memory. Bea's ranting. Elven reminding her she wasn't a cop while he rushed to a crime scene. Her anger. The bar. And Max.

And then more Max.

She rubbed her head, which still throbbed. She needed her morning pills and wondered if she could manage to slip out of the room unnoticed. It wasn't that she was embarrassed about what had happened with Max. She was an adult, one quite capable of making her own decisions. And she didn't regret the one she'd made.

The aftermath, though, as she looked at the sheets that she'd soiled... That was worth running away from.

Carolina found her bra on the floor. Her t-shirt beside it. Her jeans were half-under the dresser. One shoe was in front of the door, and the other, under the bed, holding court with enough dust bunnies to populate Watership Down.

What she couldn't find were her panties. She was still hunting for them when the bathroom room opened; Max appeared through a cloud of steam.

"Hey," he said, holding a towel tight against his waist. He wasn't wearing a shirt, and she could see his dark, defined abs. There was even a hint of what was underneath the towel, and she once again thought that there definitely wasn't anything to be ashamed about.

He cinched the towel around his waist, tight enough to keep it in place as he moved to a small table beside the door. "While you were sawing logs, I got us coffee," he said and made it half-way there when the smell hit him.

"Oh, damn." He covered the bottom half of his face with one hand as his eyes homed in on the bed. "Oh, damn!" he said again.

"Sorry about that," she said. She tried to think of an excuse but came up empty-handed. Instead, she grabbed the sheets, stripping them from the bed and pulling them into a vile ball. "I'll just put these out for the cleaning lady."

She dropped them outside the room, then closed the door.

"Should we leave a note or money or something?" Max asked.

"Like what? I puked in the sheets. Here's five dollars. Sorry."

"That would be a start," he said.

It probably would have been a considerate thing to do, but Carolina had too much on her mind. "I can't find my underwear," she said.

"Don't look at me. You think I keep 'em like a trophy or something?"

He handed her a styrofoam cup. She wrinkled her nose.

"What? You're the only cop in the history of the world who doesn't drink coffee?"

She poked a hole through the lid. "I drink it. I just hate it."

Max rolled his eyes. "You're an enigma, Carolina McKay."

He took several long swallows of his brew while she sipped hers. The silence bordered on awkward, and he broke first.

"Look," he began. "I hope that last night... well, I hope that you're okay with everything."

His face contorted as he spoke, his expressions exaggerated. She watched him with curiosity as he continued.

"I mean, things, uh, they got a little, what? I guess, out of hand, maybe?" His eyes grew wide as she watched him stumble through his words. If possible, he was even worse at this than she was.

"I mean, it was fun... from what I can remember." His hands fumbled with the towel, searching for something to do. "I mean, great. Really great. But I don't want to give you..." He shook his head. "The wrong impression."

She wouldn't have expected him to be the type to experience morning-after nerves. But it was time to let him off the hook. "Max. It's fine. I'm okay with what we did. Are you?"

He let out a long sigh of relief. "Okay, good. Yeah, I'm okay. It's just, I mean, I normally don't do this sort of thing. I would much rather have wined and dined you, and then—"

She held up a hand for him to stop. The last thing she needed right now was for Max Barrasso to think this was the beginning of... well, anything.

"Last night was nice. You were great." She gave him a thumbs up. "But don't expect much out of me right now. It was a stress reliever, a very enjoyable one. But that's done, so let's get back to business."

Harsh? Maybe, but it needed to be said.

"Oh."

His nervous smile faded, and he took on sad, puppy-dog eyes. She felt awful but couldn't dwell on that.

"Now tell me about that assault you mentioned from years back."

"Right," he said, grabbing his tablet. "It happened about four months before the first murder. Allison Petry was attacked while walking home from her Sunday-evening church service, and there was no sexual assault, which I thought matched the guy you're looking for."

"Did she identify her assailant?" Carolina asked.

Max shook his head. "She got clocked on the back of the head, then took a bad fall. She was in a coma for a few months. They didn't expect her to make it. When she did come around, she..." His words trailed off. "Well, she wasn't exactly capable of helping. Brain damage."

That was underwhelming. "No offense, but if she couldn't tell the cops anything twenty years ago, what good is that going to do me now?"

Max shrugged. "I just dug up a possible lead. How you use it is up to you."

Max was right; he couldn't be expected to do her job for her. But still, she felt a little like the girl who'd bought tickets to the circus expecting to see lions and elephants and, instead, found a donkey and a clown.

"Is she still living in Dupray?" she asked.

Max nodded. "In a group home."

"How do you find all this shit?"

He smiled, looking more like himself again. "Like I said, I'm good at my job."

"Not just some guy living in his mom's basement, right?"

He held up a hand. "Just to be clear, that was a metaphor. I don't really live in my mom's basement." But he broke eye contact when he said that, and once again, he was stumbling with his words. "I mean, not that there's anything wrong with living with your mom or anything—"

She took another sip of the coffee, which was amongst the worst she'd ever drunk. "Stop," she said. "Just stop. I don't live with my mom. I live in my van, which is occasionally and temporarily, I might add, parked in her driveway. There's a difference."

His eyes narrowed with skepticism, and she supposed he had a right. The difference was negligible.

"Speaking of my van," she said. "I have to take my thyroid medicine. I'll be back."

CHAPTER FORTY-FOUR

Carolina was half-way to her van when she saw the Wrangler, its Deputy emblem on the door, pull in beside her ride.

Shit.

Elven stepped out of his Jeep, moving to her van and rapping his knuckles against the panel door.

How was she going to get out of this without things being awkward? Where could she tell him she'd been?

She considered rushing back to Max's room and hiding, but before she could, Elven surveyed the area and spotted her.

Double shit.

Carolina increased her pace to a light jog, trying to put as much distance between herself and the motel as possible in hopes he wouldn't catch on. "Morning," she said.

Elven wore his mirrored sunglasses, making his face impossible to read. But they gave her a good look at herself. Hair disheveled. Clothing wrinkled. And she imagined her post-puke breath could put down a small animal. Yeah, she really had her life together.

"I stopped by Bea's. You weren't there; so, I thought I'd canvas the town."

"Yeah. We had a disagreement last night," Carolina said. "Decided to camp out and give her some space."

She'd almost convinced herself that she could escape from this without things getting weird when—

"I found your panties!" Max yelled.

Both Carolina and Elven's heads swiveled to find Max in the open doorway to his motel room. He held her underwear in the air like the lady liberty displaying her torch.

"They were behind the toilet," Max said.

Carolina bit down on her tongue, hoping the pain would clear her head and bring her some wisdom. That did not work.

When she looked back to Elven, his expression was steely. She could see that even with the glasses concealing his eyes.

"I see you're busy," he said. "I'll leave you be."

He turned back to his Wrangler and made it a step before she grabbed his arm.

"Wait. Why were you looking for me?"

Elven shook his arm free, then folded them across his chest. "I was going to brief you on last night's murder."

"Okay," she said. "Fill me in."

Before he could, Max's footsteps stole their attention. He'd arrived on the scene, wearing just the towel and flip flops and holding Carolina's white, satin underwear in his hand.

"Didn't you hear me?" he asked as he handed them over.

Carolina grabbed them and shoved them in her pocket. The men stared at each other for a moment; then, Max broke the silence.

"Don't you want to introduce me?"

What Carolina wanted was to kick him in the balls. Instead, she said, "Max, this is Deputy Elven Hallie. Elven, this is Max Barrasso."

Elven cocked his head. "You're that newspaper fellow Lester told me about."

Max extended his hand, and to Carolina's surprise, Elven reciprocated. "Blogger, actually," Max said.

"If you say so," Elven said.

Carolina turned to Max. "Hey, can you give me some space here? There's been a development."

Max held up his hands in surrender, reminding Carolina of when Elven made the same gesture days earlier. The thought that the men, who seemed like polar opposites, might actually be similar in many ways flitted through her mind, but she could ponder that later.

She turned her attention back on Elven. "I'll get in." She moved to circle to the passenger side of the Jeep.

"No," Elven said. "Follow me in your van."

With that, he climbed into his Wrangler. He tipped a finger toward Max before starting the engine. "You might want to put some clothes on before you go out in public. I could write you up for public indecency if I were so inclined."

"Are you?" Max asked.

Carolina ignored their dick-measuring contest, getting into her van.

"Not today," Elven said. "Bigger fish to fry."

"Well, I appreciate the leniency, Deputy. And I promise you I'll be fully dressed next time you see me."

"Good to know," Elven said. He threw the Jeep into gear and backed onto the road.

Carolina rushed to follow and, in the process, heard Max call out, "Am I ever going to hear from you again?"

She'd have to think on that.

CHAPTER FORTY-FIVE

She was two miles from home when she realized she was being followed. The ugly car made every left, every right, that she made. It slowed down when she slowed down, and it sped up when she sped up.

It's that guy.

She pedaled faster, legs pumping, muscles burning as she headed uphill. She risked a glance back and saw it lurking there, like a predatory animal. Stalking her. Waiting for the right time to strike.

She hit the top of the hill and caught her breath. On any other day, Carolina would have coasted down, letting gravity do all the hard work. But today, she needed speed. Her legs turned to a blur, and soon, she was going almost too fast to keep up.

The bike suddenly felt like a missile, out of control and on a course all its own. She gripped the handlebars, which shook as if they were going to break free. In all her years of bicycle riding, she couldn't ever remember going so fast.

It both terrified and thrilled her.

As the wind assailed her face, she couldn't breathe. This was like her own solo ride on a rollercoaster, one with no safety belts.

Another look back. The car had picked up speed, too. He was closing in. She tried to see his face through the windshield, straining to make out his features—

And then she crashed. One minute she was upright and flying. The next, she was on her side and skidding across the asphalt. She felt her skin tear away in chunks. There went a piece of her arm. A bit of her leg. Better keep your face up, she thought to herself.

The road curved, but she kept going straight, slamming into a dense hedge of boxwoods. Their branches clawed at her like skeletal fingers, slicing and dicing her flesh.

She took a moment to gather herself, to realize she was still alive, when she heard the car's engine. The door groaned as it opened.

And the driver began to whistle.

Carolina didn't waste any time checking to see how close he was. She bounced to her feet, scaled the bushes, and dropped to the other side. Then she sprinted, ignoring the blood, ignoring the pain. Because she knew that if he caught her, she was dead.

CAROLINA LOST him in the woods. One minute he was there, crunching through last autumn's fallen leaves, and the next, the only sounds were her own thudding footsteps. Even though she thought she was finally safe again, she kept running until she made it home, breaking through the trees and into her mother's backyard.

Only then did her fear begin to abate.

She scaled the steps to the kitchen and stepped inside, finding Bea sipping coffee at the sink. Her mother didn't acknowledge her arrival until Carolina spoke.

"I wrecked my bike."

Bea turned to her, moving in slow motion. Carolina expected her to scream in shock or maybe yell in anger when she saw her bloody body, her shredded clothes. But the woman barely reacted.

"Did you break anything?"

"Maybe the front wheel," Carolina said.

"I meant bones, darling."

"Oh." Carolina shook her head. "I don't think so."

"Well, that's good. Go get yourself cleaned up."

Her mother's nonchalance was a relief as the last thing she wanted to do was tell Bea what had happened and what she'd been up to. Halfway to the bathroom, she turned back.

"Can you call Lester and ask him to pick up my bike? It's beside Burke's Bend."

Bea took another sip of coffee. "I don't think he'll be able to do that."

"Why not?"

"Because they found another dead girl this morning." Her tone was monotone, matter of fact.

Carolina considered pressing her for details, but she knew better. As she moved into the bathroom and took in her battered reflection, she thought about how close she'd come to being victim number four. And for the first time throughout all of this, she was scared.

CHAPTER FORTY-SIX

Throughout the drive to the laundromat, Carolina wondered how badly she had fucked things up. She respected Elven and, despite his flaws, liked him. And there was a part of her that viewed being a woman in law enforcement as something akin to being an alien invader visiting Earth from a galaxy far away. No matter how much she tried to be one of them, she always felt like an interloper. She wanted to fit in.

Here in Dupray, despite its plethora of faults, she'd felt that acceptance. She felt respected in a way that had eluded her even as she climbed the ranks and made detective in Baltimore. Now she might have ruined all of that.

And that pissed her off. Because if she'd caught Elven or Tank, or even Johnny (the thought made her shudder) after a one-night stand, she wouldn't have judged them. But men got to live by different rules, and no matter how unfair she deemed them, it was the reality of the situation.

By the time the sign for the laundromat came into view, her nausea had returned with a vengeance. It didn't help that three oxys were dissolving in a thin puddle of coffee in her stomach, either.

So much for coming home and getting her shit together.

Yards of crime-scene tape surrounded the squat, concrete block building. There were no lookie-loos, only Lester, Phil Driscoll, and Tank. The three of them were huddled beside a battered pickup truck. That vehicle was unfamiliar, and Carolina assumed it belonged to the victim.

She stopped her van parallel to Elven's Jeep, and she was the first one out of the vehicle. If he was going to scold or judge her, she wanted it to be done right away and not in front of Lester and the others. She was prepared for a fight, but none came.

"The victim is Rita Prescott," Elven said, his voice flat and matter of fact. "This one is sloppier than the others, but it's got all the telltale signs. It's our guy."

He held up the yellow tape, and she scooted under it. She was relieved they didn't have to hash out the awkwardness, but she still had that walking-on-eggshells feeling.

"Is her body on-site?" Carolina asked.

Elven nodded. "In that copse of pines out back."

"She's the first victim that wasn't moved."

"From what we've pieced together, she was attacked by that truck." He pointed. "There's some blood there, and all I had to do was follow the trail to the body."

"So, what are you thinking?" What a loaded question.

But he didn't take the opportunity to jab at her. "Between the evidence and her 9-1-1 call, I think the killer planned to incapacitate her in the vehicle but failed. She ran, but her injuries began to take their toll. There are signs of a scuffle near the body. Maybe he got spooked that it didn't go as smoothly as usual. Who really knows?"

They reached Lester and the others.

"Morning, Carolina. Get any sleep last night?" Lester said to her. His voice carried no weight or confidence. It was like this case was sucking the life from him.

"Some." She resisted the urge to gauge Elven's reaction. "You?"

Lester shrugged. "I'm out the second my head hits the pillow these days."

"Good." She found the drops of the blood on the pavement. Her eyes followed them toward the trees, and she realized she didn't want to see what waited at the end of the trail.

"Anything out of the ordinary with the body, Doc?" she asked Driscoll.

He scratched at his wooly beard. "Not in the slightest. But go ahead and have a look for yourself."

She paused, waiting for one of the men to step up and join her. But none did. She again felt separate from them, isolated. But that was only her paranoia. She knew they'd already seen the body, and although these were seasoned law-enforcement officials, staring at a dead human being was something you didn't do any more than necessary.

So, she went alone. The droplets of blood became splatters, then small pools. She saw a blanket of pine needles kicked asunder at the edge of the thicket, red footprints marring the area. Flies skittered over the blood, gobbling up its sticky wetness.

Rita Prescott waited five yards into the trees. Carolina could have been looking at a photocopy of the other scenes. The pose was the same. The upward staring look was the same. Her eyelids had been excised.

The only difference was her head wound, which had turned her light brown hair dark with coagulated blood. That blood also saturated her clothing.

You made a mess this time, Carolina thought as she took in the scene. You got careless, and she almost beat you.

That realization gave her some hope. A belief that this killer wasn't as smart or perfect as she'd believed. That catching him wasn't just a possibility, but a reality.

Have you made mistakes before?

She thought of the girl Max told her about. In the aftermath of the fiasco with Elven, that assault had been pushed to the back of her mind, but now, it was all she could think about.

CHAPTER FORTY-SEVEN

"That was quick." Max's voice came through the speakers of Carolina's van. "The way you left, I pretty much assumed I'd never hear from you again."

"Don't get too excited, big boy," Carolina said. "I need the name and address for that assault victim."

"Sure, you got a pen?"

"I'm driving. Text it to me."

"Damn, you're bossy. You might want to remember who is doing you the favo--"

She ended the call.

After viewing Rita Prescott's body, she told Lester and Elven that she needed to follow up on another old case. With few other leads, neither protested, and she made a hasty retreat.

Her phone buzzed.

Allison Petry. Better Days Care Home, 92 Sycamore Rd, Dupray.

It ended with a heart emoji, which Carolina hoped was ironic.

BETTER DAYS WAS a two-story building with a faded brick facade. Ivy scrabbled its way up one side of the building, tall enough to reach the roof and push up the nearest shingles. The windows were old and clouded, giving little insight into what might wait inside. It looked more like an asylum than a sunny resort.

As she pulled open a steel door and stepped inside, her nose was immediately assaulted by the smell of cleaning products. Posters of flowers and too-cute baby animals and clouds adorned the walls, each decorated with inspirational messages like *Difficult roads often lead to beautiful destinations*. The combination of all of it did nothing to settle her stomach.

A worn, oak desk waited ahead, and behind it, a middle-aged woman in a peach-colored blouse. She wore thick glasses and dolphin earrings. Her smile was much too cheerful for Carolina's liking.

"Good morning, Miss. How can I help you?"

Carolina glanced at the desk and found a placard that identified the woman as Hillary Smail. She wanted to avoid making this visit official as that might get the facility's legal staff involved, which would only slow things down. All she could do was hope Smail wasn't the inquisitive type.

"I'm here to visit my cousin, Allison Petry," she said. Being such a good liar, she sold it easily.

"Oh, sure. Just sign in here." She tapped a paper with *Visitors* printed on the header.

Carolina scribbled an illegible signature on a clipboard.

"She's in the cozy craft corner," Hillary said. "Do you know your way there?"

"Can you refresh my memory?"

The woman beamed. How were people this happy? Maybe she was medicated.

"Oh, sure. Just go straight down this hall and take the second right. You can't miss it."

"Thanks."

She found the cozy craft corner, a ten-by-ten room where four women sat around a table using Elmer's glue to fasten tongue depressors into a variety of rudimentary shapes. Carolina had no idea which, if any of them, was the girl she wanted to see, and since she was playing the part of a fake cousin, she couldn't exactly ask.

The thought of texting Max to see if he had a photo crossed her mind, but before she could do anything, one of the women spoke.

"Can I help you with something?" The woman, forty-something with spiky red hair, stared at her with grade-A resting-bitch face.

She was out, probably. That left three others. One of them was in her late fifties, with a sloppy gray mane that hung in unwashed strands past her shoulders.

Two to go. Both were the correct approximate age. Both looked at her with bored, disinterested eyes.

"Excuse me," Red said. "I asked you a question."

"Sorry," Carolina said. "I'm a little deaf from my time overseas." That sounded good, as long as the woman didn't ask for details. She looked back and forth between the two possibilities, trying to decide which looked more like an Allison. But she was taking too long, and soon, it wouldn't matter if she guessed right or not.

"I'm here to see Allison," she finally said. She hoped one of the women would perk up, but neither did. "She's my cousin," Carolina added.

The woman with red hair thawed by a degree or two. She turned to Mystery Woman Number Two. "How about that, Allison," she said. "You've got a visitor." Then she looked to Carolina. "It's been a while since any family's come to see her." Her tone was full of judgment.

"I live in San Diego. It's so hard to get back," Carolina said.

"Do you want to join us in a craft hour?"

Carolina shook her head. "I'm not the crafty type," she said.

Red stood and took Allison Petry, aka Mystery Woman Number Two, by the hand. Allison rose to her feet, her movements slow and deliberate. Those of a toddler still learning how to walk. The woman led Allison to Carolina, then indicated for her to take her hand.

After the tradeoff, Red pointed to the right. "There's a new visitors' room just down the hall. There's a TV in there, too, but it only gets the locals."

"That's all right. I just want to catch up and see how this pretty cousin of mine is doing."

Until they were out of the room, Carolina expected Allison to blurt out that she was not her cousin, that she was an imposter, and blow up the entire ruse, but they made their escape without incident. Once in the visitor's room, Carolina led her to a plush, beige couch, and she eased the woman onto it. Then she sat across from her.

The woman was a brunette, her hair the color of caramel with only a few strands of gray intermixed. She would have been extraordinarily pretty if not for the blank expression on her face. An expression that made Carolina think of a department store mannequin. And now, closer up, she could see the lingering remnants of her injuries.

Allison Petry's left eye socket had been shattered and surgically repaired, but the work was poor. A pale, pink scar circled from her cheek to her temple. And her eye on that side of her face sat a few millimeters lower. Not enough to notice at first glance, but once you saw it up close, you couldn't unsee it.

As she took in the women, Carolina wondered if this was worse than death. This life of stasis. Where the highlight of her day was probably a cup of ice cream in the evening. Where she had no hope of getting better, and her future consisted of more of the same day after day after day.

Carolina knew she'd rather die than exist like this, but that wasn't her call to make. And that wasn't why she was here.

"Allison, my name's Carolina," she offered.

The woman looked up, meeting her gaze. There was no recognition in her eyes, but she put on a thin smile.

Carolina was never one to pussyfoot around and didn't see any sense in starting now. "I have to ask you some questions about what happened to you that night after church."

She reached over and took Allison's thin hands in her own.

"Do you remember that?"

Allison stayed silent so long that Carolina began to wonder if she could speak at all. But then she did, although her words came slow and halting. "He. Was. So. Mad."

"Who was, Allison? The man who hit you?"

The woman nodded. "Hurt me."

"I know he hurt you. He was a very bad man." Carolina gave her hands a reassuring squeeze. "You're doing so good. I just need to know the bad man's name."

"I can't." She shook her head. "I can't say it."

"You can tell me. It'll be our secret."

Allison kept shaking her head, whipping it side to side, almost frantic. "Said he'd kill me if I ever said his name."

"He can't hurt you here. He can't hurt you anymore. I promise."

She stopped shaking her head but didn't speak. In fact, she had her lips pinched so tightly together that they had turned white.

"I have an idea," Carolina said. "Instead of telling me his name, why don't you write it?"

She scanned the room and found a coloring book and crayons on a coffee table. She grabbed both, then flipped open the cover, revealing its blank interior side. Then she held the book and passed Allison a crayon.

"If you write it, he won't get mad. Because you didn't say it."

Allison stared at her, wary. "Are you sure?"

"One hundred percent."

The woman gripped the crayon in her fist, holding it more like a knife than a writing instrument. Then her hand dropped to the book, and she began to write. Her movement was jerky and awkward, as well as slow. But eventually, she finished, and Carolina took the book back and examined what she wrote: *JR*.

Was that Junior or initials? She wanted to ask but was afraid of ruining the thin layer of trust she'd established with the women.

"That's good, Allison. Thank you."

"Welcome."

"Do you remember what he looked like?"

Allison's eyes drifted toward the window, where a catbird pecked away at a block of suet.

"Did you hear me, Allison? Do you remember what JR looked like?"

No response.

Carolina had a feeling she was done here, but that might be okay because something clicked in her head. Words from the recent past.

"You want my brother. Ray junior."

Her heart sank. Raymond Harvey Lape, Junior. That son of a bitch.

"Thank you so much for your help, Allison." She gave the woman an awkward pat on the shoulder, then turned to leave.

She made it to the door when the woman spoke again.

"He never gave me my pizza."

Carolina turned back. "Who?" she asked. "The bad man?"

Again, Allison shook her head. "The ghost man." She squeezed her hand, snapping the crayon in half. "He said I'd get pizza if I helped. But I didn't."

Carolina had trouble paying attention to any of this. She needed to find out where Lape had been the night prior and give this information to Lester. "I'll get you a pizza," Carolina said. What do you want on it?"

"Black olives!" Allison said, with more life in her voice than at any point thus far.

"Okay, black olives, it is."

On her way out, she gave Hillary at the front desk a twenty-dollar bill and told her to have Hank's deliver the pie to Cousin Allison. Hillary promised she would, but Carolina didn't wait to find out.

CHAPTER FORTY-EIGHT

"How in the hell could you lose him?" Lester tried but failed to keep his voice down, and he didn't care that everyone in the station was gawking.

Johnny Moore sat behind his computer, looking like a rag-doll version of a man, as if every ounce of fortitude had deserted him. "I'm sorry, Sheriff. I had a good tail on him. He stopped for gas at the Quickie Mart and then went inside. I followed, and he was buying scratch tickets one at a time, then checking to see if he won, then buying another. I had the sense that might go on a while; so, I ordered a couple of wieners with chili, cheese, and onions."

Lester wanted to grab him by the throat and squeeze but resisted the urge. "And what, he slipped out while you were waiting on your goddamn hotdogs?"

"No, Sheriff," Johnny said. "After ten minutes or so, he cashed out. He hit on a five-dollar winner. I know that because I was paying real close attention, just like you told me to."

"Johnny. I'm short on patience right now, and I would be much obliged if you would get to the part of this story where you fouled up, and a man who might be a homicidal maniac got away from you."

Johnny sighed, a whiny sound that seemed to start in his toes and work itself all the way up his body before boiling over. "It was the wieners," he said. "About an hour after the Quickie Mart, I was watching Lape trim some hedges up on Bobcat Lane. That's when I felt my stomach start to protest, and I knew if I didn't get to a bathroom asap, I was never gonna get my Fruit of the Looms clean again. So, I ran over to Hank's to use theirs."

He paused, his eyes wide and on the verge of spilling tears. "When I got back, he was gone."

"And you didn't think to call in and report this?"

Johnny shook his head. "I thought maybe I could find him."

"How did that turn out?" Elven asked from the sidelines. Lester had almost forgotten he was there.

"I didn't," Johnny said.

"Enough of this malarkey." Elven grabbed his keys. "I'm going to Lape's right now."

Lester was ready to say he'd go along when Meredith piped in.

"Lester, you've got a call from Carolina. She says it's urgent."

"Put her through to my office," Lester said. He looked to Elven. "You take Tank along with you. Last thing I need's you walking alone into an ambush."

"So, you'd rather fifty percent of the force be wiped out than twenty-five?" Elven asked with a grin.

"I'm serious, Elven. Be careful; I need you." And he meant it. As much as he blamed Elven for being forced out as Sheriff, he couldn't run this station without him. And, even more than that, he cared about the boy.

"You know me," Elven said.

"I do, and that does little to put my mind at ease," Lester said.

With that, the deputy was gone.

Lester stomped past Johnny, who leaned into his desk like a grade-school student who was being forced to keep his head down during recess for misbehaving. When he reached his office, he snatched the phone.

"Hello."

"Lester, you need to get with Johnny and see where Harvey Lape was last night."

It was Lester's turn to sigh. "About that," he said. "Johnny lost him."

"That stupid mother—"

Lester pulled the phone away from his ear until she was finished. "I'm not pleased either. Trust me."

"I think Lape might be the guy after all," she said. She told him about Allison Petry, about her writing Jr. Then, "Lape is a junior. We need to head to their place right now."

"Elven's already on his way," Lester said.

"Alone?"

He thought her voice sounded worried. "No. I sent Tank with him."

"Oh. Good. You want me to join them?"

"Hell, no. I want you here with me so we can start putting together a case against this asshole."

"I like that idea," Carolina said.

He hung up the phone and closed the door to his office. Then his own tears came, and he made no effort to stop them as they were tears of relief. After almost twenty years, he might finally be able to close the worst and longest chapter of his life.

CHAPTER FORTY-NINE

"What the fuck is this shit?" Bonnie demanded, pointing her shotgun directly at Elven Hallic's chest.

Elven held one hand up but kept the other on the grip of his pistol, which was still holstered. Although he considered himself an above-average draw, he harbored no illusions that he'd be able to shoot Bonnie Lape before she unloaded both barrels of buckshot into him. And if that happened, it was game over.

"Now, Bonnie, we're only here for some questions. Nothing else," Elven said.

"I'm sick of you fuckin' pigs comin' on my property and harassing me. I got rights. You ain't the king of Dupray County, even if you think you are."

As he wondered how to reason with a crazy woman, Elven saw movement in his peripheral vision. Tank had circled around and had his pistol leveled at Bonnie. He was just waiting for Elven to give the word.

But Elven had no desire to see this end in more death.

"Bonnie, I need to talk to your brother, Harvey. Is he around?"

"Harvey ain't here. And if he was, I wouldn't tell you anyhow."

Her finger tensed against the trigger. He knew she was one twitch away from blasting him.

"You best be gettin' back into your rig. Harvey already answered enough questions the other day. He don't got to answer no more."

Elven shook his head. "These are new questions. About last night."

Bonnie didn't have a quick comeback. In fact, she seemed caught off-guard. "What of it?"

"We need to question Harvey about his whereabouts."

She was trying to think up a lie. He could see that plain as the nose on her face. But her dim mind was too slow, and he realized she had no idea where her brother had been the night prior.

"Lower that shotgun and talk to me like a civilized human being, or Hank over there is going to put you down."

Bonnie looked toward Hank out of the corner of her eye. When she saw him, she spun, aiming the gun at him. Her finger squeezed against the trigger—

But Elven was quicker after all. He drew and fired, the bullet slamming into Bonnie Lape's thigh.

She dropped the gun, then fell to the porch, both hands clutching her wounded leg. The pain did little to improve her attitude. "You cocksucker! You shot me! I'm gonna sue your ass off, you rich prick!"

Elven grabbed the shotgun, expelled the remaining ammunition, and tossed it to the ground. He stared down at the woman, who was frothing at the mouth with rage. "Then I suppose we'll see each other again in court."

He grabbed a handkerchief from his pocket and held it against the woman's thigh. It was a through and through and, he imagined, would cause no lasting damage beyond a scar.

"Get your hands off me, you prevert!" She hissed.

"As you wish," Elven said. He turned to Hank. "Search the premises. I'll call in and report this."

Hank nodded and disappeared around the trailer.

Before Elven radioed the station, he retrieved a first-aid kit from his trunk. He set it beside Bonnie, who stared at it like it was a bomb. "Use it if you so choose," Elven said.

He heard her pop the plastic latches as he returned to the Jeep, and that made him smile. He was reaching for his radio when—

"Hey, Elven," Tank said. "Come check this out."

Elven moved toward the sound of the man's voice. As he passed by Bonnie, he lobbed one more jab. "Don't you run off on me now."

"Fuck you!" She screamed as he disappeared around the hovel.

He found Tank kneeling beside a steel fire ring, staring at its charred contents. "What do you got?" Elven asked.

Hank used a long stick to pull a jacket from the pile. It was blackened with soot but intact. And even if Elven hadn't recognized the school colors, the stitching on the back was impossible to mistake: McDowell University.

On the front, the name Rita was embroidered.

"Well, I'll be dipped," Elven said. "Let's show this to our foul-mouthed friend. See if it jogs her memory."

Hank flashed a goofy grin.

Bonnie was busy wrapping a bandage around her leg when they returned. She stared with furious, beady eyes.

"This looks a might small for Harvey," Elven said. "And I don't take you for the book-learning type. Care to tell me how this ended up in the burn pit in your back yard?"

"That wasn't here until you got here! You planted that! This is a setup!" She cackled, a harsh, bird-like sound.

"You won't think it's so funny when you're charged as an accessory to multiple murders."

He saw blood on the jacket and hoped, by some miracle, some of it was Lape's. Then they'd have the bastard dead to rights.

"Throw her in your cruiser and take her to the station," Elven said. "Call Doc and have him meet you there. I'm going to see what other trophies Lape's got laying around here."

"Go ahead and look, pig! It don't matter 'cause you ain't never gonna find Harvey. He'll find you!"

Tank had her at the patrol car, the back door open. Elven motioned for him to wait.

"What's that supposed to mean?" he asked her.

Bonnie cackled again. "That bitch cop better watch her back. All y'all better watch your backs. Ain't no one fucks with the Lape's and gets away with it!"

Elven met Tank's gaze and nodded. The big man deposited her into the rear of the cruiser, then locked her in.

"Are you sure you're okay on your own?" Tank asked.

"Yeah. After listening to her mouth, I can use some peace and quiet."

Tank grimaced, as if he suddenly realized the verbal diarrhea that he would have to deal with the entirety of the ride back to Dupray; then, he climbed in behind the wheel.

Elven watched until they were heading down the driveway, then began to survey the property. It was going to take him the rest of the day to get through a fourth of it, but before he could begin, he needed to do something. He grabbed his cell and dialed. It rang four times, then went to voicemail.

"Don't leave a message because I won't listen to it. Text me if this is important," Carolina's voice said.

Despite her demands, he spoke. "This is Elven. We need to talk."

He ended the call, then texted the same message. Then, he waited.

That lasted all of twenty seconds before he was in his Jeep, pedal to the floor.

CHAPTER FIFTY

Carolina was only a block away from the Sheriff's department and stopped at one of Dupray's two traffic lights when she saw Elven's text.

We need to talk.

She didn't like the sound of that. Maybe the professionalism he'd put on earlier in the day was a ruse, and he was as pissed off and disappointed with her as she'd expected him to be. She began to type a message, something to buy time, when the light flipped green.

That was excuse enough to put it off. She set the phone aside on the passenger seat and hit the gas.

Halfway through the intersection, she felt the world explode around her.

Her body hurtled sideways, snared by the seat belt, which violently lurched her back into position. The glass in the passenger side window blew inward, raining onto her like hail.

Then the airbag blew open in her face, slamming her skull into the headrest. Her eyes burned, blurring her vision, but as her van came to a stop, she scrambled to regain her bearings and figure out what the hell just happened.

The hazy mirage of a truck came into view. She blinked. Again. Again. Her vision cleared by half, and now she could see it better. A pickup had slammed into her van, its grill catching her front end. That explained the violent motion of the crash that had spun her an almost full 360 degrees.

She took a couple of deep breaths and felt her heart pounding in her chest. She tried to focus on what was happening. To shake away the disorientation and shock.

Then she heard a man's voice. "You alive in there?"

Carolina pushed open her door and tried to step outside but immediately lost her balance and fell onto the asphalt. She worked herself into a sitting position, waiting for the waves in her head to stop crashing.

"Call nine-one-one," Carolina said, then risked standing up. Her balance wasn't great, and she kept herself upright by leaning into the van, but she remained on her feet this time.

She closed her eyes, trying to get her bearings. She had to check on the other driver to see if he or she was hurt, or worse.

When she opened her eyes, the first thing she saw was the rifle. The barrel was pointed in her general direction. As she looked beyond it, she saw the man who held it.

Harvey Lape.

A ragged gash crossed his forehead, and blood drained down his face. It dripped from the tip of his nose, ran in his mouth, and coated his teeth as he snarled.

"Time for you to die, bitch."

It seemed like everything moved in slow motioned as Carolina saw him shoulder the rifle, aim at her chest. His finger began to squeeze the trigger.

She dove to her right, and the gun went off as she was falling. She heard the bullet slam into her van at about the same time she hit the ground.

Lape jerked back the bolt, chambering another round. Instead of wasting time looking, she scrambled to the front of her van, continuing around it, desperate to get to the glove compartment, where her pistol waited.

But Lape's truck blocked her path. The bull bar on the front of his pickup was entwined in her wheel well. She had to race around his vehicle before she could get to her own.

Harvey was coming, but he was hurt. She could hear a foot dragging across the pavement.

Step. Drag. Step. Drag. Step.

She was at his tailgate, circling.

"Where you think you're gonna go, rabbit?" Lape asked. "You trying to run from the big, bad hunter?"

What a fucking lunatic.

Carolina made it to Lape's driver's side door when the second shot rang out. This one slammed into the cab of his truck, punching a hole in the frame beside the windshield. She felt the vehicle shudder under the impact.

Lape chambered another round. "You're a slippery rabbit," he said and began to whistle tunelessly.

Carolina dove for her van. The window was shattered, and she reached through the cavity, popping the switch for the glove compartment.

Her hand found her gun. She ripped it from the holster, flicked off the safety, and spun around.

She had no time to aim because Lape had a bead on her. He shot first.

The bullet whistled past her head, so close she could feel the cool breeze that broke in its wake. He missed.

Her turn.

Carolina fired, and she hit her target, but it wasn't a kill shot. The slug hit him in the left arm, around his bicep. He did something akin to a pirouette in the middle of the street, his rifle clattering to the hardtop.

But he remained upright. And he was pissed.

Despite his injuries, Lape ran at her full bore, a move that so surprised Carolina that she didn't have time to get off a second shot before he hit her. Her head bounced off the side of her van, causing the world to go black for a second, and she dropped her gun.

When she could see again, his bloody, raging face was tight against her own. He exhaled his fetid breath, bloody aerosols splattering her skin.

"I like me a girl who fights back." He grabbed a fistful of her hair and slammed her head again into the van. This time she didn't black out, but a galaxy of stars appeared in her vision.

He did that again, and she felt her equilibrium disappear. Now, she was holding onto Lape simply to remain upright and on her feet.

Lape shoved her off him. Her right shoulder - her bad shoulder - took the brunt as her body fell into the van. Fireworks of pain exploded throughout her upper body, and she felt as if she would simultaneously pass out, puke, and collapse.

Somehow, she managed to stave off all three.

Lape grabbed at her again, but she rolled to the side, using her van for support. The man lost his balance and stumbled forward in time to collide with the vehicle. Before he could turn toward her, Carolina kicked, her foot connecting with his knee, which buckled at a gruesome angle that joints aren't meant to bend.

He grabbed his wounded appendage, as if he could heal it with just a touch. "I ain't going back to prison. Not because of some cunt like you." He spat a mouthful of blood in her direction. "You wanna see a murder? I'll show you one."

He launched himself at her, tackling her to the ground and landing on top of her. He flailed with his arms, a right catching her in the eye. A left in the gut, knocking the wind from her.

Then he grabbed at her face, his fingers closing over her ear. It felt like he was going to tear it off her head, and she felt a hot burst of blood as his ragged nails sunk into her flesh.

Lape's grip slid to her neck. His strong hands closing over her throat. Thumbs digging into her windpipe. She felt her lungs seize and burn as they fought for air that wouldn't come.

The fucker's going to kill me. Right in the middle of the street.

If Dupray weren't such a shithole, someone would have come to her aid by now, but it was, and no one was going to help her. If she wanted to survive this, she had to do it all by herself.

Her right arm felt as useless as a stump, so she used her left.

Carolina slammed her fist into Harvey Lape's face, bending his nose sideways. A geyser of blood burst from his nostrils, raining onto Carolina, who clamped her mouth shut to avoid swallowing it.

Lape released her throat, both of his hands going to his broken nose. It was enough of a distraction for Carolina to slide out from under him.

She spotted her pistol by the wheel of Lape's truck. It was within reach, and she grabbed it, then rolled onto her back to better position herself.

Lape saw her. He reached toward his belt, where the hilt of a knife protruded.

As soon as his hand closed over the weapon, Carolina put two rounds in his chest.

Lape slumped sideways, propped up against the van. His breaths came in deep hitches that shook his entire body. Blood seeped from his open mouth. Despite it all, he never stopped glaring at her.

Carolina kept the gun trained on him until she was sure he was dead.

CHAPTER FIFTY-ONE

AS FAR AS CELEBRATORY PARTIES WENT, THIS ONE WAS PRETTY low-key. All the employees of the sheriff's station, plus Bea, Meredith's husband, Phil Driscoll, and his wife had gathered together at Minnow Point, Lester's lake house, which was far less luxurious than it sounded.

The log cabin was more of a hunting camp than a house. A single-story, four-room building with no heat or AC, no running water or plumbing, and no electricity. Despite all that it lacked, Carolina had nothing but fond memories of the place.

She'd spent countless weekends there during her childhood, learning everything from how to whittle to the best time of day to fish on the lake. Occasionally, her mother and Scarlet would join them, but neither enjoyed *roughing it,* and they had spent most of the time complaining about the bugs, having to use the outhouse, or being bored.

None of those things bothered Carolina. In fact, she loved the break from regular life. She relished the slow pace of the days at the lake, where Lester was not only her teacher and mentor but the father she'd never had.

"Food's up," Johnny called as he turned away from the charcoal grill to face the middling crowd. He wore a grease-and-barbecue-sauce-stained apron that he'd brought along to the party, along with the hot dogs and hamburgers. It declared him the *Grill Master* and, from the smell, Carolina might have to agree.

The past week or so had been anything but easy as she recovered physically and mentally from her altercation with Lape. With her van out of commission, she'd spent most of the days in her childhood bedroom, lost in a sea of pain and pills.

She'd still be there if Lester hadn't organized this gathering: "a party in your honor," he'd called it. She didn't exactly feel worthy or up to it, but the man was finally looking alive again, and she wasn't about to disappoint him.

Meredith handed out paper plates and plastic utensils at the head of the makeshift buffet line. There were potato salad and deviled eggs, watermelon and cantaloupe, baked beans dressed up with bacon and sausage, three varieties of chips, and all the condiment options you could want.

"You're looking good," Meredith said as she handed Carolina her plate and cutlery.

Carolina appreciated the lie. She looked like hell. In addition to the bruises, scratches, and scrapes, she'd lost twelve pounds in the last week from not eating. And although Bea had asserted, "Skinny looks good on you," Carolina knew better.

She hadn't realized how hungry she was until she smelled the food, and she loaded up the paper plate to a near-critical level, topping it off with two hot dogs and a burger so thick it must have weighed half a pound.

Johnny grinned at the sight of her haul. "Glad you brought your appetite," he said. "You need to put some meat back on those bones."

Men rarely knew how to give a compliment, but she smiled and nodded. "It looks delicious," she said as she layered onions and tomatoes on top of her patty.

"The secret's using ground chuck. Eighty twenty. That lean hamburger gets too dry on the grill. You need the fat to make it good."

As she looked the portly man up and down, she thought that might be his motto in life. But she also knew fat cooks were the best cooks, and she couldn't wait to dig in.

Two picnic tables, both painted forest green, sat beside the lake. At one, Bea was holding court, regaling Tank, Driscoll, and Meredith's husband with anecdotes that she thought were hilarious. Bea was always at the top of her game, like an emcee at a nightclub around men, and this was no different.

Carolina went to the other table, where Elven sat alone, picking at some potato salad and deviled eggs. His plate was conspicuously absent of meat.

"Don't you trust Johnny's grilling?" Carolina asked as she sat across from him.

"I'm sure he's perfectly adequate," he said. "But I don't eat meat."

She narrowed her eyes, inspecting him. Surely, he was joking. "You had a chicken sub that night at Hank's."

"Chicken is different."

"How so?"

"Have you ever looked into a chicken's eyes? If you do, all you'll see is feral stupidity. They have no soul. And they're cannibals, too." He cut a deviled egg in two and popped half in his mouth. "Cows and pigs, they have feelings and emotions. Personalities."

When Carolina bit into her burger, grease squished out and dribbled down her chin. She wiped it away with the back of her hand. "You've put a lot of thought into this."

"Common sense, really."

She traded the burger for a hot dog. "Are you judging me right now?" She took a bite.

Elven shook his head. "It's not in my place to judge anyone."

The way he looked at her when he said it, the earnestness in his eyes, she believed him.

Carolina carried two bottles of vaguely cool beer as she approached Lester, who sat on a wood bench and stared out at the lake. The sun was on its downward decline, tossing brilliant orange rays onto the gentle waters. It looked like a scene straight out of a Bierstadt painting.

Yeti bounded into and out of the water, rushing to her as she walked and jumping in excitement, a tennis ball in his mouth. She managed to pull it free and chucked it into the lake. The dog chased after, and Carolina sidled up beside Lester.

"Room for two on there?" she asked.

He looked up at her, a soft smile on his face. "Always."

She handed him a beer and sat beside him, dragging her fingers across the bench. It was constructed from hand-hewn pine, perfect in its rusticness, and would have looked at home in a high-end ski resort or maybe a ranch out in Montana or Wyoming. "This is nice. Did you make it?"

"A little project some years back."

"You could go into the furniture-making business after you retire." She paused, trying to read his face, to see if the thoughts of retirement still affected him so. But Lester appeared peaceful, a foreign look compared to how he'd been in the weeks before the case was closed.

"Maybe I'll do that," he said. "See if I can get a booth at the farmer's market and peddle my wares beside Abigail Chalmers and her ginseng."

Carolina spilled a small laugh. "Golden years dreams."

Lester laughed, too, now. She reached over and took his hand in hers, loving its rough texture against her skin. Yeti plopped down beside them, panting with jubilant exertion.

"Or maybe I'll just sit here," he said. "And enjoy this view."

Even though she was a little drunk, as they stared across the lake, Carolina thought that sounded like a fine plan.

CHAPTER FIFTY-TWO

THE TOWER OF PAPERWORK ON HIS DESK WAS NEARLY A FOOT-and-a-half in height. Lester stared at it, wary, as if a strong wind might come along and collapse the pillar onto him, trapping him under his shirked responsibilities.

"Lester?" Meredith asked from the doorway, startling him.

"Sorry," she said. "Didn't mean to sneak up on you."

"That's all right. Come on in."

She did, and he noticed that she held a piece of paper in her hand. "I suppose this is a moot point now after that mess with Harvey Lape, but I finally got the records back from the DMV about that Pacer. The one you asked me to look into a couple weeks back."

"And?"

"I found one."

His annoyance and worry over the less interesting duties of his job vanished. He reached for it.

"Took some digging. The registration hasn't been renewed in a long time. But it's the only one that's ever been registered in Dupray."

Lester examined the document. It was faded, a copy of a copy.

But he could decipher the important parts. The owner's name and address.

She was right; it was probably a moot point, but he didn't like leaving knots untied, and besides, he welcomed a break from the office.

As he rolled down a long, gravel driveway, a farmhouse came into view. Its white paint had long ago flecked away, leaving bare wood the color of lead. Ornamental flourishes, such as the gingerbread trim, had fallen prey to wind and time—now, only scraps of wood fastened to the porch and gables.

The barn was in equally poor condition. Several boards had gone missing in the siding, and sheets of tin roof flopped in the wind, creating thunderous booms on an otherwise sunny day.

In front of the open barn doors was an International Harvester tractor, and a man almost as old as Lester stood on a wooden crate, using a ball-peen to beat the machine's engine into submission. As the wheels of the car crunched through the rocks, the man turned to see who had invaded his space.

Lester stepped out of the car, plopping his hat on his head. He glanced at the passenger seat, prepared to tell Yeti to be patient and wait, only to recall that he'd left the dog at the office. With no one to say goodbye, he closed the door.

Rulon Munroe, the farmer, took a careful step off the crate and watched Lester approach. He was bald and tan with a craggy face etched with wrinkles deep enough to lose spare change. He wore faded overalls and a white thermal shirt. As he approached, the old man snagged a dirty rag from his pocket and wiped his blackened hands on it.

"If you came to talk about my boy, you're too late."

Lester had no idea what the man was talking about. "Pardon?"

Rulon spat tobacco juice into the dirt. "My son, John Munroe.

He was missing, but out of the blue, he called me about a month ago. Told me not to worry anymore. That he was fine."

Lester hesitated, racking his tired mind. Had he been here before? Nothing about this place, this man, felt familiar.

The farmer realized he was clueless. His worn face twisted into a sneer. "You don't even remember him, do you?"

"I apologize, sir. But I do not."

Rulon shook his head, disgusted. "Can't say I'm surprised. Never did trust your kind."

"My kind?"

"Police." Rulon took a step toward him. "If this isn't about my son, then why the hell are you here?"

Lester steeled himself, trying to get this conversation back on track. To be the one asking the questions and not answering them. "I'm looking for the owner of an AMC Pacer. It might've been used in the commission of a crime."

"Jesus Christ," the old man said. "You lose your marbles or something? That was John's car."

"I don't suppose you still have the vehicle?"

Rulon Munroe nodded. "I do. It's in the barn."

He turned and stomped toward the barn, passing through the cavernous opening and into the shadows. Lester remained where he stood until Rulon turned back to see where he was. "You coming or not?"

He followed, all the while trying to conjure up some memory of the farmer and his son. It was beginning to come back—broad strokes anyway.

It was summertime when Rulon had reported his son missing. The farmer's fields were full of eight-feet-tall corn—so tall it made the homestead seem like it existed on its own island. An oasis against the green sea surrounding it.

They passed by a variety of farm implements and tools. A hay wagon. Two tractors. A vintage Harley Davidson XL Sportster which was probably quite the machine in its day but to which time had been unkind.

Munroe approached a car-shaped mound that was covered by thick, blue tarp weighed down by two metal wheels. "Don't stand there like you got a cock up your ass. Make yourself useful and give me a hand."

Lester grabbed one of the wheels while the farmer took the other. They set them aside, then Rulon grabbed the tarp and slid it off the vehicle. As it came free, it revealed a Pacer so pristine it looked fresh off the showroom floor.

Lester's shock must have been obvious as Rulon commented, "I give it a coat of wax once a year. Armor All the dash so it don't crack."

Lester reached for the door handle. "May I?"

Rulon nodded.

As Lester pulled open the door, the stale aroma of time filled his nose. The interior was almost as clear as the outside, with only some wear on the driver's side floor mat revealing it was used.

He popped the glove box and fished out the paperwork. There was an owner's manual, a bill of sale. The buyer was listed as John Robert Munroe. Address the same as the farm's. There were a few receipts for oil changes and service work, but that was all. He looked deeper. There was a hand-held ice scraper. A few packs of matches. A small sewing kit.

That last item caught his attention. He opened it. It contained thread, a few buttons, and needles. No scissors, though.

That absence seemed too serendipitous. He took the case in his hand and retreated from the vehicle.

"Remind me when you last saw--"

He turned to face Rulon Munroe just in time for the ball end of the hammer to catch him in the cheek.

Lester fell onto the barn floor, feeling the old straw pricking through his shirt. Hot wetness spread across his face, seeping into his eyes. His vision became a red haze. He tried blinking to clear the blood, but it did no good. There was too much.

Rulon stepped over him, straddling him. He spun the hammer in his hand. "John told me to keep an eye out for you. Said you'd come poking your nose around again now that he was home."

He reared back with the hammer, readying himself for a second strike, when—

Lester kicked with his right leg. His foot planted square where the old man was split, sinking into the soft mass between Rulon's legs.

Munroe sucked in a mouthful of wind, making a pained *Ahhhh* sound in the process.

The hammer slipped from his hand, the head landing on Lester's thigh before bouncing to the floor. Lester pushed himself onto his side, then grabbed the strap of the farmer's overalls, jerking him sideways.

The farmer toppled over, and Lester slammed his fist into Rulon's jaw. A second punch resulted in a crunch and, when Munroe's mouth sagged open, Lester saw a broken dental plate jumbled inside his bleeding mouth. Rulon's eyes had gone unfocused, and Lester knew this was his best chance. Maybe his only chance.

He lurched to his feet, the act making his head feel as if it was going to float off his body like an untethered balloon. Only the pain kept the connection active.

Lester staggered out of the barn toward the undercover car. He fumbled with the handle, missing on his first attempt. The second was more successful.

He reached for the radio, punched all the buttons. No response. He tried again with the same lack of results. Then he saw the frayed wires and realized mice had put it out of commission. The way his luck was going, that seemed about right.

The reflection in the rear-view mirror was that of a monster. His cheek was flayed open under his eye, revealing a glimpse of bone as a shocking amount of blood drained from the wound.

Lester explored it with his fingers, then applied more pressure. It hurt like hell, but nothing underneath seemed to move. He was confident his face was broken.

A glance at the barn showed that Rulon Munroe was still prostrate on the floor. Lester knew he should go back and cuff him, but that barely-there feeling in his head was getting worse, not better. He needed to get out of there.

After starting the engine, he whipped a U-turn and sped up the drive. The rear end fishtailed as he made a left onto the main road, and he almost lost control.

He was fading.

The world ahead of him was a crimson blur, and Lester squeezed one eye closed, hoping that would improve his vision. It did not.

He made it the better part of five miles before the Crown Vic drifted off the road, onto the berm, and collided head-on with a telephone pole.

CHAPTER FIFTY-THREE

The cerulean warbler stalked a wasp that danced between the purple aster flowers. Carolina was almost finished with her sketch; so, she ignored the annoying buzz that indicated she'd received a text message.

I'll check it later.

Buzz number two.

It can't be that important.

She continued to draw as the bird caught the wasp in its beak, shook its blue-and-white head side to side, and devoured it. Hardcore.

Buzz number three.

Shit.

She gave up and set her sketch pad and pencil aside, trading them for her cell. All three messages were from Elven.

It's Elven. Pick up.

9-1-1. Pick up.

Lester's been in an accident. Injured.

She let the sketch pad and pencil lay as she raced around the house and toward the Blazer. She dialed Elven as she climbed inside.

"It's me," she said. "What happened to Lester?"

CHAPTER FIFTY-FOUR

She found him in Phil Driscoll's medical office, where he sat on the exam table as Driscoll poked a needle through his face. A large gash marred his cheek, but it was half-stitched shut and oozing blood.

His eye on the wounded side of his face was red as a fireball. His uniform shirt was saturated, stained so dark she'd have thought he dumped an entire thermos of coffee on himself if she didn't know better.

All things considered, she'd expected worse.

Elven sat in a metal chair nearby, hat in his lap, head in his hands.

"God, Lester," Carolina said as she entered the cramped room, drawing the attention of all three men.

Lester sat up straighter, the move causing a scowl from Driscoll, who pinched the suture needle between his thumb and forefinger.

"If you keep moving, you're liable to lose that eye," Driscoll said.

"Only if you're careless," Lester said.

Carolina wormed her way into the mix and hugged him, drawing an exasperated sigh from the doctor, who slid his wheeled chair backward.

"I'll give you a minute," he said, leaving the needle behind, skewering Lester's cheek.

"I'm all right," Lester said, returning the embrace. "Don't know why Elven had to tell you about this in the first place. Gave you a bad scare over nothing."

"He should be in Charleston. In the hospital," Driscoll piped in from the peanut gallery. "Grade two concussion would be my guess. And that eye socket might be cracked."

"Oh, shush," Lester said as he pulled back from Carolina. "Even if it is, that are they gonna do? Put a cast on my face?"

Carolina hurriedly wiped budding wetness from her eyes, then checked to see if Elven had noticed. If he had, he didn't make a spectacle of it, and she appreciated that. "What happened?" she asked.

Lester filled her in on what he could remember, which wasn't a lot. All he could recall was arriving at the farm and Rulon Munroe bitching about his once-missing son, then seeing the Pacer. After that, it all went blank. Then Elven added what he knew, informing her of the 9-1-1 call that came from a concerned motorist.

"He saw all that blood and thought for sure you were dead," Elven said.

Lester tried to smile, but his swollen, damaged face refused to cooperate. "I'm not that easy to kill."

"What about the farmer? Has anyone brought him in?" Carolina asked.

"I sent Tank and Johnny out there. Waiting to hear back," Elven said.

"Maybe I should head out there," Carolina said.

"No," Lester and Elven replied simultaneously.

"Fine," she said.

With all that out of the way, Carolina let Driscoll get back to work and finish stitching shut Lester's cheek, complaining all through the procedure. "I'm not a damnable plastic surgeon. I shouldn't be putting sutures in someone's face."

"I didn't expect to win any beauty pageants anyway, Doc."

Just then, Elven's phone went off.

"That's Tank." He put his finger in his ear and slipped out of the exam room.

"What's the story with these Munroe's?" Carolina asked Lester. "The old bastard wouldn't attack you for no reason."

"Maybe Tank can get something out of him," Lester said.

"I rather doubt it," Elven said from the doorway.

They looked at him. His usual cocksure grin was gone, his expression sober.

"Why not?" Carolina asked.

"Because Rulon Munroe is dead." Elven stepped into the room. "Choked to death on his own dentures."

"I need to get back to that house," Lester said. "Find out what the hell's going on."

"Maybe they will." Driscoll nodded toward Carolina and Elven. "But you're not going anywhere but your own house." He tied off the suture thread and pressed a bandage over the mess.

Lester opened his mouth to protest, but Driscoll held up a finger for silence.

"Don't you give me grief, Lester. I can have you admitted to the hospital against your wishes, and if you push me, I'll do just that. You were attacked and in a serious accident. You can rest for one damned day, and the world will go on. I promise."

Carolina saw the frustration in Lester's eyes. She turned to Elven and Driscoll, her face angled away from Lester's, and raised an eyebrow. They took the hint.

"Elven, did I ever show you my collection of fishing flies?" Driscoll asked.

"No, sir, Doc, I don't believe you have."

"Come with me."

They left the room.

"Very discreet," Lester said. "That act wouldn't have fooled an inebriated six-year-old."

"They mean well."

"I'm sure." He met her eyes, his own gaze flagging, eyelids drooping. "I should be out there."

"No. You *want* to be, and I understand that. But what you *should* be is home. Doc's right."

His shoulders sagged, and his chin dropped against his chest. She hated putting him on the sidelines. He deserved to be in the thick of it, in the action, but this was for his own good. At least, that's what she told herself.

"Goddamn," he said. "I shouldn't have turned my back on him. How'd I get so dumb?"

"Like you were supposed to know he was going to brain you?" She put her hand on his shoulder. "Any one of us would have done the same in your position."

He risked a glance up, and when he did, she saw a myriad of exhaustion, frustration, and hurt on his face. He looked not only tired but fragile.

"You always did look out for me, didn't you, hon?" he asked.

"I try." Her fingers became entwined in his long hair, which was so soft it felt like strands of silk against her skin.

He reached up and placed his plus-sized hand over hers. He pulled her hand off his shoulder, then took it between both of his palms, staring at it. "You're such a good girl, Diana."

Carolina inhaled sharply, choking on the air. She swallowed away the resulting cough and told herself that she'd misheard him. That he hadn't just called her Diana. That he hadn't confused her with his long-dead daughter.

But she knew better. And she saw it in his eyes. He'd always been something of a surrogate father to her, but the look in those eyes at that moment transcended their actual relationship. He was living decades in the past.

Carolina pulled away, startled, more roughly than she meant.

Lester's suddenly empty hands fell into his lap, and his focus fell to them.

"I'm going to see if Doc can give you a ride home," she said, backing away from him.

The commotion seemed to bring him back to the present, and when he looked up, he was himself again. "Okay," he said. "But I want you to call me if you find anything, no matter how inconsequential it seems."

She was able to breathe again.

Don't freak out; this isn't a big deal. He's exhausted. He has a concussion. And he just inadvertently killed a man. He was allowed to be flustered and confused.

That was a lie she would tell herself as long as possible.

CHAPTER FIFTY-FIVE

The scene in the Munroe barn was, in a word, sickening. Rulon Munroe laid on his back, face twisted and vaguely blue in color. His open mouth overflowed with vomit and blood. Some of each had leaked down each side of his face and into his ears, resembling a sort of vile warpaint.

"Jesus," Carolina said. "Lester did a number on the guy."

"Can't say that I blame him," Elven said. He rummaged through Rulon's pockets, pulling out the contents. Tums. A dirty rag. A keyring with enough keys to manage a large hotel. Loose change. His wallet.

"Let me see that," Carolina said, and Elven handed it to her. The brown leather was worn to a light tan, the seams splitting.

When she opened it, she found sixty-eight dollars in cash, a variety of cards, his driver's license, and a concealed carry permit. She reached into the inner pockets, the ones where people usually store receipts and other things they don't want to lose.

It was there that she found three photographs. One was Rulon Munroe as a very young man, barely twenty by her guess. He was dressed in a suit and posing beside an equally young woman in a nice dress. She flipped it over and found written, in neat, block font - *Our Wedding Day.*

The next photo was the same man and woman sitting on a porch. The same porch she'd seen at the front of the farmhouse upon her arrival. This time, they were joined by a toddler, a boy who looked about five years old. All were dressed in their Sunday best. Written in the same handwriting was - *Easter Sunday,* along with the year.

Photo number three was of a stranger. A young man, maybe sixteen or seventeen. It was a formal portrait, the kind taken in a studio with all the falsehoods that went along with such a picture.

The teen had a *Say Cheese* grin that displayed a front tooth that was broken in half, but there was no cheer in his eyes. He wore a poorly fitting suit jacket and tie. The back of the photo read, - *John's Senior Portrait.*

She pushed the photographs back into the dead farmer's wallet, thinking that the entirety of his life was likely summed up in those three small prints. That struck her as depressing, which seemed doubly so when she considered how empty her own life was. She didn't have a single person's photo in her billfold.

"I'll take that back if you're finished," Elven said, snapping her out of her brief pity party.

"Sure," she said as she handed it over.

With the dead man telling no tales, her attention went to the AMC Pacer. The sight of it took her breath away because it looked identical to the vehicle she'd seen that day in the cemetery and again on the road, only then, her teenage brain had no idea of the make and model of the hideous automobile.

When she tried to convince herself that this was all a bizarre coincidence, it wasn't hard to do. Besides, she had no proof that the man in the cemetery had anything to do with the murders. For all she knew, he was an old boyfriend who didn't appreciate her spying and wanted to give her a good scare.

Still...

A slip of paper discarded on the floor beside the Pacer drew her attention. She picked it up and saw it was an old vehicle registration card that listed the make and model of the car: the insurance information, the VIN, and the owner.

Munroe, John Robert.

She read that name a second time.

John Robert.

J.R.

Her breath caught in her throat. This went beyond coincidence now.

She wanted - needed - to tell Elven. But not just yet, not when the whole county was still riding high over the death of *Serial Killer Harvey Lape*. She couldn't kill that buzz without proof.

And she was going to find it.

CHAPTER FIFTY-SIX

THE FOLLOWING MORNING, CAROLINA SCOURED THE CHURCH logbooks and found several mentions of the Munroe family. It was all coming together, to her anyway, so she got the keys and went to the basement of the Sheriff's Department, where the old files were stored. The room smelled like mildew and armpits. A dense, secretive aroma that seemed meant to ward off intruders.

But Carolina wouldn't be deterred. She'd gone through shelves filled with filing boxes, skimming through every single folder, and after more than four hours, her search had yielded no results. There wasn't a single mention of John Robert Munroe.

She had four more rows to go when she heard the door above open, then close. Footsteps approached, the hard heel of a man's boots echoing off the metal steps.

"Carolina," Elven called. "Meredith told me you've been down there for half the day. Thought I better make sure you didn't lose your mind trying to make sense of her filing system and hang yourself from the light cord."

He appeared at the bottom landing, and when he saw her, he grinned.

"What are you smiling about?" she asked, sensing it was at her expense.

"You've got a little…" He wiped at his face, and Carolina found the nearest reflective surface. She saw dirt smeared across her cheeks and forehead, making her look something like a coal miner at the end of a long shift underground.

"Doesn't anyone ever clean around here?" she asked, then spit into her palm and tried to wash the filth off herself.

"Not really. Not since Johnny was promoted anyway."

Carolina checked her reflection again. Not perfect, but better. "Maybe you should put that on your to-do list for when you take over as sheriff."

"I'll prioritize that." He moved toward her, having to walk partially hunched over due to the low ceilings. "Did you find whatever the heck you were looking for?"

Carolina glanced around the dim room. "No. But I don't know how you people find anything down here."

Elven gave a little laugh. "Sometimes Meredith files according to the date. Others alphabetically. And occasionally, she breaks it down by location. It's a mystery, really. I think she does it on purpose as job security. She's the only one that knows where everything is."

"Good for her." Carolina pulled an unexplored box from a shelf, resulting in a category two dust storm.

"I can help you look if you'll stop being so close-mouthed."

"What are you talking about?"

"You barely said ten words to me on the ride back yesterday. I thought maybe my presence offended you."

"It's not that," she said. She examined the hodgepodge of files. "I'm looking for a missing persons report for John Robert Munroe. If one was ever filled out anyway. Lester didn't take it, and neither did Tank."

"Maybe Anse Medley handled it," Elven suggested. "Though, from what I've seen, Anse and paperwork were not friends."

He pulled open a drawer, ready to help her search. "What do

you want it for, anyway? With the old man dead, I don't see that his son matters all that much."

Carolina had a feeling this wouldn't go well, but she saw no sense in dragging him along blind. Time to spill the beans.

"You're going to think I'm crazy," she started.

"That horse has already left the barn."

She gave a fake laugh. "Funny."

"I try."

"Rulon Munroe's son is named John Robert. J.R." She watched him, trying to gauge his reaction, but the man was an enigma.

"And he owned a Pacer, the same model that Driscoll saw picking up Darlene Mason after her abortion inquiry. Then you have Rulon going apeshit and attacking Lester for no reason…"

She wanted him to complete her thought, but he didn't give her the satisfaction, and she had to say it herself.

"What if John Robert Munroe is the real killer. And Harvey Lape was just some half-crazy motherfucker with a hair-trigger temper like we all thought at first?"

"Like you thought," Elven said. "You're the one that dismissed him as not fitting your *profile*, like you were fresh off the bus from Quantico."

He'd lost his smile and didn't make an effort to hide his annoyance.

"The man gave you fake names as alibis. He ditched the tail we had on him, and that same night, a girl was killed. The next day, we found her bloody jacket in his burn pit. And soon thereafter, he tried to murder you in broad daylight!"

That last sentence was as close as she'd ever come to hearing the man yell. She knew bringing it up was a gamble, but now, she wanted to melt into the carpet.

When he said all of that out loud, it made her theory sound like something cooked up by a conspiracy nut on Reddit, and she half-expected him to offer her a tinfoil hat. She waited to see if he was done. He was not.

"I understand that your life is in a challenging place right now. Maybe you're trying to find a purpose. But don't do that by bringing up these crackpot notions of yours. My lord, if what you're saying got out, half of Dupray county would storm this office demanding justice for Harvey Lape, and the other half would run us out of town for being the most inept law enforcement officials since Barney Fife."

She waited again. This time, he was done.

"I'm sorry," she said.

Elven waved his hand. "Don't apologize. You're just... being you."

She didn't know if that was a compliment or insult and didn't press her luck by asking.

"Oh," he said. "They called from the garage. Your van's fixed."

Finally, some good news. But there was one problem. The garage was ten miles outside of town. She could drive Lester's Blazer there, but then she'd have two vehicles and no means get both back.

Elven seemed to read her mind. "Do you need a ride?"

She gave her most winning smile. "Do you mind?"

He turned away from her, ascending the stairs. "Of course not."

CHAPTER FIFTY-SEVEN

"We didn't have that exact shade of paint," Brett, the mechanic, said as he displayed her freshly-repaired van. The front fender on the passenger side had been replaced and now stuck out like the proverbial sore thumb.

"White?" she asked, hoping she had worked a heaping amount of sarcasm into that one word.

"Old," he said.

"Oh."

Aside from the fender looking like a new penny in a handful of twenty-year-old change, he'd done good work. She couldn't even see the bullet hole.

"Well, thanks," she said.

He handed over the keys.

The best part of having her van back was having her freedom. The van meant she didn't have to stay in Bea's house. Hell, she could drive out of the state. Out of the damn country if she wanted.

After the mess of the last few weeks, she was untethered; so, why was she still in Dupray?

Because as batshit insane as Elven had made her feel, she knew she wouldn't be able to put this case to bed until she knew whether there was any connection between John Robert Munroe and the murders.

And to do that, she needed help.

Max's rental car was parked outside his motel room. She knew he'd been hitting dead ends on getting info on the murders for his blog, and she'd been ignoring his text messages. Hopefully, he wouldn't hold that against her.

She was halfway between a second and third knock at the door when he jerked it inward.

"You look like shit," he said.

Her bruises were fading, and she didn't think she looked too bad until that remark. "Gee, thanks. That's what every girl wants to hear."

"No, I didn't mean it like that. I just meant... Damn, that bastard really did a number on you."

"I'm aware," she said. "Can I come in? I need some of those computer skills you're always bragging about."

He stepped aside to grant her access, and she saw his luggage on the bed, packed and ready to go.

"You're leaving town?" she asked.

He sat on the bed. "That's the plan. No one here will talk to me, including you. I can finish my report back in New York."

She felt a little sorry for leading him on, then blowing him off. He had been helpful to her, and she failed to live up to her end of the deal.

"What do you want now?" he asked, his tone curt.

"Can you help me find someone?"

"Depends. What's in it for me?"

"The personal satisfaction that comes with knowing you did a good deed?"

He scowled, a foreign expression on his typically jubilant face. She expected him to kick her out. Instead he grabbed his tablet.

"Give me a name," he said.

CHAPTER FIFTY-EIGHT

Despite all of Max's efforts, he couldn't find a scrap of information on John Robert Munroe after the time of the first murders. No criminal activity, no income, no utilities in his name. It fit with the theory she'd created, where Munroe had changed his identity to escape his past.

Sometimes, she hated being right.

With Munroe a dead-end, at least temporarily, she had him get an address for Anse Medley, the retired deputy who may have taken the missing persons report. He was easier to track down, but Max refused to give her the address, instead insisting that he take her there and join in on the interview. Carolina was in no position to refuse.

Medley lived in a decrepit, 12 x 60 house trailer that occupied lot number nine in the deceivingly named Pleasant Meadow mobile-home park. An Oldsmobile station wagon with two flat tires occupied the patch of dirt that served as a parking space.

They didn't need to knock because a shirtless Anse Medley was push mowing his lawn at approximately half a mile per hour. Smoke billowed from the engine of his mower, and when he shut it down upon seeing them, it sputtered and coughed for a good ten seconds before dying.

He was in his eighties, with a potbelly that hung low over his belt. A faded tattoo of a bald eagle adorned his shoulder. His weathered face was partially hidden by a patchy beard, but his expression was clear enough. Distrust.

Carolina gave a nod and wave. The man returned neither. Great.

Max stayed on her heels as she approached, and she thought most of Medley's wariness was directed at him. But it was too late now.

"Anse?" Carolina asked. "I'm not sure if you remember me. I'm Carolina McKay."

He peeled his focus off Max and examined her. His blue eyes softened with recognition. "Well, I'll be damned," he said. "You grew up good."

She took that as a compliment, but it was an awkward and unwelcome one. "Thanks," she muttered.

"I thought you got out of this God-forsaken place. Why in the hell are you back?" As soon as he said that, he paused, eyes growing wide in mild alarm. "Did something happen to Beatrice?"

"No," Carolina said. "I'm convinced she's indestructible. I'm actually helping out Lester with the murders. I don't know if you've been keeping up with the news."

Anse shook his head. "The less I know about what's going on in the world, the better I am."

"You remember Diana, though?"

"Of course." He motioned to two concrete blocks in the yard. "Sit with me. This sciatica is kicking my ass."

He flopped onto one of the blocks. Carolina took the other. And Max was left standing. Medley still hadn't acknowledged the man's presence.

"Some other girls were killed recently. And we're sure there's a connection."

"Okay?" Medley sounded and looked uncertain. "You know I've been retired for over a decade though, right?"

"I do," Carolina said. "I'm actually here about a man named John Robert Munroe."

His eyes were blank.

"He went missing around the time of the first murders. His father, Rulon Munroe, was a farmer out near Effing." She thought about telling Anse about the altercation between Rulon and Lester but knew that would drag out this conversation for longer than she preferred. "We're trying to find out if there was a missing persons report filed on the son."

Anse thought about it, his gears turning as slowly as the wheels on his mower. Then he gave a curt nod. "The son had one of those shit ugly cars. A Gremlin, right?"

"It was a Pacer, actually, but you're close enough."

He smiled with the satisfaction of knowing he still had it. "Yeah, he called the station and said his son had been gone a few weeks. I drove out and took the report."

"Did you file it? Because there's nothing in the database," Max said.

Anse looked at him, peeved. "Who's he?" Medley asked Carolina.

"Max Barrasso. He's my research assistant."

The old man huffed. "What would your dad say about you associating with a negro?"

Carolina knew she needed Medly's help, and that was the only thing that kept her from raging at him. "Seeing as how he took off before I was born, I wouldn't know. But Max is the best damned researcher I've ever found, and he's been a tremendous asset."

That seemed to put a pin in the man's prejudice.

"Son," he said to Max. "Things worked different back then. We aren't talking about a boy. That fellow was in his late twenties as I recall. And if a man wanted to disappear, that was his right."

Max snorted but didn't respond verbally.

"You never had any leads on what might have happened to him?" Carolina asked.

"Nothing in particular. His old man wasn't exactly pleasant. And the boy had lost his job around then, so I figured he took off for greener pastures. Who could blame him?"

Medley put his hands on his knees and pushed himself into a standing position, his face a mask of pain from the exertion. "I don't want to talk about this anymore."

"Anse, this is important. It might be related to Diana and the others. And the recent murders."

"Then talk to Lester."

"Lester's... slipping," she said. "He forgets a lot these days."

Anse Medley stepped toward his mower and grabbed the starter rope. "Sometimes, forgetfulness is a blessing."

She knew this discussion was over but got out one more question. "You said Munroe had lost his job. Do you remember where he worked?"

He gave the cord a yank, and the engine roared to life in a cloud of black fog. "Sure. The college," he said.

CHAPTER FIFTY-NINE

McDowell University was typical of rural colleges. Unassuming buildings scattered across a flat lot. A large courtyard where students studied, smoked, and socialized. Plenty of tree-lined brick walkways. It was charming, in its own way.

Max let her drive his rental, giving him time to do a deeper dive into Munroe's work history. The reason they hadn't connected him to the college where all the murdered girls had been enrolled was because he was officially employed by Broughton Security, a now-defunct company that had handled the campus' security.

Since Lester never reclaimed his badge, Carolina used it to bluff their way past the secretary and get into the office of Rodger Wilk, the current head of security. The man was nearing retirement age but filled out his uniform in all the right places. His buzz cut and posture made her think he was once in the military. And he was black, a fact that made Max smile at the sight of him.

She'd explained that they were looking for information on John Robert Munroe, and as soon as the name came out of her mouth, Wilk's expression turned sour.

"That one," he said. "Yeah, I remember him."

"Forgive me for making assumptions, but I'm guessing those aren't good memories?"

"Anything but." Wilks took a seat at his desk and continued speaking as he typed at his computer. "I wasn't in charge then, just a regular grunt. Munroe had been hired a couple years before me, and let me tell you, he always let me know he had seniority.

"He was one of those guys who became a security guard because he needed his ego stroked. You're cops; so, I'm sure you know the type."

Carolina saw Max smirk but ignored it. "Absolutely. We were told he was fired. Do you remember why?" she asked.

"That's what I'm trying to pull up," Wilks said. "I don't know that I ever heard an official explanation, but I can tell you from personal experience that Munroe was a scumbag of the first class. Always using the job to push around the students, especially the guys. The women, well, he was too friendly with them. Offering to escort them to their dorms. Volunteering to work all the female sporting events. And if he'd have been even a halfway-normal guy, he probably could have got all the ass he wanted. The cliché about women liking a man in uniform exists for a reason."

Carolina raised an eyebrow. "You have experience?"

If a black man could blush, Wilks did. "I'm married. And my wife would castrate me if I so much as cast a lascivious look at another woman."

"Good to know some men have morals," Carolina said.

Max barked out a surprised cough, which she ignored. In the corner of the office, a printer clanked to life.

"Guys like Munroe, it's like they must put off pheromones or something. A warning signal to the opposite sex to stay far away. Because they all seemed to know he was an odd duck."

Wilks rose from his chair and moved to the printer. He grabbed the two sheets of paper it spit out, skimming them. "Huh," he said.

"What is it?"

"I guess I was wrong. Munroe was never fired. Not officially anyway. He just stopped showing up for work."

He handed the papers to Carolina who gave them a speed read. There had been three complaints about Munroe. Two from males who claimed he was bullying them. One from a female who said Munroe had asked her on a date and became belligerent when she declined.

His last day of employment was a few days after the final murder.

When she finished, she handed the papers to Max. "Did he have any friends on campus that we might connect with?" she asked.

"Munroe didn't have friends. Sorry, I know that doesn't help you out."

"Yeah, not really."

Max held up one of the papers, pointing to a line at the bottom. "What's this mean?" he asked. His finger was beside a line reading: PE. There was an unchecked box beside it.

Wilks looked. "His personal effects were never picked up. Probably the contents of his locker."

"Any chance you still have them?" Max asked.

"After nineteen years?" Wilks sighed. "I believe it's more likely I could find the Willie McCovey rookie card I traded a week's worth of lunches for back when I was eleven."

"Can we at least try?" Carolina asked.

Wilks grabbed a set of keys off his desk. "Why not? This is the most interesting thing that's happened on campus since I caught that bird professor lady and the basketball team captain bare-ass naked behind her desk."

In her peripheral vision, Carolina saw Max's mouth drop. She gave him a look that said it all.

Don't even think about it.

"Well, shit," Rodger Wilks said as he pulled a plastic tote from the bottom row of storage shelves. "I was sure you folks were going to get my allergies fired up for nothing."

He wiped dust off the container, clearing the label: *Rmunr-Unclaimed.*

"May I?" Carolina asked, motioning to it.

"That's why we're here."

She popped the top, coughing as nineteen years' worth of grime puffed in her face. The contents were sparse. A set of clothing - black slacks and a polo shirt. A lunch box, empty aside from a thermos. A Kentucky Wildcats cap. A composition book.

She opened the latter, finding the pages filled top to bottom with block printing. It included names, all women's names, and beside each name were notes.

Tanya Petras—20—Wore a loose-knit pink sweater and no bra. Could see her nipples. Complimented her. Didn't respond. Cunt.

Angela Neilson—18—Likes tight jeans and crop tops. Brunette but would look better blonde. Uppity bitch.

Cindy Phillips—18—Does laundry Wednesday evenings, leaves clothes in dryer, and goes out to smoke. Took a pair of her panties. Smartmouth doesn't know her place.

It went on and on, page after page. Carolina handed the notebook to Max.

"You want a look inside the mind of a maniac? Here you go."

At the bottom of the tote was a small pack of polaroid photographed, held together by a rubber band. Carolina went to remove it, and the band crumbled. She flipped through the stack.

They were photos of college girls, taken without their knowledge as they walked to classes, chatted with friends. Each photo had a name and hand-drawn stars ranging from one to five. The bastard's own personal rating system.

She was nearing the end of the stack and hadn't seen any of the murder victims. Maybe he kept those somewhere else, she thought, and she wondered if he took photos of them during and after their murders, too.

The images changed from spy pics of students to nature shots. A squirrel under a rhododendron bush. A chipmunk with cheeks packed full of acorns. A rundown cottage in the woods. A lake.

She almost set them aside, but that last snapshot, something about it, drew her back. It probably could have been any of the hundreds of lakes or ponds in West Virginia, but it looked familiar.

Then it hit her.

CHAPTER SIXTY

Carolina made Max take her straight to the motel. She didn't say a word on the ride back or as she exited his car and headed to her van.

"Carolina," he said. "Are you all right?"

She paused, fingers on the door handle. "I have no idea."

"You recognized something in those pictures. What was it?"

"Probably nothing," she said, pushing open the door and dropping a foot outside.

"Don't stonewall me. It's not fair."

He was right. He deserved better. "Will you do me one more favor?"

Max nodded.

"Can you check and see if Rulon Munroe or John Robert owned any property aside from the farm?"

"I can. It'll take a bit, though, as I'll need to hac—" He stopped himself. "Access the tax records."

"That's all right. Text me if you find anything." She was out of the vehicle.

"Let me come with you."

Carolina didn't look back. "I can't. I'm sorry, Max."

SHE BANGED on the front door to Lester's house, a small ranch home which was located three blocks up and one over from the sheriff's station. There was no answer, but she knew he might be sleeping, recuperating from his attack.

But she had to talk to him. To tell him everything she found out.

She felt above the door frame for a spare key, but nothing was there. Under the mat was empty, too. Then she had another idea and tried the knob. It was unlocked and swung open. Small town living.

"Lester?"

No answer.

She stepped into the house, which smelled of his aftershave and dog. That made her realize the house was empty; Yeti would have tackled her if he and Lester were home.

Carolina pulled her cell from her pocket and dialed.

"Dupray County Sheriff's Office."

"Meredith, this is Carolina. Is Lester in?"

"No, hon; he took the day off."

"Did he say where he was going to be?"

"Home, I'd assume."

So much for that. "Okay. Thanks."

"Is everything all right?"

"I'm not sure. Probably."

"Well, if you need anything, I can get Elven on the radio."

She was tempted to take Meredith up on the offer. As a cop, she should bring Elven in on this. But she wasn't ready yet. Lester deserved to be the first to know what was going on.

"No, it's fine. Thanks." She ended the call.

Before leaving, she decided to check Lester's bedroom. Maybe he had a planner where he kept track of appointments.

When she entered the room, she saw his Sheriff's uniform shirt draped over a chair and his hat sitting on the dresser, which meant he wasn't attending to anything job-related. There were no schedules to be found. Back to square one.

On the mirror, she saw a myriad of photographs held in place with masking tape: Lester and Bea at some type of formal event, Carolina and Scarlet in costumes for Halloween, Carolina as a police officer, Scarlet as a belly dancer, and Lester and Carolina at the lake house.

That one stopped her. She peeled it off the glass, examining it closer. She wasn't even a teenager when it was taken, and Lester was still in the prime of middle age. God, he was so full of life then.

She pushed the photo into her pocket and headed out of the house. She knew where she had to go.

CHAPTER SIXTY-ONE

A third of the way to the lake, Carolina's phone rang. She saw it was Max and answered.

"What did you find out?"

She heard his sigh through the speakers. "Can't you even humor me with some small talk? Make it seem like you actually give a crap about me?"

"I'm sorry, Max. I'm under a bit of stress here. How's your day going? Did you find any bedbugs at the motel yet?"

"You really suck at this," he said.

"Sorry. I tried." She passed a sign reading *North Spectacle Pond —8 mi.*

"And I appreciate that. Anyway, I did some deep diving. There has never been property in John Robert Munroe's name in the state of West Virginia."

"What about the father?"

"Only the farm."

"Shit!" She banged her fist against the steering wheel.

"Hold up; don't freak out just yet. I've got something for you." He took a dramatic pause. "Rulon's wife, John Robert's mother, was

Erline Chabol. Hey, what's up with all the weird-ass names around here anyway? It's like J.R.R. Tolkien started a country-music band."

"I don't know. Must be something in the water."

"That's why I drink bottled. So Erline came from a big family: four brothers and seven sisters."

"Jesus," Carolina muttered.

"Yeah. Ouch, am I right?"

"Sure. But hurry up with the relevant part."

"Alright. Alright. The Chabol family formed a trust after the parents died off. And part of that trust was approximately fourteen acres of property and one dwelling."

"Can you give me the address?"

"One sixty-six Tecumseh Lane. I checked on Google maps, and that's a on a lake ne--"

"I know where it is," she said.

"You do?"

"Yeah. I'm almost there."

"You want me to come?"

"No. I'm good."

Even she didn't buy that lie.

CHAPTER SIXTY-TWO

The driveway to 166 Tecumseh Lane was blocked by a simple steel gate in which a metal pole extended from side to side. Carolina pulled the van close enough for the bumper to touch before coming to a stop. Then she exited her vehicle and approached, hoping that it was unlocked.

Those hopes were dashed as a padlock, still shiny and new, held the gate closed. But it was clear the path had been used recently, as the previous season's weeds had been smashed down by tires.

She had gone straight here, abandoning her original mission to see if Lester was at his camp. And despite knowing she should have someone along for backup, she plunged forward.

It was a quarter-mile before the house came into view—if you could even call it a house. Time had ravaged the abode, leaving it leaning to the side as if it were in the middle of a long, slow process of toppling over. The roof sagged while the wood siding was black with mildew and mold.

A quick scan of the area revealed no one in view. Nonetheless, she took her pistol from its holster but kept the safety on. She felt better with it in her hand as she approached the building.

The porch was rotting, and she stepped lightly, trying to land on the joists as she moved to the door. She made it there without falling through and breathed a little easier.

Two quick raps against the door were met with no response, so she moved to a window, peering inside. And that's when she saw the clothing.

Scattered about the floor was a variety of women's clothes and accessories. A purse. A scarf. A cardigan. Some looked new, whereas others featured outdated styles and a dense coating of dust.

This was the proof that she wasn't crazy. She held her phone against the glass, snapping photos of the trophies. The images looked like crap, but they'd be enough for Lester and Elven to get a warrant.

As she pocketed her phone, she heard one of the rotten planks creak behind her. She began to turn, but it was too late. There came a flash of pain in her head, and it all went black.

CHAPTER SIXTY-THREE

The GPS app on Max's phone showed he'd reached his destination, but he didn't see anything but dirt road and trees. It ended up being off by about half a mile, and he soon spotted Carolina's van abandoned down a narrow lane. He pulled in behind it, then hopped out of his car.

When he saw the gate and the wooded drive that disappeared down an embankment beyond it, he didn't need to be a detective to deduce where she'd gone. He wanted to follow that same path, but his instincts told him that would be unwise, and he wasn't one to ignore them.

He grabbed his phone and dialed. It rang twice before the call was answered.

"Hey, it's Max Barrasso. No, don't hang up; just listen, okay?" He didn't wait for another word before starting up again. "Look, Carolina's on to something here. About the murders. I'll text you the address."

He paused, listening.

"Yeah, sure, I'll wait for you."

He hung the phone up and typed a quick message, sending over the address. Then he waited.

That didn't last.

While he trusted his instincts, he knew his friend might be in danger, and he wasn't going to stand there and wait for the cavalry to arrive, doing nothing to help. Even if it meant risking his own life.

CHAPTER SIXTY-FOUR

The world returned in gradual waves, light and images ebbing in and coming into focus, then fading back out. Her point of view was ground-level. She saw boots in front of her. Their wearer stepping around her.

Then all went black.

Someone grabbed her under the arms and dragged her through a doorway and into a dim, foul-smelling room.

Black.

She was dropped onto the floor. Her head thudding against the hardwood.

Black.

Now she was propped against a wall. The woozy feeling lessened, and her vision came into focus. The scene before her was the inside of Munroe's cottage.

God, her head hurt. It was more than the usual dull ache that came from her pills wearing off. This was acute, like an ice pick was embedded in her skull. She reached to check, to pull it out if it was indeed there, and her fingers found a sticky, walnut-sized lump. When she looked at her hand, it was wet with blood.

She snapped her head from side to side, an act that caused both pain and nausea as she took in a 360-degree view of the one-room cottage. It was empty, save for an eclectic assortment of furniture. One lawn chair. One wicker rocker. A metal desk. An end table with a radio on top. Two stained mattresses that, sans frames, sat on the floor. It was like someone had picked up the junk that was leftover after a yard sale and thought, *This will do.*

She saw a glass jar on the desk. The small, pint-sized kind used to can jelly and jam. Only this container didn't house condiments.

Slivers of what looked like pistachio shells covered the bottom of the jar, but although Carolina was a yard away, she knew they weren't shells. She crawled to the desk and, her hand trembling, picked up the container.

Light spilling through the window highlighted the contents. It glistened off the fine hairs that grew from the tan, leathery things.

From the eyelids.

Several looked almost mummified, withered, and desiccated. But the top layer was still fresh. Blood tinged their cut edges, a hard crimson against the pale flesh.

Carolina made sure the lid was on tight and shoved the jar into her coat pocket. She wasn't taking any chances on Munroe coming back here and making the evidence vanish. Not when she was so close to ending this madness once and for all.

She knew she needed to get up and out of this place, but her brain was underwater. She made it to one knee when—

"Carolina? Are you in there?" The voice outside was Max's.

"Max!" she screamed. "Munroe's here!"

She forced herself to her feet, holding her arms at her side for balance and closing her eyes to stop the world from spinning.

And then came Max's voice again. Louder. Panicked. "What the fuck?"

She heard someone hit the side of the cabin. Scuffling. A punch.

Then a gunshot.

CHAPTER SIXTY-FIVE

When Carolina stumbled out the front door, her foot immediately plunged through a weak spot in the wood. She went in hip-deep, the jagged edge ripping through her jeans and carving divots in her thigh.

"Max!" she yelled.

As she pushed herself loose, she wondered if he was dead. Would this be another death on her shoulders? How many more could she bear?

Finally, she freed herself and moved more carefully as she scrambled off the porch and into the dirt. She hobbled to the rear of the cabin, the area from which the shot had come, steeling herself for what she might find.

But there was nothing more than disturbed leaves, the signs of a struggle. Neither Max nor Munroe was anywhere to be found.

Maybe he got away, she thought. And maybe Munroe's chasing him.

Her gun was gone, as were her phone and keys, all stolen while she was knocked out. She saw little sense in returning to the van or making a run for the road. It seemed the natural place for Munroe to wait to ambush her, if he were still around.

Instead, she circled the pond on foot, an act that took the better part of half an hour and left her so winded and exhausted she could barely remain upright. The wound on her leg was worse than she'd first thought and had spilled enough blood that her leg was red from thigh to foot. A chunk of wood as thick as her thumb protruded from the gash, and she felt it moving inside her with every step. A splinter from hell.

By the time Lester's camp came into view, the sun was dipping behind the mountains, halving the light of day. The sky had gone tangerine orange in the sunset, and the resulting reflection off the lake gave the landscape a surreal, atomic look. Like she was alone in a world post-nuclear apocalypse. It would have been beautiful under other circumstances.

As she closed in on the lake house, she reached the bench first. The exertion from the jog had left her gasping for air. The cabin was still a hundred yards away. She had to keep moving, but she knew she'd never make it there if she didn't stop and recuperate.

When she tried to sit on the bench, she was so tired and unsteady that she missed it, hitting the ground hard. Her entire body felt like one throbbing ache. If she'd had her pills in her pocket, she'd have downed the whole bottle.

But she didn't. She had to get up. She had to get to Lester so they could find Max and Munroe.

Carolina planted her hands in the dirt, pushing to get herself back to her knees, when a new, sharp pain screamed in her palm. She jerked it back and saw a bloody puncture. Then her gaze went to the ground to see what had stabbed her.

An object jutted from the indentation her hands had made in the dirt. A dull, white stick.

That's what a normal person would have assumed, anyway. Someone who didn't go through life with death on their mind 24 hours a day. That person didn't see a stick. That person - Carolina - saw a bone.

Now she scooped at the ground. The soil was loose and sandy and made for easy digging, and she quickly realized she was right. It was a bone.

What am I doing? This is the wilds of West Virginia. This could be the remains of any animal, from a porcupine to a white-tailed deer.

Then she thought about Lester's previous dog. Ghost. If she unearthed the remains of his old best friend, she'd feel like the biggest asshole in the history of the world. And this being the dog's grave would make sense. Lester could have buried him there, then built the bench so they'd always be together.

Ghost.

Something about that gnawed at her. It seemed like more than the dog's name. She closed her eyes, trying to concentrate. Trying to remember.

Ghost man.

Allison Petrey's voice was in her head.

The ghost man. He said he'd give me pizza if I helped.

She'd thought the woman was rambling at the time, but what if she weren't?

Carolina dug faster, handful after handful. A growing pile of ground formed on one side while an increasing number of bones grew on the other. She was no forensic anthropologist, but she soon realized they weren't those of a dog. Or a porcupine. Or a deer.

They were human.

She exposed the disarticulated rib cage, then moved upward on the remains. She saw vertebrae and kept digging.

Another few handfuls of dirt, and the skull was revealed. There was a hole above its right eye socket. A bullet hole.

As she traced her finger around that mortal wound, her eyes examined the face, anonymous in death. Only it wasn't. Because amongst a row of otherwise perfect choppers, she saw the broken front tooth. The same one she'd seen in John Robert Munroe's senior portrait.

"Oh God, Lester," she said to herself. "What have you done?"

CHAPTER SIXTY-SIX

It felt like her world had imploded, like nothing made sense anymore. She ran for Lester's house and could see his Blazer parked on the upper side. What would she say to him?

She didn't bother knocking, instead pulling open the screen door and slipping into the cabin. And there he sat in the recliner, an oil lamp illuminating his poor, mangled face. His feet propped up on an ottoman. A Louis L'Amour western in his hands. Yeti dozing at his side.

Upon her entrance, he looked up. And smiled.

"Carolina? By God, what a nice surprise."

Yeti lazily climbed to his feet and trotted to her as Lester set aside the book that he'd been reading - *The Proving Trail*. The dog stuck its nose into her leg wound and brought Lester's attention with it.

"You're bleeding," he said. "What happened to you, now?"

He didn't wait for an answer, hurrying to the kitchen where she heard a cabinet open. A moment later, he came back with a first-aid kit that he'd already opened. He pulled out antiseptic and gauze.

"Lester, I think Max might have been shot. I was attacked at a cabin across the lake. It was full of trophies from the murder victims. Proof that John Robert Munroe was the killer."

He had crouched to care for her leg but then looked at her, eyes panicked. "I'm calling Elven. We need to get everyone out here right away."

He discarded the first-aid gear. He moved to the door, but Carolina stopped him.

"Lester, wait. Listen to me. That's not all," she said. She swallowed hard, unsure if she'd be able to get out the words. "I found what was under your bench."

"Pardon?" he asked.

"What you buried there." She reached out and took his hand. He turned back and they were face to face. What a sorry pair we make, she thought.

"*Who* you buried there," she said.

Confusion filled the man's eyes. Not the overly dramatic act of someone trying too hard to put on a show. This was genuine bewilderment.

In that moment, she would have welcomed death because she didn't want to be the one to tell this man, whom she respected more than anyone she'd ever known, whom she loved more than anyone she'd ever known, that he was a killer.

But there was no way around it.

"Lester, you killed John Robert Munroe." Her voice cracked, and she knew she was seconds away from crying, but she tried to stay strong. For him.

"What are you talking about?" He leaned back, away from her.

"He's buried under your bench. There's a bullet hole in his skull."

Lester stood up, putting more distance between the two of them. "Why would you say that?"

"Because it's true. You must have found out that he was the killer. The man who killed Diana."

Now, Lester was on the verge of tears. He crossed his arms over his chest, swaying side to side like a longshoreman struggling to stay afoot on high seas. "Carolina, you know that's not true. I couldn't do that; I'm not a murderer."

Her throat was on fire. It took every ounce of strength she possessed not to sob, not to pull a U-turn and tell him he was right and that she was playing the worst practical joke in the history of mankind.

"It's okay. I understand. And I might have done the same thing in your position." She took a step toward him, reaching for him, wanting to console him, but he backed away from her.

"You're wrong," Lester said, his voice rising and bordering on a wail. "I'm not that kind of man. I can't be."

He spun away from her, retreating back into the kitchen.

Then came a gunshot.

The bullet soared past her, slamming into the cabin wall. She skittered sideways in instinct even though the shot wasn't close to hitting her, and as she did, the wood in her leg shifted, digging into muscle. The pain dropped her to a knee.

And then she heard footsteps. Boots against the hardwood floor.

She looked up and saw Lester, his .357 in his hand. Only the man looking at her was no longer Lester Fenech. He hunched over, jutting his jaw forward. Just like the man she'd seen that day at the cemetery.

Just like John Robert Munroe.

He aimed. Fired. And this time, his shot hit its mark.

CHAPTER SIXTY-SEVEN

THE BULLET HIT HER, RESULTING IN A LOUD POP.

Carolina felt a stab of pain in her side, felt blood running down her hip.

She reached for the wound to gauge its severity and, in the process, sliced open her hand. It took her a moment to connect the dots, but then she figured it out. The shot had shattered the mason jar of eyelids.

There was only a moment of relief before the reality of the situation rushed back. Lester - or the alternative personality inside his body - was trying to kill her. She spun away from him and ran.

Another shot blew out one of the front windows. A third hit the oil lamp, which burst into a small fireball. Flaming fuel washed off the end table and onto the floor, setting a braided wool rug ablaze.

The missed shots proved to her - if she'd had any doubts - that this wasn't Lester putting on a show. He was a crack shot, and if he'd been the one firing, he wouldn't have missed.

That was little solace.

As he chased her out of the cabin, she heard him toss the gun aside, and they dashed into the diminishing light of dusk. Her only chance was the Blazer, and she sprinted toward it.

"Don't run from me, you whore!"

She was at the vehicle, grabbing for the door handle. It was locked.

Behind her, Lester laughed, a sadistic, joyless noise. "Bitches always think they can get away," he said. "But in the end, they're too fucking stupid."

Carolina turned toward his way. The sunset backlit him, making it hard to see his physical features, to see the real Lester. His silhouette was almost identical to the day the fifteen-year-old version of her had seen Munroe in the cemetery. The way he stood, the way he walked. It was uncanny. And terrifying.

"Don't do this, Lester. I know you're still in there."

He whistled tunelessly and kept coming.

"I had to put Lester to bed. He's not capable of doing what needs done."

She was pressed against the Blazer, and there were maybe two yards between them. She thought about diving to the side and making a run for it, but she was tired of running. Finally.

"It's John, right?" she asked. "John Robert Munroe."

He clapped his hands together. "You got it! Took you long enough though to figure it out, though. Might want to stop believing your own press."

"I saw your little notebook, the one you kept when you worked at the college. Your stalker ramblings about those girls."

"What of it?"

"The rantings of a little man," she said. "I thought it was kind of sad, really."

"Oh, yeah?" He took another step. "You bitches think you're smart, but you don't know shit. Like my daddy always said, a woman's place is on her knees."

It made her skin crawl to hear those words, John Robert Munroe's words, coming out of Lester's mouth. She knew Lester would never hurt her, physically or emotionally. And she had to break this imposter to bring him back.

Carolina inched away from the truck, closer to Lester/John. When she did that, he stopped forward movement, staring.

"And you put them on their knees, didn't you, John? Only once they were down there, you couldn't get it up. Your limp noodle was as useless as tits on a turtle."

The man sneered, nostrils flaring. "Maybe I'll show you what I can do," he said. "Course, you're old and used up. Ain't good for much of anything." He pulled a small pair of sewing scissors from his pocket.

"All these years, I wondered what the deal was with the eyelids," she said, taking another step toward him. This time he stepped back. "But now I understand. Women never paid attention to you. They never acknowledged you. They never looked at you. And you decided to change that, right, John?"

"Damn straight."

She laughed.

"What's so funny?"

"You," she said. "You did all this for attention, but you've been dead for almost twenty years, and no one even knows your name."

"You shut your whore mouth!" He screamed.

But she wasn't going to do that. "In life, you were just a pathetic, impotent, piece of shit. And in death, you've been completely forgotten."

He charged, head down. As stupid and unthinking as a bull rushing a matador. And Carolina was ready. She sidestepped him and shoved him in the back, pushing him headfirst into the Blazer's door, which indented with a dull thud.

He tumbled to the ground, falling awkwardly and putting his arm out to catch himself. She heard it snap in the fall.

Then she was on top of him. "Why did you do this?" She grabbed his broken arm, twisting and bending it. He howled in pain.

She screamed in rage and sadness as she wrenched his arm to and fro. "Give me back, Lester! Give him back, you motherfucker!"

Jagged bone broke through the skin of his forearm, blood gushing from the wound. It was only then that she realized he'd gone limp.

Her chest rose and fell with heaving breaths, and she looked down on his placid, unconscious face. Was Lester still somewhere in there?

She couldn't take any chances and unbuckled her belt, pulling it free. Then she turned Lester onto his side and pulled his arms behind his back. She looped the belt around his wrists and cinched it tight.

Behind her, the amber glow of the flames intermixed with the sunset and turned the world into a fireball. As a siren wailed in the distance, she wondered who could have called it in.

Then Yeti trotted over, laying down beside his master, their heads aligned. The dog licked Lester's wounded face—as if that could make everything better.

Carolina wished life could be that simple.

CHAPTER SIXTY-EIGHT

The sirens were closer now. Less than a mile away, from the sound of it. Her heartbeat had finally dropped to a semi-normal level when she heard branches snap.

Carolina and Yeti both spun toward the sound. The dog unleashed a ferocious bark, his hackles raised, but he stayed beside Lester, protective and guarding. Meanwhile, Carolina scanned the area for anything she could use as a weapon but had little luck.

"That dog isn't gonna rip my throat out, is he?"

It was Max's voice. He pushed through the trees and into the open. Carolina sighed, relieved he was alive, relieved this wasn't some new, unexpected danger. She'd had her fill for the night.

"I can't make any promises," she said.

Max approached, wary, his eyes darting between her and Yeti, but the dog remained in place.

"Good dog," Max said.

As he moved to Carolina, she saw the side of his white sweater was saturated with blood. And he saw her noticing.

"You just let me there to bleed out," he said. "Thought you were supposed to be a hero." He sat beside her, wincing.

"I was preoccupied," she said.

"Excuses." He shook his head. "Can't believe I grew up in the projects and never have an ounce of trouble, then I come to West fucking Virginia and get my ass shot. How's that fair?"

She lifted his shirt and found a long divot where the bullet skimmed across his side. "It's just a flesh wound," she said. "You'll be fine."

"What are you, like an expert on getting shot or something?"

"I have some experience."

Red and blue flashing lights spilled onto them, and Carolina saw Elven's Wrangler barreling down the drive. It skidded to a stop behind the Blazer.

"I may have made a call," Max said.

"I won't hold it against you," she said.

Elven was out of the Jeep and rushing toward them. He hadn't even seen Lester or the dog. Tank was close behind.

"What happened?" Elven asked.

Carolina wanted to explain but couldn't. "Lester," was all she could manage. She pointed to where he laid bound.

By the time the fire trucks arrived, the lake house was no more than rubble and ash. It seemed just as well, as the serene beauty of the place, the happy memories they'd shared there, were gone forever.

CHAPTER SIXTY-NINE

CAROLINA AND MAX RODE WITH ELVEN AS THEY FOLLOWED THE ambulance to the hospital in Charleston. Lester hadn't come around by the time they arrived; so, they sat together in the waiting room. Even Max was speechless.

A few hours later, Dr. Ahluwalia, a female physician with a strong Indian accent, stepped into the room. "Are you Lester Fenech's family?" she asked Carolina and Elven.

Without a beat, Carolina nodded. "I am."

"Let us speak in the hall," the doctor said.

"Is Lester going to be okay?" Carolina asked as they slipped outside the waiting area.

"Physically, I would say yes. He's suffered a concussion, and the orthopedic team had to perform surgery on his arm, but he will heal."

She motioned to a row of blue, plastic chairs, and the message was clear enough. Sit down, bad news is coming.

"From everything you told me about what happened, I believe Mr. Fenech suffered severe trauma after taking the life of his daughter's killer. The extreme stress from that, compounded by his daughter's death..." She paused, searching for the correct word. "Fragmented his sense of self."

"So, he had multiple personalities?"

The doctor pinched her lips together. "We actually call it dissociative identity disorder. But yes, in layman's terms, it would be similar. When Mr. Fenech's psyche was unable to cope with what he had done, he created this caricature of his daughter's killer as a way to absolve himself of his own guilt."

Carolina nodded. It made sense, she supposed. "Why now?" she asked. "What made him start killing these girls?"

Dr. Ahluwalia looked down at her hands. "Psychiatry is an inexact science. It's impossible to say with certainty, but the MRI of his brain shows significant atrophy. His deteriorating mental status, coupled with his pending retirement, might have brought all that past trauma to the forefront. But we'll never truly know."

That seemed to be the totality of the situation, and Carolina saw no point in pressing for details or speculation.

"Can I see him?"

The woman nodded. "Of course. He regained consciousness about an hour ago."

CHAPTER SEVENTY

Lester smiled when he saw her. And it was Lester, not the killer who'd taken up residence inside his head. But his grin was full of sadness.

"Surprised you want anything to do with me," he said.

She sat beside him and took his hand. "You shouldn't be."

They both searched for the right words, even though there was no such thing. He ended up going first.

"Those doctors told me a little about what happened. They used lots of fancy words, but I got the gist of it. I'm crazy. And I'm a murderer."

She squeezed his hand tighter. "You're sick."

"That's no excuse," he said. Tears rolled freely from his eyes. Carolina took a tissue from the box on the nightstand and handed him one. He didn't bother using it. "By God, I don't understand how any of this is possible."

She didn't either.

"Why didn't I shoot myself after I shot John Munroe?" he asked. "Would've solved everything."

"Don't say that. Don't think like that."

"He shook his head. It's true."

"No, it's not."

He turned away from her, ashamed. She took his chin lightly in her fingers and made him look at her.

"I couldn't have handled losing you back then," she said. "And I can't handle losing you now."

They both fell silent; then he broke the silence.

"I'm so sorry, Carolina. All I ever wanted to do was help people."

"I know that. I know you're a good man. I'm always going to be here for you, Lester."

She wrapped her arms around him, for once not even caring about the throbbing pain in her shoulder. She just wanted to feel him in her arms.

"I love you so much," he said.

"And I love you. No matter what."

He hugged her back, and they stayed like that for a long while. For one more night, at least, she could tell herself everything was okay.

She was nothing if not a good liar.

If you enjoyed book 1 in the Carolina McKay series you can dive into book 2 - Her Killer Confession - now.

FROM THE AUTHORS

Thank you for reading book one in the Carolina McKay series! We hope you enjoyed it. Carolina is a wonderfully fun character to write and we have so many stories planned. Hopefully you decide to stick along for the ride. It's definitely going to be bumpy!

Her Killer Confession

Her Deadly Double Life

As authors without million dollar ad budgets or huge publishing houses at our backs, reviews are very important to both the success of the book and our careers so, if you enjoyed the book, please consider a quick jaunt to Amazon or Goodreads to share your thoughts.

Again please accept our most sincere thanks & happy reading!

-Tony

-Drew

Join Drew's mailing list - http://drewstricklandbooks.com/readers-list

Join Tony's mailing list - http://tonyurbanauthor.com/signup

MORE FROM TONY & DREW

Hell on Earth

Within the Woods

Soulless Wanderer

Patriarch

A Land Darkened

Printed in Great Britain
by Amazon